From Sinner to Saint

From Sinner to Saint

Janice Jones

www.urbanchristianonline.net

Urban Books, LLC
78 East Industry Court
Deer Park, NY 11729

ISBN 13: 978-1-60162-876-3
ISBN 10: 1-60162-876-5

First Printing April 2010
Printed in the United States of America

10 9 8 7 6 5 4 3 2 1

Distributed by Kensington Corp.
Submit Wholesale Orders to:
Kensington Publishing Corp.
C/O Penguin Group (USA) Inc.
Attention: Order Processing
405 Murray Hill Parkway
East Rutherford, NJ 07073-2316
Phone: 1-800-526-0275
Fax: 1-800-227-9604

Dedication

I dedicate *From Sinner to Saint* to the First Institutional Baptist Church of Phoenix, Arizona, where Dr. Warren H. Stewart, Sr. is our Senior Pastor. Words cannot fully express how much I love you all. You have embraced and supported me and my literary works, *His Woman, His Wife, His Widow* and *Still Standing*. You have promoted, given glowing recommendations, kept the bookstores sold out, and shared with your families and friends all across the country the books I have written. I just pray that I continue to live up to the standards you have all set for me with this work, *From Sinner to Saint*. And thanks again for the tremendous pressure you have put on me to put out a sequel to *His Woman, His Wife, His Widow*. (HUGE SMILE)!

Acknowledgments

I can never start an acknowledgment of thanks without first starting with God, who makes all things possible. Lord, I give you all the thanks, honor, and praise. I worship and adore your name. John 15:5 says, "I am the vine, you are the branches. *If a man remains in me and I in him, he will bear much fruit; apart from me you can do nothing.*" This is the scripture by which I write. Not a single word could be written without you, and it is all done to bear fruit and win souls for Christ.

To my husband, David Jones: It was mistakenly printed on the back of *His Woman, His Wife, His Widow* that we were still married at the time of its release. I guess we can look at the error as prophecy because here we are married again. You are my soul mate and the love of my life.

To my children and grandchild respectively, Jessica Jones, Jerrick Parker, Chalise Jones, Derrick Parker, and Jevon Parker: I thank God every day for your very lives. You all are my greatest blessings. I love you.

My father, Harold Bumpers: Thank you again for always being there wearing your proud Daddy smile as I continue to do my thing. I love you and I am blessed that God chose you to be my father.

My siblings, Sherrie Roberts, Darrius Bumpers, Linda Gard-

Acknowledgments

ner, Darrin Bumpers (Main) and Darnella Bumpers: You all made growing up wonderful. You make being grown exciting. Thank you with much love for all of my nieces and nephews.

To Denise Franklin and Monique Gaskin: You two are the greatest friends and fans I could ever have. You are so loyal that some would probably think I pay you all to help me the way that you do. But you are both wonderful to do it for free. Thank you for your love.

When mentioning friends, I can't forget Sonya Allen and Georgia Harris. You both are my sisters here in Arizona. You are proof of how awesome the God we serve is, because He made sure that I am covered with love no matter where I live. Thank you for serving Him proudly.

To Janell Walden Agyeman, my agent: Thank you for your loyalty, advice, and hard work. I can see us working together for many, many years to come.

To my editor, Joylynn Jossel: You are wonderful and wise beyond what I believe you even know. I love the way you can disagree with me and do it without animosity. That takes true talent.

To my readers and burgeoning fan base: Thank you for the wonderful words of praise and encouragement. I do this all for you. I just pray that God will continue to allow me to make you proud. You all are the best.

Prologue

Thirteen-year-old Antonyo, or Tony, as he was dubbed by everyone but his mother, sat at the kitchen table, constantly checking the window to see if his father had arrived. He was scheduled to pick up Antonyo at 3:00 P.M. That was forty-five minutes ago.

"Boy, I don't know why you get yourself so worked up over something your silly daddy has told you. How many times has he said he would come and get you, then never bother to show up?" Antonyo's mother, Trina, asked with little concern. She was baffled by and tired of her son's confidence in his father.

"But, Mama, he knows I really need to get new gym shoes to play in my first basketball game tomorrow. Daddy said he would take me to get them and that he couldn't wait to see me play."

In the thirteen years since Antonyo's birth, Trina could probably count the number of times Sheldon had actually come through for his son.

"So what you gon' do, sit there in the window until he shows up? If you do, your butt is going to be as stiff as my ironing board."

"He'll be here. You'll see." In spite of his mother's lack of faith, Antonyo still believed his father would keep his word . . . this time.

"No I won't. I'm leaving for work in five minutes. So, if

by some miracle that deadbeat does show up, make sure you lock my doors and take your key. I'll see you when I get home tonight. Hopefully you won't still be glued to that chair like you waiting for Jesus," Trina said as she kissed Antonyo's forehead and walked away.

Antonyo did indeed sit in that chair by the window for six consecutive hours, moving only to answer the ringing telephone on the kitchen wall, hoping the caller was his dad saying he was on his way. Being that it was Sunday and the stores closed at six, one would think the boy would have given up by then, but no. He stayed put, holding fast to his faith in his father to not let him down this time.

Antonyo wondered if perhaps Sheldon had somehow gotten hung up and couldn't pick him up. Maybe he went to get the shoes himself. He would arrive any minute with the brand new shoes in hand.

However, by 9:00 P.M., Antonyo had lost all hope of seeing his dad or his new shoes that day. At around ten-thirty, he fixed himself a sandwich, watched a little television, and then put himself to bed. It would be sixteen days later before he heard his father's voice again. Not once would Sheldon mention the shoes.

Antonyo did not bother showing up for the game after school the following day. He refused to play in the beat-down shoes he owned. Instead, he ducked out after sixth period, skipping his last hour class, which was gym. He knew he could not show up at home early, so he headed for one of his favorite hangouts, Auntie Treecie's, a place where anything went.

Trina left for work worried about her son and his state of mind as it related to what she knew would end up being a no-show visit from Sheldon. Time and time again, Sheldon had led Antonyo to believe that he would do something for him or come by to visit him, only to leave him sad and disappointed at the end of the day. Each time she learned of Sheldon's pending promises, she tried to warn Antonyo not to put too much faith in his actually coming through for him. Each time, her warnings had gone unheeded. She felt so powerless to protect her son from the ensuing pain of each disappointing let-down; her powerlessness, in turn, left her defeated.

As she stood at the bus stop waiting for her chariot to arrive, she reflected on how the state of defeat had been a constant companion in her life. Though she did not have a fancy college degree or even a high school diploma, she was smart enough to know that life just had to have more to offer than the hopelessness she felt now and, quite frankly, more often than not.

Just as the bus pulled to a stop in front of her and the one other waiting passenger, she was, for some reason, drawn to a beautiful white Cadillac as it passed in front of the bus. She continued to watch as the car passed the bus stop, and just before she boarded the freight, she read the personalized license plate that said TRY GOD.

Chapter 1

LaTrina and LaTreece Simms were beautiful, identical twins. They were tall, five feet seven inches, slim and curvy. They were medium brown in complexion, with big brown eyes. The only difference in their appearance was their hair. LaTrina kept her sandy brown locks long and naturally wavy, while La-Treece wore hers cut short and chemically straightened. The women's looks, however, were where the similarities ended.

Antonyo was LaTrina's only child. She worked very hard to raise him by herself. Sheldon, Antonyo's sometimes to mostly-no-time daddy, barely put in an appearance. His financial efforts were laughable. Trina did the best she could, at times working up to three low-paying, menial jobs to support herself and her son, leaving very little personal time for the two of them to spend together.

LaTreece, on the other hand, had nothing but time. Even though she had three children to support, she had never worked a real job in her twenty-nine years. Treecie was a hustler. She sold marijuana from her home, styled hair in her basement without a license, was a welfare recipient, and always had a man or two on standby. Treecie had no earthly idea who fathered her youngest child, and there was no shame in her game about it.

LaTreece was all about the good time. Her small, rarely clean, but always crowded home was known as the party house. This was where Antonyo loved to be.

Since his mom worked so much, Antonyo often found himself in Treecie's care. Trina was well aware of her sister's derelict lifestyle, but daycare choices were limited for the impoverished single mother. The twins lived only three blocks from each other, one on Bentler and the other on Trinity, nestled in the Brightmoor Area, one of the worst neighborhoods in Detroit.

The mean streets of Detroit had not yielded any kindness to these ladies. The sisters had no one other than each other. Their mother had been beaten to death by a man who was fifteen years her junior, four days prior to Antonyo's fourth birthday. The girls never knew their biological father, only a series of "uncles" that flitted in and out of their mother's life.

Linda Simms, their mother, had been far from a shining example of motherhood. The twins practically raised themselves while their mother traveled from bar to bar searching for a sponsor for her and her daughters. And while there was never a shortage of men in her bed, Linda's home had lacked everything else but roaches. At least two or three times a year the electricity and/or gas were shut off, the telephone stayed disconnected about half the year, and Trina and Treecie were lucky to receive one square meal a day.

Childhood was harsh and brief for these girls. By age fifteen, both girls had become pregnant and were forced to grow up quickly. School became a hindrance, as they needed the time allotted for class to figure out a way to make money to feed their babies. Welfare was their primary support system. Babysitting, braiding hair, delivering newspapers, working fast food, and seducing older men were secondary sources of income.

Trina eventually tired of the going-nowhere lifestyle after having her third abortion. Recognizing that she could barely take care of Antonyo, having another child was out of the question for her. While she was smart enough to identify her limitations as far as raising children, she was not as crafty about preventing the pregnancies from occurring.

When they left the clinic, she cried on the shoulder of her sister, older than her by seven minutes, who had accompanied her to her appointment. "Treecie, I can't believe I just did this again. What kind of horrible person am I to kill three babies?"

"It's okay, Trina. We all make mistakes and have prob-lems. Just be glad God offers us solutions to help us fix our prob-lems," Treecie crooned as she rubbed her sister's shoulder.

"Girl, you better stop. We may not be all holy and spiritual, but we both know that God does not want us to have abor-tions. No, Treecie. It is not that simple and I know it. Other women have normal lives, with normal families. They have husbands, good jobs, and they get excited when they find out they're pregnant. I believe that is what God is about."

"How would you know? You ain't never set foot inside a church one day in your life. Mama's funeral wasn't even at a church; it was at the mortuary." Treecie sucked her teeth and rolled her eyes at her naïve sister.

Becoming annoyed with her cynical sister, Trina lifted her head from Treecie's shoulder and dried her eyes. "Well, that could be part of the problem. Maybe we should start going to church. Maybe somebody in there could teach us how to do life better than we are right now."

At age nineteen, the day after she left the clinic follow-ing abortion number three, Trina enrolled herself in G.E.D classes and began trying to better her life. After obtaining her certificate, she was able to get work in the small factories that paid a little more than the fast food establishments. She found welfare demeaning, seeing as how it was never enough when she was a child, so she got off the system and instead worked her tail off to support herself and her son.

Approximately one year after receiving her G.E.D., Trina went to work at a video manufacturing plant, where she met a woman named Louise Fletcher. Ms. Louise was one of the kindest people Trina had ever encountered. No matter how bad the circumstances of her life, Ms. Louise never frowned, never seemed sad, never had a cross word for anyone. Even when her grandson was killed in a drive-by shooting, Ms. Louise managed to handle his death with courage and great strength.

Louise Fletcher was a confident child of God's Kingdom. There was no shame in her game. While she was not pushy or preachy, she would tell anyone willing to listen how wonderful her Savior had been to her. During her work breaks and at lunchtime, people could always find Ms. Louise reading her Bible, some other spiritually educational material, or a Christian novel.

Trina found Ms. Louise's pleasantness to be such a contrast to the world in which she lived and interacted; so much so that Trina's curiosity was piqued. She found herself often wondering if being a Christian truly offered the contentment she saw in Ms. Louise.

While Trina admired the older woman's confidence and strength from afar, she never had the nerve to inquire of her how she could go about achieving these qualities for herself. She did, however, purchase a King James Bible for herself at a dollar store, and tried reading it at home with the intention of starting at the beginning and working her way through. Unfortunately, she found the language hard to understand, so she quickly grew disinterested in what she was trying to accomplish. Trina assumed her inability to relate to what she read stemmed from her only having a G.E.D. versus having completed high school in the normal manner.

One afternoon during their shared break, Trina took a

look at the Bible Ms. Louise was reading, finding a difference between her own and her co-worker's. This she was bold enough to ask about.

"Ms. Louise, I bought a Bible the other day that says King James Version on it. I notice that your Bible says New International Version. Is there a difference between the two books?" Trina asked timidly.

"Both Bibles have the same information," Ms. Louise told her, "but mine has been translated into a simpler language to read, is all. I would recommend all beginning Bible readers to start with a version other than the King James. It is good to have the original translation handy, but it sure is tough to understand sometimes."

Ms. Louise was thrilled to hear that the young woman had begun reading the Bible, and she felt compelled to help her. "Here, you take my Bible. I have plenty more at home. This one is a little marked up, but you should find it much easier to read than the one you have."

"I can't take your Bible, Ms. Louise," Trina stated, trying to refuse the generous offer.

"Oh, yes, you can. I insist. God wants us to help others to learn about Him. This is the best way I know for you to start and for me to help. I will also suggest you read the book of Proverbs first, then move on to the Psalms, which is right before the book of Proverbs. I think this is where all new learners should begin."

Trina felt it would now be disrespectful not to accept Ms. Louise's offer of assistance. She took the book and began studying in the exact manner Ms. Louise had recommended. Approximately two weeks later, Trina had left the video manufacturing plant for a better paying job at a different facility, but she took the memory of Ms. Louise's disposition, as well as her advice on beginning Bible study, right along with her.

Her twin sister was less ambitious on both the career and spiritual levels, however. Treecie had her second child by age eighteen; number three by age twenty. These children were born in addition to three abortions of her own.

Darnell, her oldest and only son, was the same age as Antonyo. His father, Darryl, was about as supportive as Sheldon. Taraija (Ta-ray-ja) was ten. Her dad, Marcus, was a good man, a constant fixture in his daughter's life. Eight-year-old Tianca was the baby and had no man laying claim to her as his child. Oddly, Treecie found this aspect of her and her daughter's life amusing.

"Girl, I can't tell you which one of them trifling Negroes I was dealing with at the time is my baby's sorry daddy. That was a particularly busy time in a young pimpstress's life. I was juggling three or four of them fools back then." This was the reply she would give with a laugh to anyone who inquired about Tianca's paternity.

Treecie would drink and smoke weed on any given day, but not every day. Despite her obviously rowdy lifestyle and her questionable ways of providing, she loved her children and her nephew. They were her first priority.

Treecie temporarily lost custody of her children as a result of a Child Protective Services investigation. The kids were placed in the care of their aunt Trina for three days while Treecie awaited a hearing with a judge regarding the incident that led to the children's removal.

Treecie's boyfriend, Tevin, had been visiting when the police and Tevin's ex-girlfriend came to Treecie's home with an arrest warrant for Tevin. While Treecie watched television in the living room and the children played in the back bedroom, Tevin was in the basement making crack cocaine.

Treecie opened the door at the insistence of the police officer's knock, and the first thing she saw as she looked beyond the officers was Caryn, Tevin's ex, sitting in her car directly in front of Treecie's home.

"I know that heffa did not roll up to my house like she a welcome visitor. I just know she didn't." She immediately disregarded the officers standing on her porch, along with anything they had to say, setting her sights on getting to the woman who had nerve enough to show up at her home, with police escorts, no less. Needless to say, there was bad blood between the two females.

Treecie approached Caryn's vehicle, tongue ablaze. "Did you forget your address, wench? 'Cause if you did, I'm here to set you straight. You don't live here, so you better get going before I let loose and act a fool out here in front of these police officers."

"Ma'am, I need you to go back inside of your house," said the officer who followed Treecie to the car.

"I am not afraid of you. I am here to make sure that your boyfriend is arrested for putting his filthy hands on me. So, unless you want to join him in jail, I suggest you get away from my car, stupid," Caryn shot back boldly, feeling brave because of the officer's presence. She and Treecie had exchanged unpleasant words before over Tevin, but never had Caryn been so courageous.

Her new bravado only served to infuriate Treecie. Before the officer who followed had a chance to stop her, Treecie pulled Caryn from the car and the two started fighting. The police officer immediately got between the scuffling women. When he looked to the porch to summon his partner's assistance, he discovered that he was no longer there. He assumed correctly that he had gone inside the house, where he found Tevin with his stash.

Tevin was arrested and charged with assault and battery on his baby's mama, the initial reason for the police visit, and possession with intent to distribute drugs. Treecie was also arrested and charged with assault on Tevin's baby's mama, and conspiracy in the drug-related charges against Tevin. The children were taken into protective custody, where Trina was able to retrieve them after several hours.

After posting bond on the criminal charges, Treecie was released the following day, but was unable to get her kids back until she saw a judge two days later. During the hearing, she convinced the judge she was unaware of Tevin's activities in her basement. Treecie told the judge she would never approve of such behavior while her children were home. The family court judge gave Treecie the benefit of the doubt and returned the children to her, pending the outcome of the criminal charges.

In the criminal case, the conspiracy charge was dropped and Treecie was eventually given six months probation on the assault charges. Tevin was sentenced to a much harsher punishment, and Treecie never saw him again.

Shortly after Treecie's brush with the law, Taraija's dad sought and won physical custody of his daughter. Marcus used every negative aspect of Treecie's life against her in family court. The facts of Treecie's life were his weapons. His attorney told the court that fact one: all three children had different fathers, one unknown. Fact two: Treecie had no actual job to speak of and no education. Fact three: there was always a constant barrage of men in and out of her home and around his client's daughter. Fact four: the child's mother was now a convicted criminal. Treecie tried denying the validity of Marcus's claim, but proved less successful in family court than she had been in the initial protective custody hearing. These four truths were all the ammunition Marcus needed to gain full custody of his daughter.

When Taraija left to live with her dad, Antonyo took it especially hard. The two were very close.

This was life for Antonyo, minimal stability on the part of his dad and aunt, and minimal quality time spent with his overworked mother. School was not challenging enough, offering only a part-time distraction, and Antonyo had seen and heard too much about the mean streets to even consider taking the route to thug-dom. Still in his early teens, young Antonyo waded in limbo, bored, confused, and in search of a beginning to his identity.

Leave it to Aunt Treecie to help him discover where his true talents lay. . . .

Chapter 2

Antonyo was a very handsome boy. His female classmates and all the young girls in his neighborhood all agreed that he was the cutest boy in both places. He stood tall for his thirteen years, almost six feet. His skin was deep brown and flawless, something else unusual. Most boys his age were plagued by acne. He wore his hair cut short and tapered close to his head. Antonyo possessed the most expressive big brown eyes and a million-watt smile.

Antonyo had yet to realize the power he carried as a result of his physical beauty. The genuine cluelessness he wore like cologne only fueled the underdeveloped desires of the adolescent groupies in school and around the neighborhood. His naïve demeanor kept him approachable and down to earth. Even at his tender age, he garnered a great deal of attention— attention he was oblivious to.

Treecie recognized her nephew's potential and talents and insisted that he take full advantage of his capability. Treecie took it upon herself to clue Antonyo in to his magnetism during one of his visits to her home.

"Yo', Tony! Auntie need to holler at you for a second. You know that cow Jasmine that be trying to hang around here?" Treecie asked him as they sat on the sofa watching television. Antonyo nodded his head, acknowledging that he knew her.

"Well, she been asking about you like she want to get with you. Now, that girl is too old for you, and she nasty. She done already slept with all the boys around here her own age, so I guess she trying to find her some fresh meat."

This bit of news excited Antonyo to no end. He thought Jasmine was very pretty. He really enjoyed seeing her when she would come over to hang out with his aunt and watch music videos on television. She always got up and danced around the living room, imitating the moves she saw the females performing on the screen. In his opinion, Jasmine was fabulous.

"How old is she, Auntie?" he inquired innocently.

"She sixteen, why? You want to holler at her?"

"If she likes me, why not?"

"Uh-oh! Look at my nephew trying to be a young pimp. Look, li'l man, if you do get with that tramp, make sure she gives you some of the McDonald's money she making. Since she the one interested in you, make her take care of you. Know what I mean?"

Antonyo stared at his aunt, baffled. Though his knowledge of women was limited and secondhand, he was sure it was supposed to be the other way around. In his estimation, the man should take care of the woman.

"Auntie, I thought the guy was supposed to lace the girl. I don't see you running around giving guys no money."

"And you never will. However, nephew, you got *it*. You have something special that make these young chicken heads want to fight over you, throw themselves at you. You might not realize it yet 'cause you still young, but Auntie Treecie gon' school you on the fine art of pimping."

That day, the lessons began.

Three days later, Treecie arranged a date between thirteen-year-old Antonyo and sixteen-year-old Jasmine. They met at Treecie's house, where she set up a romantic scenario in her basement. She made a small dinner of fried chicken, boxed macaroni and cheese, a tossed salad, and 7-Up soda. The pop looked like champagne in the plastic cups. Treecie covered a card table with clear plastic plates, utensils, and a cheap floral tablecloth.

Antonyo neglected to inform Trina he would be experiencing his first date this evening. She was working again. Antonyo only told her he would hang out at his aunt's house until she got off work, and asked her to pick him up on her way home.

Antonyo arrived at Treecie's before Jasmine. After inspecting his aunt's handiwork, he found himself truly impressed with his aunt's decorative work and choice of foods. Armed with the ammunition Treecie had given him in the form of information about women, Jasmine in particular, he was sure he was ready to win her over with his charm.

When Jasmine arrived, Antonyo greeted her at the door with a slight kiss on the cheek. He took her by the hand and led her into the house. "Auntie, Jasmine is here. Please come and say hello."

"You look nice, Tony," Jasmine said as they waited for Treecie to come from the back room, where she and her children were watching television.

"Thank you. So do you. You smell very nice, too," he replied as he gave her a small peck on the lips.

Treecie caught this action just as she stepped into the living room. "All right. All right. Don't be freaking each other all up in my living room. Y'all can take that mess in the basement." She gave them both a hug then ushered the two kids downstairs.

In the basement, Antonyo turned on the charm. He held Jasmine's hand and led her to the chair, pulled it out for her, and helped her into her seat. After settling himself into his own chair, he started small talk while he prepared each of their plates. He played the part of the perfect gentleman, just as his aunt had taught him.

"How was school today, Jasmine?" he asked his date as they ate.

"Don't know. I'm not really in school right now."

"Why not?" Antonyo asked innocently.

"I got kicked out about a month ago for cussing out my English teacher. I just never bothered to get back in," she said nonchalantly.

"Does your mother know you don't go to school? My mother would kick my butt if I stayed out of school a month."

"Well, my mother doesn't really care what I do. As long as I go to work and give her some money from time to time for her beer, she straight." Jasmine laughed lightly. "Besides, school is no big deal to me anymore. I've already completed up through the tenth grade. How much more can they teach me?" She shrugged her shoulders casually and went back to eating her meal.

Antonyo thought about not being in school, being free to do whatever he wanted all day long. He then pondered the beat-down his mother would give him and realized those thoughts were too costly.

Trina may not have been too strict on him in other areas, but she was adamant about school. She was determined that her son receive a high school diploma, even if it meant beating him through every class, every year until he graduated. As a matter of fact, any whippings he ever received were a result of something he did or did not do in school. He would skip a class or two on occasion, but he made sure it was never enough to warrant his teachers having to call his mother.

They finished the rest of their meal mostly in silence, with the exception of Antonyo making the small talk his auntie had told him to make. Antonyo removed the used dishes from the table and took them upstairs to the trash. He returned and made a big show of clearing the table of the plastic cloth and wiping it clean. This was not part of the game he learned from Aunt Treecie, though. It was a lesson he had acquired from his mom. He was great at keeping their home clean.

Jasmine was very impressed with the actions of this young boy. "Can I help you do something?" she asked.

"No. You are my guest. It's my job to serve you today," he smoothly replied.

Once he completed the minor cleaning, Antonyo escorted Jasmine to Treecie's beat-up sofa nestled in the basement area designated as the den. When they were comfortably seated, he located the remote control and turned on the television.

"Is there something you want to see on TV, or would you prefer to watch a DVD?" he asked.

"What movies do you have?"

"I need to go upstairs and check in my aunt's room. I'll be right back." Antonyo went to Treecie's room to inquire about her movie collection. "Aunt Treecie, she wants to watch a movie. What should we watch?"

Treecie got up from the bed and went to her closet, where she pulled out a box containing a vast array of movies. She had just the title in mind that would play into her scheme of teaching her nephew to mack a young girl. As she rummaged through the box, she hoped she had not misplaced or loaned out the particular movie she had in mind. She searched the box, thrilled when she was able to locate her prey.

True Romance, written and directed by Quentin Tarantino, who was known for his violent, action-packed thrillers, had just enough sex to stir the youngsters' libidos. Treecie owned the unrated version, which was a little raunchier than the normal R rating shown in movie theaters.

Trina usually forbade Antonyo to watch R-rated movies. She would allow him to see only those that she watched first and deemed not too bad. *True Romance* was one of those on the prohibited list after she had borrowed and viewed Treecie's copy. It was also one that Antonyo was dying to see, simply because it was forbidden. Auntie Treecie was never as strict as his mother. She always treated him as a young man, not a little boy. Almost everything was cool with his aunt.

"Thanks, Auntie. This is the bomb." Antonyo snatched the DVD and bolted for the basement. He was so anxious to see the movie that he nearly forgot Jasmine was down there.

Treecie halted Antonyo's hasty retreat. "Wait, boy. Don't forget what we talked about. That trick gon' probably want to get cozy after watching Clarence and Alabama doing their thing, but don't give in. Not tonight. Just let her kiss you and show you how to do that. Then flip the script on her. Tell her you really like her, but you're not ready to go any further with her because you don't want to rush her."

"But I do really like her, Aunt Treecie," he stated openly and honestly.

"Yeah, okay, whatever. But you still want her to kick out some of that cash. Now, do what I said. Hold off a day or two before you let Jasmine sleep with you."

Tony took in what his aunt said, deciding to follow her lead. He went back to the basement and started the movie.

Just after the first sex scene, Jasmine started massaging Antonyo's thigh. He, however, was totally into the movie. He barely noticed her hand gestures until she actually became a little bolder. Startled, he gave her his full attention. Jasmine smiled, pleased at his reaction, but downplayed her intentions.

"I'm sorry. Did I hurt you?" she asked slyly.

"Uh, no. I kind of liked it," Antonyo replied naïvely.

"Good. I'm really glad to hear that." The two continued to play touchy-feely. She kissed him seductively and he responded in kind. When the kiss ended, Jasmine was impressed.

"Okay, Tony. You can really kiss. It is not that often I find a boy I like to kiss, but you're different."

Antonyo smiled. His young ego swelled by leaps and bounds. He now began to really believe what his aunt had told him about having "it." He also remembered she said to play it cool and not let on that he knew Jasmine was all in to him.

"Thank you, Jasmine. I enjoyed kissing you too," he replied coyly. The two continued to kiss for a few more moments.

Even in his excitement, Antonyo somehow managed to hold on to his composure, remembering that he was supposed to be in control of the situation, not let it control him. Though his mind was thoroughly clouded, he had sufficient enough poise to interject his mack and put his and Treecie's plan into motion.

"Jasmine, hold up. I'm still a virgin," Antonyo announced, then shyly added, "I don't know if I'm ready to have sex yet. But if I were ready, I would definitely want it to be with you. I think you are so special."

Jasmine stared, stunned by Antonyo's words. She took a good look at Antonyo, overwhelmed with the spoken words of her young paramour. Nobody, not even her own mother, had called her special before.

"Wow! Thank you, Tony. That was so sweet. I respect your not wanting to rush your first time, and I am happy that you want it to be with me." She was smiling from ear to ear, cheesing as if Antonyo had proposed marriage.

Antonyo eyed Jasmine in amazement. Aunt Treecie was right. Jasmine ate his words like chocolate.

"Well, sweetie, I think you should get ready to go," Antonyo told Jasmine. "My mother will be here soon to pick me up. Tomorrow her schedule is the same, so maybe you could come to my house. We would be completely alone. Perhaps then I will have more courage and things can go as far as you want them to. I really do want to be with someone as pretty as you." He gave Jasmine one last kiss then escorted her, hand in hand, to the front door.

They walked out the front door just as Trina stepped on the porch. Seeing his mother startled Antonyo. He immediately snatched his hand from Jasmine's and addressed his mom with a kiss as she approached the door.

"Hi, Mama," he said tensely.

Trina received her son's kiss with apprehension. She then started with the questions. "Who is this young lady, Antonyo?"

Jasmine answered for him. "Hello, ma'am. My name is Jasmine. I'm Tony's new girlfriend."

Trina stared at Jasmine like she suddenly turned into an alien creature from another planet. She rolled her eyes away from the female, directing her venomous stare on her child. "Antonyo, you need to tell this . . . young lady that you are too young to have a girlfriend. You might also want to inform her that even if I did let you date at thirteen, she looks to be too old for you."

Again, Trina stared sneeringly at Jasmine. She eyed the girl from head to toe with pure nastiness, then sarcastically added, "Now that *you* have told her all of this, you can say goodbye to your *friend* and make your way back into this house." Trina walked into her sister's house without another word or a backward glance.

Antonyo was thoroughly embarrassed as he tried to apologize for his mother's behavior, hoping she had not ruined his chances with Jasmine. "I am so sorry about the way my mother acted, Jasmine. I had no idea she would behave so mean toward you."

"It's okay, Tony. I'm cool. I just hope you still want to kick it with me. What your mother said doesn't bother me as long as we can still see each other," Jasmine whispered. The last thing she wanted was for Trina to hear what she said, just in case she was eavesdropping.

"Like I said, she will be at work tomorrow, so you can come by after I get out of school. Be there about four o'clock," he replied, careful to keep his own voice down. He leaned in to give Jasmine a peck on the cheek, but decided against it and pulled away just in case his mother was lurking nearby. She totally understood his action and smiled. She left the porch and headed home.

When Antonyo entered the house, his mother and aunt were arguing.

"Why do you constantly let my child come over here and do what he wants? He only brought that fast-tailed girl over here because he knows I would not allow him to have female company in my house," Trina stressed to her sister.

"Girl, give it a rest. Tony is not a baby. What is wrong with him kicking it with females? It's not like they were having sex up in here. I was here with them the whole time," Treecie defended.

"Look, Treecie, how you choose to raise your children is your business, but leave the job of raising my son to me. I do not think his behind is old enough to have a girlfriend. If you can't respect my policy on this, then he won't be allowed to come over here anymore."

"Yeah, okay. Whatever, Trina." Treecie kept her tone flat and agreeable just to end the argument.

Midway through her sister's first sentence, Treecie had tuned her out. She had heard the speech about keeping Antonyo away far too many times. She was sick of listening to it. Because she never wanted Trina to enforce a ban on her nephew coming to her home, Treecie would agree to whatever terms her sister set—then totally ignore them.

Trina took her son and drove the three blocks home, lecturing him all the way about not being allowed to have a girlfriend.

"Boy, you need to be concentrating on your school work only, not worrying about these little fast-tailed heffas. That girl Jasmine looks to be at least sixteen or seventeen, so what does she want with a boy your age? You don't have a job or a dime to your name. Please! Leave these little tramps out here alone."

Antonyo followed his aunt's example of nodding, agreeing, and ignoring, all the while thinking how he couldn't wait until tomorrow so he could finish his plan for Jasmine.

Chapter 3

The phone rang, waking fourteen-year-old Antonyo from his sleep. It was three-thirty in the morning. Unfortunately, Antonyo was sure he was not the only one disturbed by the ringing noise. Trina would be screaming her way to his bedroom any minute.

Antonyo checked the caller ID on his receiver and found the caller had blocked their number. He knew, however, from past experience that it was Jasmine, sweating him. This had been the problem for the past three weeks, ever since Antonyo stopped spending time with her. The girl simply would not go away. As amazing as it sounded, a fourteen-year-old boy was being stalked by a seventeen-year-old psycho.

Antonyo ignored the ringing phone, but his mother did not. He could hear her yelling from her bedroom.

"Who is this calling my house this time of morning?" he heard her scream. He figured from the silence that followed that Jasmine had hung up, as she usually did when his mother answered the phone. But that was definitely not going to be the end of the discussion. He heard Trina stomping down the hall a few moments later.

"Get up, Negro, 'cause I know you ain't 'sleep. You heard the phone ringing just like I did," Trina said as she pushed open her son's bedroom door.

"I don't know who that was, Mama," he replied nonchalantly, acting as if he truly had no clue.

"Boy, don't lie to me. I know who it was, so I know you know who it was. It was that stalking little trick, Jasmine," she screamed. "Look, Antonyo, you got one day to straighten out this mess. I mean it. If I have to change my phone number to get that cow to stop calling here at all hours of the day and night, I'm gon' kick your tail with *almost* every ounce of strength I've got, saving just enough energy to kick hers too. Then you're going to use some of that money the stupid little fool gives you to pay for the phone number exchange."

For just over nine months, Jasmine and Antonyo had been a couple. Initially Trina was against the relationship, but after a month, she gave in, letting her son have his little girlfriend. She saw how her son was maturing in his association with an older girl—or so it seemed—and she liked the growth in him. She was also proud of Jasmine's decision to go back to school, assuming it was a result of her interactions with Antonyo. For the past three weeks, however, Trina wished she had followed her first mind and put a stop to this little courtship in the beginning.

When they initially started seeing each other, the two were inseparable. Jasmine continued to work at McDonald's during the daytime, while Antonyo attended school. After classes and work, the two would meet at Antonyo's house each day when he was done with his homework. Then the couple would leave and walk to his Aunt Treecie's house, spending most of their time together hanging out with her.

On some occasions, usually when Jasmine got paid, they would go to the movies, shopping, or to the arcade, then sneak back to his house to have sex. Antonyo strategically arranged it so the pair was only intimate when Jasmine spent some money, and the poor girl was totally unaware of it. Antonyo had her feeling like the sex was sporadic because he did not simply see her as a sex object, but someone he really cared about. In the months they were together, she purchased clothes, shoes, and video games for him. Treecie had trained him well.

When the fall semester for school began, Antonyo entered his first year of high school, and Jasmine started adult education classes. This meant she had to cut the amount of time she spent with Antonyo, the hours she worked, and the amount of money she had available.

Antonyo's reputation of going with an older girl preceded him to high school. Every female, it seemed, from the freshmen to the seniors, was aware of his involvement with a seventeen-year-old. News of his conquest made just enough of them curious. They wanted to know what was so special about Antonyo. From day one, the girls flocked to him, most under the guise of wanting to just be his friend. The fact that he had grown even more handsome weighed heavily to his advantage as well.

Jasmine found the competition to hold on to her man incredible. Everywhere they went, some hoochie or group of hoochies were either staring at him from across the room or going out of their way to make conversation. Most of them were girls from school; a few were the younger females in the neighborhood.

Antonyo realized that his stock was on the rise, and used his newfound popularity to his advantage. When Jasmine's usual showers of cash became more like a drizzle, he started using his charm to get what he needed from other admirers.

Tianda Davenport, a junior, had no problem whatsoever giving him lunch money, even though he was part of the free lunch program. Monique Mitchell, a fellow freshman, loved helping him with his homework. The sophomore, Kelly Lewis, whose brother, Kelvin, was well known as the school's marijuana supplier, always made sure Antonyo had a little pocket change. Each of these young ladies was aware of his relationship with Jasmine, but they were all subtly bidding to take her place.

Jasmine noticed things with Antonyo were beginning to change. As a result of her new schedule, the amount of time available to spend with Antonyo had decreased. In addition, she noticed that Antonyo had put extra restrictions on their time as well. It soon became apparent to Jasmine that he only wanted to be with her on the days when she received a paycheck.

Jasmine decided to skip her classes one day because she knew Antonyo had a half-day of school. Her intention was to catch up with him at his mother's, then spend the entire day with him, since she was also not scheduled to work that evening.

"Hey, Ms. Trina. Has Tony made it home yet?" Jasmine asked as she arrived at their home and found Antonyo's mother on the porch, retrieving the mail.

"Why would he be here now? You know he doesn't get out of school until two forty-five, girl," Trina replied.

Jasmine quickly realized that Antonyo must have neglected to tell his mom about his shortened school schedule for the day. She tried to hurry and cover before Trina figured out something was going on.

"I'm sorry, Ms. Trina. I just assumed since I had a half-day today at my school, Redford High School did too. I'm going to go on home and help my mama do some housework. I'll catch up with him later," she said, hoping she had convinced Trina that she'd made a mistake.

As she began her retreat from the porch, Trina stopped her in her tracks. Jasmine just knew she had busted on her man.

"Jasmine, come here for a minute."

"Yes, Ms. Trina?" Jasmine said as she turned around apprehensively.

"I just wanted to tell you how proud I am that you decided

to go back to school. A lot of young girls put their relation-ships ahead of their futures. I know because I did it myself. You just make sure you stay in school and finish your educa-tion. It's the best thing you can do for yourself." Trina gave Jasmine a big hug and an inadvertent boost of self-esteem.

"Thanks, Ms. Trina." Jasmine walked away feeling like a million dollars as she headed for Treecie's house, knowing Antonyo must be there. Once she got there, that million-dol-lar feeling quickly depreciated.

The front door to Treecie's house was unlocked as usual. Jasmine walked in and down to the basement where Antonyo always hung out, figuring she would catch him watching an-other movie his mother did not allow him to see. What she actually saw was something else Jasmine was sure Trina would surely not approve of.

"Tony!"

Antonyo and Kelly both jumped from the sofa and reached for their clothing spontaneously and simultaneously.

"What are you doing here, Jasmine?" Antonyo asked while doing his best to put his legs in his pants.

Jasmine never bothered to answer the question her boy-friend asked. She, instead, went after Kelly, who also strug-gled, trying to get into her sweater. While Kelly's head was still lodged beneath her clothing, Jasmine grabbed her in a headlock hold with one arm, and commenced to swinging wildly with the other.

"Why are you here sleeping with my man, trick? You know he's my boyfriend. You should have stayed away from him," Jasmine yelled between the blows she threw at Kelly.

Kelly was caught totally off guard. She fell hard to the hard basement floor while her arms and head were still bound by the cute pink sweater. Jasmine remained all over her, pum-meling, kicking, and shouting.

"Tony, help me!" Kelly screamed as she did her level best to get away from the brutal beating.

"He has helped you to everything you gon' get from him, tramp," Jasmine yelled, continuing to do serious damage to the young female she'd caught with Antonyo.

Antonyo finally found his way into his pants and went to assist Kelly. Treecie came downstairs to witness the melee going on in her basement just as Antonyo was able to sufficiently dress himself. The two of them pulled Jasmine off the screaming, bloody young woman. Antonyo dragged Jasmine until he had her all the way up the stairs and out the front door, while Treecie stayed in the basement to help Kelly.

"Why are you here with her, Tony? Why are you here with her?" Jasmine yelled in her brokenhearted rage.

Antonyo knew there was nothing he could say to Jasmine that would make sense. He decided it was best to just cut the ties and be done with her. He'd actually become tired of dealing with her since the money had stopped flowing like it used to. Between Kelly, Tianda, and Monique, he knew he would get all of his needs met without having to put up with his overly emotional and newly dubbed ex-girlfriend any longer.

"Look, Jasmine, you might as well go home. You and me are finished. I didn't want you to find out this way, but I'm not really feeling you the way I used to, since we don't get to spend as much time together," Antonyo stated emotionlessly.

"Oh! So, what? You're gon' quit me for that little heffa in there? Is that what you're trying to say, Tony? Since I decided to go back to school to better myself, you ain't got time for me no more?" Jasmine was yelling and crying so loudly she could be heard all over the entire block. This was evidenced by the neighbors making appearances on their porches or peeking through their curtains.

"Girl, just go home. It's over between us," Antonyo said casually, never raising his voice.

Treecie was now in the living room, standing at the front door, listening to the conversation between her protégé nephew and his ex. After she helped Kelly get herself together, she sent her out the back door so she would not run into Jasmine and another beat-down. The scene she witnessed on her front porch was better than her daytime soap operas.

"Nooo, Tony. You can't quit me. I love you. You can't quit me. I'll stop going to school and spend more time with you. Please. I'll do whatever you want me to do. Just don't quit me," Jasmine wailed as she tried to wrap her arms around Antonyo for emotional and physical support. All of her bravado had escaped her. She was now a desperate young woman trying to hold on to her man at all cost.

"Now you're just acting stupid, Jasmine. You need to stay in school so they can teach you not to be so dumb. And it really doesn't matter whether you quit or not. It's just over between us. I'm not into you anymore." Again Antonyo spoke with the same cool distance as he grabbed her arms and held Jasmine away from his person.

Jasmine was dumbfounded as she stared at the young boy in front of her. She could not believe he was the same virginal thirteen-year-old she had hooked up with initially. Before her stood a cold, calculating man in the body of fourteen-year-old Antonyo. She became utterly humiliated as she noticed Treecie standing in the doorway, laughing at her.

With a wave of his hand, Antonyo turned to go into the house, dismissing Jasmine as if she were nothing. Jasmine, however, refused to go away so easily. Gone was the sniveling, begging, despondent female; she was replaced by a bitter woman scorned. Her wrath had returned, and she clawed at Antonyo's face with a vengeance. Before he realized what happened, he'd sustained several gashes in his near-perfect skin.

Treecie burst through the door to help her nephew free

himself from the grip of the contemptuous woman. It actually took more effort to get her off of Antonyo than it had to pry her away from Kelly. Jasmine had become untamed and out of control. In her hurt and despair, she meant to make Antonyo pay for every bit of pain he had caused her that day.

By the time the two family members were finally able to get the alley cat away from Antonyo, his face was bleeding terribly. Treecie pushed Jasmine down the four steps that led to her porch, and she landed smack dab on her behind. The fall must have jarred some sense into her. She jumped up immediately and ran away from the house. Unfortunately, this would not be the last they would hear from the distressed girl.

Jasmine resorted to prank phone calls, waiting for Antonyo outside of school, and following him around. Whenever she would see him with either Tianda or Monique, she would attempt to provoke a fight with the young ladies, but Antonyo would somehow always prevent the girls from coming to blows. Jasmine never again started trouble with Kelly. Her brother, Kelvin, paid two girls to jump her after he learned of the whooping she put on his little sister.

That had been three weeks ago. In that time, Jasmine had become a constant nuisance. Antonyo began to worry he would never be free of her bothersome behavior. He also had to deal with his mother constantly on his case because Jasmine repeatedly called the house and hung up on her. Antonyo knew his mother was as good as her word when she said she would kick his and Jasmine's tail if the phone calls did not stop.

As Antonyo prepared to leave for school later that morning, none other than his friendly neighborhood stalker met him on his front porch.

"You know what, Tony? I decided that I am going to finally leave you alone. I ain't even here to start no mess with you," Jasmine announced.

Trina heard Jasmine's voice outside her door and decided she was going to give little Ms. Telephone Woman a piece of her mind. As she approached the front door, she stopped at hearing Jasmine's next words.

"All I want from you is the money, clothes, shoes, and games I gave you, and you won't ever have to worry about seeing me again," Jasmine stated.

"Girl, get away from me. I ain't giving you nothing. You want it back? Take me to Judge Joe Brown and sue me for it." Antonyo laughed at his own joke as he walked past Jasmine. Her next words startled both him and his mother.

"Oh! I will do better than sue you. I will have my brother and his boys beat the dog stew out of you. Watching you get your butt kicked will be all the compensation I need. So what you gon' do, punk? You gon' pay me or take a beat-down?"

After hearing Jasmine threaten her son, Trina came through the door in a heartbeat. "Listen here, little girl! I'm gon' say this to you one time and one time only. If anything happens to my son, I'm coming looking for you," Trina shouted.

Jasmine stood shocked with her mouth hanging open. She was not prepared for a verbal confrontation with Antonyo's mother, especially after hearing the woman give her such high praises just a few weeks ago. However, she was also not prepared to back off easily.

"Don't come out here yelling at me, threatening me, Ms. Trina. You need to be talking to your son. Tell him he best be finding a way to pay me my money. I ain't scared of you or him," Jasmine replied boldly with both hands on her hips, her neck swaying.

Trina was fed up with all of this Jasmine business. She wanted to smack the crap out of her right then and there. Instead, she used all of her resources to remain as calm as possible. Getting right in Jasmine's face, she reiterated her words. "I don't give a hot ham sandwich who you are or are not afraid of. You heard what I said. As a matter of fact, if *you* come near my son again, you're going to have problems with me. And trust me when I say you don't want those kinds of problems in your life." Trina stared at Jasmine, daring the young woman with her eyes to utter another sound.

Jasmine could read the rage in Trina's face. She decided it was best to leave the matter with Antonyo for a time when his mother was not around. Silently she turned and left the porch.

"Antonyo, come in the house now," Trina yelled after Jasmine retreated.

The second her son entered the house and closed the door, Trina gave him a quick shot to his mouth with her fist. She took out her frustrations with Jasmine on Antonyo using one punch.

"I told you I was going to kick your tail if I had to deal with that girl, didn't I?" Trina spat.

Antonyo knew better than to answer the question, being that it was rhetorical. He just held his stinging jaw and listened to his mother rant.

"I'm telling you right here and now, Antonyo, you better stop running around thinking you can just play with these girls and use them to get what you want. I am not going to have this kind of mess around my house every time I turn around. All these knuckleheaded girls that call here for you think you really care about them. Jasmine is not the only crazy girl in this world. Mark my words; if you keep treating females the way you do, it is going to come back and haunt you." Trina picked up a book of daily devotions she'd begun reading about a month ago, and flipped back a few pages. "I just read about this same principle in this book. The scripture says in Galatians 6:7-8, 'Do not be deceived: God cannot be mocked.

A man reaps what he sows. The one who sows to please his sinful nature, from that nature will reap destruction; the one who sows to please the Spirit, from the Spirit will reap eternal life.' So you see? You better get it together, Antonyo, because sooner or later you are going to have to pay for your behavior if you don't turn it around. Now get out of my house and go to school."

As Antonyo walked to school, he thought about what his mother said, concentrating hard on her words. Then he remembered the actions of the other three girls he kept company with. Neither Tianda, Kelly, nor Monique had a problem with him on any level. Each realized that he was not dating either one of them exclusively. They were all content to get whatever time he allowed them to have. He then reconciled that his mother was old fashioned and unaware of what she was talking about. From now on, he would make sure to keep his business away from her to avoid having to hear her preach to him.

After school that day, Antonyo planned to stop by Treecie's house before going home. During lunch, Kelly had informed him that she purchased a brand new pair of Timberland boots for him and she wanted to bring them by. Normally he would have Kelly over to his home, but since his mom was currently tripping, he figured he needed to give her time to cool down. He and Kelly agreed, instead, to meet at his aunt's.

Antonyo told Kelly to meet him at 4:30 P.M., giving himself plenty of time to call Monique and get assistance with his English homework since it was now only 3:15. However, as he approached the house, he found Jasmine sitting on the porch, presumably waiting on him. Dreading having to deal with her, his first thought was to turn around before she noticed him. The thought of missing out on his new boots quickly changed his mind. He decided it was best that he just ignore her and go straight into the house.

Antonyo walked to the steps and tried to continue up without uttering a word to the stalking lunatic.

"I know you don't think you gon' walk in that house and act like you don't see me. I ain't standing for that kind of disrespect, boy." Both she and her voice rose as she spoke the last sentence.

This was the first time since he'd started seeing Jasmine that she made reference to him being younger and/or less mature than her. Her calling him "boy" stung his ego just a bit. He had to retaliate.

"Oh, I'm a boy now? I guess that would make me kind of like your son, since you were taking such good care of me, huh, trick?"

"Screw you, Tony!"

"You did that too, so I guess that would make you some kind of child molester or statutory rapist also, right?"

Antonyo thought his retorts to be hysterical. He responded by laughing in her face. Jasmine thought his reply to be hurtful. She responded by hurting him the only way she knew how. She slapped the crap out of him. Trina had instilled in Antonyo from the time he was a small boy to never hit a woman, even in self-defense. Heeding his mother's teaching, Antonyo just stood there stunned, holding his stinging cheek.

"Laugh at that, punk!" Jasmine screamed.

Treecie heard the commotion from inside the house and came to investigate.

"I know you ain't bring your raggedy tail over to my house after you had the nerve to threaten my nephew and disrespect my sister." Trina had called Treecie that morning after her fight with Jasmine and Antonyo to give her the 411.

"Treecie, your nephew and your sister disrespected me.

Antonyo thought he could get away with using me, and your sister came all out of pocket and threatened me. So how you gon' take their side?"

"Stupid girl, please! That's my blood you messing with. You just some hoochie my nephew done dissed and dismissed. You best be up and away from my house now before I lodge my foot in the crack of your behind."

For the second time in the same day, Jasmine had been outnumbered in her attempts to convince and strong-arm Antonyo into re-entering her life. Her earlier threats were simply a weak effort to mask that very fact. She actually had not spoken to any guys about having him beaten up. She just wanted to be his girlfriend again. Jasmine figured she could scare him back into their previous relationship.

Now, even with her limited education, she could see that Antonyo had lost all respect for her. Without respect, he could never actually love her. He had everyone in his corner and she stood all alone. She felt more unworthy at that very moment than any time in her entire life. What was the point of finishing school and getting a decent education when she was such a pathetic person?

Jasmine stared at Treecie and Antonyo one final time, then silently turned tail and left the house. Antonyo, in his arrogant and uncaring manner, called after the defeated girl with a final barb.

"Ain't nothing in this life free, baby. You got to pay to play. The minute you started coming up short with the money, you were dismissed. I just wanted to wait until I had you properly replaced before I gave you the official boot," he said to her.

And that was the way the burgeoning hard-hearted lady's man ended his first official entry into the world of being a heartbreaker. Suddenly, however, the words his mother read from her book this morning surfaced in his mind.

Chapter 4

Trina sat straight up in bed, startled by a surreal dream. While the dream was strange in nature, it was far from being unpleasant. As a matter of fact, as she lay back down and stared at the ceiling, processing as much of her night vision as she could remember, Trina actually felt something akin to peace.

It had been several years since Trina began sporadically reading the worn Bible given to her by her former co-worker. She had finished the entire book of Proverbs and read all of the Psalms as Ms. Louise suggested. She would also read from different sections on her own, and she would sometimes go home and study from the sections referenced in the few services she attended while visiting various churches. Over the years, she had purchased several daily devotional books and other sources of scripture reading. She was working diligently on engraving God's Word in her heart.

Last night's dream brought back to memory the sermon she heard this past Sunday while visiting the church of a co-worker. Pastor Mitchell of The New Trinity Praise, Worship & Learning Center preached on letting go of the past in order to move forward and into the things God has in store. He spoke about each person being born with a purpose, distinctly created for that person by God. Pastor Mitchell's referenced text came from Jeremiah 29:11-14 and Philippians 3:13-14.

In her dream last night, Trina recalled Pastor Mitchell's especially pretty wife speaking with her. Mrs. Mitchell told her that God specifically had a purpose for her life, but in order to walk in the fullness of life, she had to let go of the mistakes she had made in her past. She said that she had to put behind her the hurt she had experienced with the failed relationships with Antonyo's father and other men she had been involved with over the years. She had to release the distress of growing up poor without the proper supervision of her own parents.

"Trina, when you decided to get off welfare, get your G.E.D., and find better employment to support yourself and your son, that was the God in you rising up to take hold of a part of the abundant life that Jesus came in order for each of us to have. As long as you keep your hand in the hand of God, your latter days will be greater than your former," Mrs. Mitchell said in a soft, maternal tone.

During her dream, Trina wondered how Mrs. Mitchell had known all those things about her, since she had never met the woman before that time in Sunday service. But now that she was fully awake, Trina realized that her sleep had been invaded by an angel of God, the One who knew everything about her.

Now a senior in high school, seventeen-year-old Antonyo was more the ladies' man than ever. He was even more handsome, more charming, more persuasive, more experienced and . . . more promiscuous. He had never had a job, yet he owned a decent car, purchased with money he received from various girls at one time or another.

For the past three years, he had been in and out of more flings and relationships than some men twice his age. Now, as a result of his dating status, he faced what some would call a serious issue; however, Antonyo simply viewed it as a minor annoyance.

The senior prom was two weeks away, and he was currently involved with three different females, leaving him with the dilemma of choosing only one of these girls to be his prom date. Two of the girls were his schoolmates at Redford High School. The other he knew through his cousin, Taraija.

Brittany was a junior, and Taylor was a senior. Both girls realized they were involved with the same guy, and neither was seemingly bothered by it. Yet, they refused to attend the prom with him as a trio.

Kayla, Taraija's best friend, was a sophomore, and the two girls attended Mackenzie High school together. Taraija and Kayla met about a year ago, when Kayla moved next door to Taraija and her dad. Antonyo met Kayla while visiting his cousin.

Taraija and Antonyo had always been the closest of the four first cousins. When Aunt Treecie lost custody of his cousin and she moved away from the neighborhood, Antonyo was crushed. He made it his business, though, to visit Taraija as often as possible. Antonyo saw his cousin more often than her own mother.

Of the three young women currently keeping company with Antonyo, he had to admit he liked Kayla most. They had been going together for five months. While the other two girls were aware of each other, neither of them knew about Kayla, nor she about them. Kayla assumed that Antonyo belonged to her alone. The fifteen-year-old beauty was totally captivated by the smooth antics of her best friend's cousin, so much so that she gave him her virginity three months after they started dating.

Being that Taraija and Kayla were best friends, Antonyo also neglected to let his cousin know that he was seeing anyone other than her girl. The two usually never kept secrets, but Antonyo figured that under the circumstances, his duplicity would hurt his cousin as well as Kayla.

Antonyo sat in the kitchen with his mother having breakfast while pondering his small prom date quandary. Trina could see the stress in her son's face and questioned its existence.

"What's bugging you, Antonyo?" Trina asked.

"Nothing much, Mama. I'm just trying to decide on who to take to my senior prom. Not anything for you to worry about."

Antonyo knew his mother had a problem with his playboy-style behavior. She had become increasingly more vocal in expressing her displeasure since she started going to church occasionally. Therefore, he regretted telling her his problem the moment it left his mouth. The last thing he needed was to hear one of her sermons. However, Trina's response surprised him.

"Well, which one of your *four hundred* girlfriends do you like the best?" she asked sarcastically.

"Ha-ha, Mama. There are actually only three to choose from." Antonyo made a guttural sound then shook his head. Again he immediately hated that he had opened his mouth.

Trina laughed at her son. She knew why he was reacting this way, but she decided she would genuinely try to give him some helpful advice with his predicament.

"Okay, baby. Like I said before, which one of these *lovely* young ladies do you like best?" she asked sarcastically, and they both shared a laugh.

"I like Kayla the best. She's Taraija's best friend. She's also only fifteen and attends a different school." He almost told his mother that she didn't have a job, so she could not help him pay for anything, but he stopped himself in time this go-round. "Taylor is a senior and we have two classes together. Brittany is a junior who I share no classes with, but she also attends Redford."

"Boy, you mean to tell me that Taylor and Brittany *both* go to school with you?"

Antonyo gave his mother a lopsided glance. He was about to start begging her not to harass him, but Trina relinquished first.

She threw her hands in the air and said, "I'm sorry. I'm not going to criticize. I just want to help."

Antonyo looked at his mom skeptically, but decided to give her a chance. "Thanks, Ma."

"Here's my advice: I say take Taylor. She's a senior, and this will probably be her last opportunity to go the prom. Brittany and Kayla will have other chances. They probably won't be going with *you*, since I have yet to meet a girl that has lasted more than three months, but there will be other chances for them." Trina tried to stay away from the sarcasm, but she just couldn't help herself.

Antonyo ignored his mother's mockery, but not her advice. He decided she was right. He would take Taylor to the prom. Besides, she had the most money anyway.

Three days before the senior prom, Antonyo visited Kayla at her home. The two of them were in the basement watching music videos on television and doing some heavy duty petting in between songs.

Kayla, having been a virgin when she and Antonyo started having sex, was still pretty inexperienced. She often found it hard to respond to his advances because she was always so nervous about getting pregnant. The two of them never discussed birth control. Yet, she loved Antonyo. She wanted to please him, so she went along with his program each and every time he wanted her. Kayla knew there were plenty of other girls who would be more than willing to do whatever it took to get their hands on Antonyo.

Without warning, Taraija came running into the basement to hang out with Kayla and her favorite cousin, interrupting their current make-out session and preventing Kayla from having to go all the way with Antonyo this time.

The moment Antonyo heard her at the top of the stairs, he stopped his advances on Kayla and did his best to give the appearance that they were only watching television.

"Hey, lovebirds," Taraija sang as she sat on the sofa next to the couple.

Kayla, grateful for the interruption, gave her friend a welcome reply. "Hey, best girlfriend."

Antonyo simply grunted his response. He was unappreciative of the intrusion.

"So, girl, why didn't you let me help you pick out your dress for the prom? I can't believe you haven't said a word about going," Taraija said as she slapped Kayla's thigh in mock anger.

What in the heck did Taraija just say? Antonyo thought as he nearly passed out on the sofa after hearing his cousin's question. How in the world did she find out about him attending the prom? He figured he would wait to hear more of the conversation between the two females before he offered any explanations or excuses.

"What are you talking about, Tee? I'm not going to the prom, and neither is Antonyo. He got in trouble for cussing out his English teacher. The principal told him the prom was off limits as part of his discipline," Kayla explained.

"But I just got off the phone with my brother Darnell. He said that he and Antonyo were sharing a limousine. My mother and Aunt Trina are paying for it."

Sweat began to pour profusely from Antonyo's armpits. He knew he had to come up with a believable lie to cover what Taraija told Kayla, and he had to do it quick. Both women were probably about to get very upset with him.

"What is she talking about, Tony?" Kayla asked. She looked both confused and saddened by the information she just learned.

"Darnell was probably so caught up in bragging about the limo to Tee, he forgot I wouldn't be able to go. He is right, though. My mother is still going to help Aunt Treecie pay for the car. She didn't want him to miss out just because I messed up."

Antonyo knew the lie was weak, but he was counting on Kayla to be weaker. Up until now, she had believed whatever he told her, no matter how stupid it sounded.

"See, girl. You know I would not have been preparing for my first prom without your help," Kayla replied without the least bit of doubt in her voice. Antonyo released the breath he had been holding since he uttered his last syllable.

Taraija was not as easily fooled as her love-struck friend, however. She had known her cousin all of her life, and they were very close. She knew he was playing Kayla, and she was not happy about it in the least. Taraija, being well aware of her cousin's doggish behavior, stupidly believed Antonyo when he told her that he was only dating her girl, and his lie made her angry. Taraija also felt badly for her friend because she knew Kayla had given her all to him.

Antonyo knew his cousin as well as she knew him, and right now he was totally alert to Taraija's disappointment. He sat for a second debating whether or not he should tell Tee the truth and swear her to secrecy, or keep up his current pretense. It only took him a moment to decide that he would leave things the way they were and just hope that his cousin's loyalty would lie with her blood.

After having dodged the prom date bullet, Antonyo needed to get away from these two females, so he decided to make an excuse and leave. His next move would be to head over to

Brittany's house. She was never too busy for him, and she had more experience than Kayla. He just happened to like Kayla more. Antonyo sensed that his sentimental side was becoming a hazard to his Mack Daddy lifestyle, but what could he do? Sometimes even the best of pimps got caught off guard momentarily.

"Kay, I'm going home now. It's getting close to finals, and I really need to get caught up on some English work. Ever since me and Mr. Flannery got into it, I've been behind in his class." Antonyo leaned over to give Kayla a good-bye kiss once he stood up from the sofa. Turning toward his cousin, he offered her a kiss on the cheek as well.

Taraija gently moved away, and Antonyo's kissed barely caught her on the ear. She didn't want Kayla to notice her action and question her about it, so she was subtle, but the last thing she wanted was a kiss from Antonyo. Still furious at him for cheating on Kayla, she vowed she would somehow get back at him.

Antonyo again noticed his cousin's attitude, and prayed she would not dime him out. Again, his mother's voice rang in his head: *You reap what you sow, Antonyo,* he heard her say. Just as quickly, his mind countered with, *That is just old-fashioned thinking. You cousin has got your back.* He left the basement confident that she would not tell, and headed over to Brittany's for a little fun in the back seat of his car.

Taraija started hatching her plan the moment she heard the side door close.

Chapter 5

That evening after Antonyo and Brittany were done with their little romp, they relaxed in the back seat of his car, still sitting at the park. Antonyo decided now was as good a time as any to tell Brittany he was taking Taylor to the prom and explain his reasoning behind his decision. He knew it would not be too much of a problem, but he wanted to be gentle.

"Brittany, baby, I have something I want to tell you. I know you are going to be a little upset, but I want to be honest with you."

Brittany snuggled closer to Antonyo and braced herself for what she was about to hear. The only thing he could say that would really bother her was that he no longer wanted to see her. She hoped that was not the news.

Holding her breath, Brittany asked, "What is it, Tony?"

"I've decided to take Taylor to the prom," he announced. He then went on to explain to her the logic as his mother had explained it to him.

"So you see, I will take you to your prom next year. I promise," he finished.

Brittany was so relieved. While she truly did want to go to the prom with him this year, she was cool with him taking Taylor. His promise to take her next year meant that he would be with her for at least another whole year. The prospect of him being a part of her life throughout the duration of her senior year was wonderful to her.

"I understand, Antonyo, and I don't mind. Taylor is cool people. I'd even like to come and get a few pictures of you two before you leave, if that's all right with you."

"That's cool with me. You can meet us at my mother's house. After I pick her up in the limo and we take pictures at her mother's house, Taylor and I will go back there to do the picture thing."

Antonyo was happy that there was absolutely no drama with Brittany. With her and Taylor, he could be completely honest because they were both content simply to have a part of him, as opposed to having none of him at all.

He just wished things were as simple with Kayla. The situation with her was difficult because she offered so much when she gave him her virginity, thus expecting much in return. Antonyo respected Kayla. He prized her innocence and naïve nature. It was that part of her that touched his heart; yet it was also the same part he took advantage of. He often found himself wrestling with conflict and guilt after spending quality time in Kayla's presence. It was like sitting between the white-clothed angel with a halo and the red-covered devil with the pitchfork.

After dropping Brittany off, Antonyo drove home, reflecting on words that were a part of his aunt's lessons: *Love has no place in the life of a mack. A pimp, on the other hand, has to sometimes show love in an effort to keep his whore, because he needs her. A mack, however, can keep his heart guarded at all times, because he should never deal with a female that is not disposable. A little interest is all the energy a true mack should ever have to exert.*

Was Kayla disposable? If so, why did he feel the need to lie to her?

***

"Hey, son! How you doing?" Sheldon asked his oldest child over the phone.

Antonyo and Sheldon were more like acquaintances than father and son. Sheldon only showed up sporadically. Whenever he did make an appearance, he always made a big deal about the few dollars that the state garnished from his paycheck for child support. Complaining about money he paid seemed more important than actually spending time with his son; therefore, Antonyo had come to dread the encounters.

"What up, Dad?" he responded unenthusiastically. He only called Sheldon Dad because his mother insisted that Antonyo always respect him.

"So, my boy is going to the prom. That's so cool. I bought you a little gift. I want to bring it over tonight before you leave, if that's all right with you."

Antonyo knew not to expect much of anything, if Sheldon even bothered to show up at all, but he agreed. "Sure. Everybody will be meeting here around seven to take pictures and stuff. You can come by then."

"Good deal. I guess I'll see you then."

Antonyo recognized *guess* was more than likely the operative word. The moment he hung up the phone, it rang again. "Hello," he answered.

"Tony, dude! What time are we supposed to hook up? Which girl are we picking up first?" Darnell's voice raised an octave from his excitement over the prom and the limousine. Antonyo found his cousin's excitement both amusing and aggravating.

"The limo will come here first; then we will come and get you. We can figure out which female to pick up from there. Calm down, cousin."

"Hold on a minute, Tony. The other line is ringing." Darnell clicked over. When he came back to the line, Antonyo overheard him yelling a message for Aunt Treecie. "Ma, Taraija said her daddy will drop them off at five."

"Taraija's coming to spend the weekend over there?" Antonyo asked with a little apprehension. For some reason, the thought of his cousin being there this weekend made him somewhat uncomfortable.

"Yeah. She'll be here later this afternoon. She wanted to see her big brother off to the prom."

Something was up. Antonyo could feel it deep down in his bones, but could not exactly pinpoint why his senses were on full alert. He became agitated trying to figure out what Taraija was up to. "Dang!"

"What's wrong, man?" a confused Darnell asked his cousin.

"Nothing. I just banged my toe," Antonyo lied. "I've got some things I need to finish around here, so I'll see you later, Darnell." He hung up abruptly before his cousin could say anything else.

Antonyo sat on his bed, thinking about why he felt so uneasy. After sitting for only a few minutes, he realized it made perfect sense that Taraija would come over this weekend. The prom was a big event for her brother. He decided to let go of his angst and finish getting ready for his prom.

Just as Antonyo and Trina were putting the final touches on his hair and tuxedo, mother and son heard a knock at the front door. Trina left the bedroom to investigate.

"Antonyo, your father is here," she yelled to him after a few moments.

Antonyo was somewhat stunned. His dad had actually come through as he said he would. Antonyo joined his parents in the living room and found his father shamelessly flirting with his mother, while Trina dissed him like a snaggle-tooth orangutan.

"Thank God my rap is not as weak as his," Antonyo mumbled as he approached his parents.

"Did you say something, Antonyo?" Trina asked.

"No, Ma," he replied then looked to his father. "What up, Dad?"

"Hey, son! I brought this for you." Sheldon handed Antonyo a gold-colored gift bag.

Antonyo, surprised, took the bag from his father's outstretched hand. He could not remember the last time Sheldon had given him anything. He opened the bag and removed a nicely wrapped box. Inside the box was a stylish new watch.

Both Antonyo and Trina stood mesmerized, looking back and forth between each other and the gift he held in his hand. Each was impressed by the watch, but more intrigued by the gesture itself.

"Well, what do you think? Do you like it?"

Not wanting to let his father know how awed he was by the watch, Antonyo opted to downplay his emotions and gave only a minimal response.

"It's cool, Dad. Thanks."

"Cool!" Sheldon repeated.

Trina could read her son like a book. She knew he was pleased with the gift and the giver.

"Dad, my graduation is in two weeks. I want you to promise you'll be there. I'll call you later in the week to give you the details."

"I promise. I wouldn't miss it for the world."

Antonyo smiled at his father. As hard as he was trying not to let Sheldon's appearance and gift get his hopes up, he found himself eager over the possibility that the two could begin to build a closer relationship.

When the limousine arrived, Sheldon and Trina stood outside and took a couple of pictures of their son. They did not want to waste too much film because he and his cousin were due back to the house with their dates before they actually left for the event.

"You'll be here when I get back. Right, Dad?" Antonyo asked.

"I sure will. I've got a quick errand to run, then I'll come right back," Sheldon said. Antonyo again smiled at his father and rode off in the limo, believing his every word.

The limo went to pick up Darnell then headed to get Darnell's date, Ebony. As they pulled away from Aunt Treecie's, Antonyo inquired about Taraija's whereabouts. "D, where is Taraija? I thought you said she was spending the weekend."

"She went to visit an old friend in the neighborhood. She said she would catch up with us at your house once we got back there," Darnell answered.

At Ebony's house, they took a few pictures then headed over to pick up Taylor, where the flashbulbs were again in full effect. Finally they made their way back to Trina's house.

Treecie and Trina greeted the limo and helped the two couples out of the car. Antonyo's mother's pulled her son aside to whisper something in his ear. "Antonyo, Brittany is in my house. She swore that you said it was okay for her to come over here and take pictures. Is that true? If it's not, I'm going in there and smack the taste out of her mouth for lying."

"It's cool, Ma. I told her she could come over," Antonyo assured his mother, who looked at him with veiled contempt.

Brittany came from inside the house, first greeting Taylor, complimenting her on how wonderful she looked, and then acknowledging the rest of the prom party. Trina and Treecie stood watching with different emotions on how Antonyo could entertain both women at the same time and get away with it. Trina was afraid for her only child and how his behavior was going to affect his adult life. Treecie was inspired by her protégé and how much better he was at macking than she thought he would ever be.

"My nephew is one bad li'l Negro," Treecie professed.

"I'm glad you are so proud of how he is paving his road to hell," Trina replied sarcastically. Treecie, in an effort to avoid a sermon, kept her mouth closed. She simply rolled her eyes at her sister.

Antonyo looked around the yard in search of his dad as everyone milled about. He then noticed his car was not there.

"Mama, where's Dad? Did he come back yet?"

"No, not yet, Antonyo. He'll probably be here any minute." Trina did not have the heart to tell her son that his father was more than likely going to be a no-show. Sheldon was Sheldon. Nothing other than God could change him. She had hoped Antonyo would have come to understand that by now, but her son obviously still craved his father's love and attention.

Antonyo trotted off to get in the pictures. Every few seconds, Trina would catch him glancing up and down the street, knowing he was looking for Sheldon. Her heart broke for him.

During one of the photos Trina took of Antonyo and Taylor, she again caught him searching the block for Sheldon. Suddenly, his eyes got big and he looked as if he were going to faint. Trina looked in the direction of her son's focus, hoping to see Sheldon coming down the block; however, she only saw her niece, Taraija, walking alongside another young girl. Why would seeing his cousin cause him such shock?

Antonyo could not believe his eyes. There came Taraija with a big ole grin on her face, while Kayla walked next to her with an even bigger scowl on hers. How could Taraija do this to him? How could she betray him like this? How was he going to explain this mess?

As if reading his mind, Kayla asked, "Tony, what are you doing? I thought you were not going to the prom. What lie are you going to tell me now?" She now stood directly in Antonyo's face, her arms folded across her chest, with her lips poked out two miles in front of her.

Antonyo was speechless. Not one word left his lips, no matter how hard he tried to speak.

Taylor stepped between the two, alleviating the closeness of Antonyo and Kayla. She was the first to break the silence. "Look, little girl, it's obvious that you're another one of Antonyo's playmates, and now you have an attitude because he's taking me to the prom. But let this be known: tonight Antonyo is *my* man. He is going to the prom with me, so back up."

"AARGHHHHH!" Whack! Kayla let out a loud howl, and then punched Taylor in the face with all her might.

Everything after that happened very quickly. Taylor grabbed Kayla, and the two began an all out fistfight. Taylor was a couple of years older, three inches taller, and about ten pounds heavier than Kayla, and using all of that to her advantage . . . long gown, high heels, and all. Kayla was definitely losing this battle.

Taraija saw how badly her best friend was being defeated and jumped in to help Kayla. She grabbed one of Taylor's discarded shoes and began pummeling her in the head with the thick heel. Darnell saw his little sister get in the scuffle, so he stepped in to grab her away. Before her brother could get to her, though, Taraija caught a solid blow to the chin.

Seeing her child get hit sent Treecie into the brawl; however, instead of acting like a grown-up and trying to pry the fighting girls apart, she, too, joined in on the beat-down against Taylor.

Trina, being the only obvious adult-minded person present, tried her best to bring control to the disaster in her front yard.

She screamed, yelled, and did her best to grab a swinging arm in an effort to break up the fight, but there were too many hands, feet, and shoes flying for her to gain any momentum.

Antonyo and Ebony stood watching the fiasco while Brittany positioned herself so she could photograph the whole thing. Antonyo was too spellbound to move, and Ebony wanted no part of any of it, since it had nothing to do with her.

Antonyo finally broke his trance when he heard his mother yell, "Antonyo Ian Demonté Sims, get your butt over here and help me break up this mess."

By the time it was all said and done, a badly beaten Kayla was seated on the front porch with Taraija, who only had a bloody lip. Taylor, who had taken the worst beating, was sitting in the limo, being tended to by the driver while awaiting her mother's arrival.

Trina, Treecie, Antonyo, and Darnell were talking to the police, who had been called by Ebony. She and Brittany were now gone because Ebony's mother had already picked up both girls and left. The police left, only warning the adults to control their children. No one made it to the prom.

Antonyo went to the limo just as Taylor's mom arrived. He wanted to apologize for everything. "Taylor, before you go—" he began, but was unable to finish.

"Antonyo, get away from me before I kick you. Don't ever speak to me again. When you see me in school, pretend like you don't know me." She then got in the car with her mother and they drove away.

Antonyo went to join Kayla and Taraija on the porch, but he had to bypass his mom first. She was still standing on the sidewalk waiting for him. She grabbed his arm as he tried to pass her.

"Antonyo, I am sick and tired of this crap. Here I am all scratched up because of your wannabe mack-daddy drama.

This is the final time I am going to tell you not to bring it to my house again."

"Yes, Mama," Antonyo replied as his mother and aunt retreated to the house. He then went to try to talk with Kayla.

As soon as he approached, both Kayla and Taraija started yelling at him.

"I can't believe you lied to me, Tony. Why did you do that?" Kayla screamed through her tears.

"You ain't nothing but a punk, Tony," Taraija added.

Treecie overheard Taraija's intervention and instructed her to come into the house and stay out of their business.

"I'm sorry I lied to you, Kayla. I had a perfectly good reason for taking Taylor to the prom, and I should have simply explained it to you." He gave her a doctored-up version of the spiel that his mother's advice produced, minus the inclusion of the fact that he had been dating Taylor and Brittany. "Taylor is just a good friend and classmate, and she had no one to take her to the prom. Since this is her last year of high school, I wanted to do her this favor. I lied to you because I just didn't want to lose you, baby." Without even realizing it, he was back in mack mode.

"I'm glad to hear that, because I found out I was pregnant yesterday." Her tears had momentarily stopped, but the moment she shared her news, she began bawling again.

Shock was barely an adequate enough word to describe Antonyo's state after Kayla's announcement. He became sick to his stomach, nearly throwing up on the front porch. This could not be happening to him. He had always been so careful not to get anybody pregnant. He wore condoms for protection against STDs; killing the chance of fatherhood was a bonus as a result. Kayla, however, was the first virgin he had been with. Since he didn't have to worry about disease, he never even thought about birth control.

Trina appeared in the doorway just as Kayla made her declaration. She became ill as well. Here was her son, the cause of World War III breaking out on her lawn and everybody missing the prom. He was only two weeks from his high school graduation, and now some fast-tailed heffa was sitting on her porch, telling him she was pregnant.

"How far along are you, little girl?" Trina stepped on the porch, startling both kids.

Antonyo really wanted to puke now that he knew his mother had overheard Kayla. He just knew he surely would be evicted before the night was over.

"I'm seven weeks pregnant, ma'am," Kayla replied.

"Does your mother know you are pregnant?" Trina asked.

"Yes, ma'am. She took me to the clinic yesterday."

"Do you plan on keeping this baby?"

"My mother said she doesn't want me to keep it, but she's not giving me any money for an abortion because I shouldn't have been so stupid. She said I have to give it up for adoption."

"Well, I guess today is your lucky day. I'll pay for the abortion. Antonyo, that will be your graduation present, so don't ask me for anything else." Trina retreated into the house and slammed the door.

Ten days later, Kayla aborted the pregnancy. Two days following the termination, Antonyo graduated from Redford High School.

Sheldon was a no-show.

Chapter 6

The day started out like every other day had since Antonyo received his high school diploma one month ago: He and his mother argued about him not having a job.

Antonyo wanted to chill before he started the fall semester in community college. Trina debated that thirty days was a long enough vacation for her playboy son. If he had time and ingenuity enough to juggle his mini harem, he could apply some of that effort toward earning a living. She felt he should now help out with the tasks of running the household. Antonyo was an eighteen-year-old man now, and it was time for him to learn some responsibility. The two stood in the kitchen, feuding as they had been for the past few weeks.

"Antonyo, I am sick and tired of supporting you while you run around trying to sleep with every little thing in a skirt. If you want to continue to stay here, you have to get a job and help pay the bills."

"Mama, you act like you have to take care of me. What do you mean, support me? I don't ask you for anything."

"Oh! So I guess the rent and utilities on this house get paid by the bill fairy. The food that you eat enters the refrigerator through osmosis."

"You would have to pay the bills and feed yourself even if I didn't live here, Ma."

Trina fell into a chair and buried her head in her arm on the kitchen table. Exasperated with her only child, she took deep breaths to calm herself, in an effort to keep from pounding him upside his thick skull. She then began to pray. She asked God to give her patience and to restore to her some peace. After a few moments of feeling no peace, she prayed that when she again lifted her head, Antonyo would be gone, because she was truly tired of talking to him. But alas, when she reopened her eyes, he was still there. She assumed God wanted her to handle this with her son.

Antonyo waited for his mother to dismiss him before he left the room. He assumed she was praying, something she had been doing a lot of lately. Out of respect, he courteously waited for her to finish.

"You just don't get it, do you, son? I am trying to teach you to be a man, Antonyo. You're right; I don't need you to help me take care of myself. I just want you to learn how to start taking care of yourself."

"Ma, I'm doing just fine, but if you want me to start pulling my own weight around here, cool. Come up with a fair amount and I'll pay it."

Of course he was talking about giving her money that he scammed out of some or all of his female friends. That, however, was not going to teach him responsibility. Trina wanted her son to stop using and abusing the young women he dated, but she was simply not getting through to him again today.

"Fine, Antonyo! I want you to give me two hundred and fifty dollars a month. Now, get out of my face."

Antonyo nodded his head in agreement. He left the house without a worry as to how he would handle his new fiduciary responsibility. Between India, Ashley, and Bianca, covering it would be absolutely no problem.

Since the night of the prom, Taylor had remained true to her word and had not spoken to him ever again. Brittany decided Antonyo was not worth all the drama he caused, and cut ties with him as well. After his mom bailed him out and gave Kayla money to terminate her pregnancy, he decided he wanted nothing else to do with her. He just wished his mom could have forgotten about Kayla as easily as he did. Trina ragged on him for more than two weeks about putting her in such an awful position. She yelled and screamed at him, vowing to never do anything like that again. She continually told him about how guilty she felt for betraying God by paying for the abortion. He couldn't understand why she took it out on him. Though he was grateful to not have to deal with becoming a father, he never asked her to give Kayla a dime.

For the life of him, Antonyo could not comprehend his mother's aversion to his lifestyle. Since he'd turned sixteen, he never had to ask her for anything other than the obvious food and shelter. If the females he dealt with did not have a problem sleeping with him and giving him money, each knowing he was not seeing any of them exclusively, then why should she? In his opinion, Trina acted as if she believed he beat these girls into submission. In reality, however, he had never hit a female in his life.

If his mother thought that he was going to settle down and do the straight monogamous commitment thing with any one female, she had another think coming. It mattered not that she kept quoting scripture and verse to him about disrespect, fornication, arrogance, and greed. He was having entirely too much fun in mack-daddy mode. Why settle for one when he could get away with having them all?

Two weeks after his mother gave him the duty of paying room and board, Antonyo handed her his first payment. And like clockwork, he paid her on time for the next three months. While Trina accepted the money from her son, she was still appalled that he had learned no real life lessons. Antonyo had not earned one red cent of the money he gave her. She could, however, take a little solace in the fact that her only child was at least attending community college and doing seemingly well in his three classes.

Trina awoke early one morning, her day off, deciding to prepare her and Antonyo a big breakfast. This being the one day during the week that Antonyo had no classes, she decided the two could spend the morning in each other's company. While in the kitchen, she looked through the front window and noticed an unfamiliar car parked in her driveway. Antonyo's car was parked in front of the house. Trina went to his room to investigate.

She knocked on the door, awaiting his response. Upon receiving no answer after the third knock, she determined that he was probably sound asleep, so she went in to wake him. There he lay in bed, snuggled closely to a human figure with honey blond braided hair peeking from beneath the covers.

Trina stood in the doorway dumbfounded, but the moment she got her bearings, she began yelling. "Antonyo Ian Demonté Sims, you and your little hoochie hooker can get out of that bed right now!"

Antonyo bolted upright at his mother's voice. Her loudness woke him like a bucket of cold water. "Ma . . . What–what's the problem?" he stammered.

At the sound of Antonyo's voice, his female companion slowly slid her head from under the covers. "What's going on, Tony?" she asked sleepily.

Hearing this tramp speak as if she had every right to be in her home, in her son's bed like they were united in holy matrimony and Trina was an intrusion to their slumber, sent Trina into a fit of rage. "AAAAARRGH!" she yelled just before she leapt onto the bed. She began pummeling and choking Antonyo with every ounce of strength in her body.

Antonyo was stunned by his mother's actions. He had no idea why she was trying to kill him with her bare hands. At first all he could do was try to protect his head with his arms. When his mother reached for the handset to the cordless phone that sat on the nightstand to use it as a weapon, he took the split second to grab her, trying to restrain her swinging arms. Bianca, Antonyo's companion, had long ago fled the bed. She sat crouched naked against the wall, fearing for her own life.

Antonyo and Trina were now standing, him naked as a jaybird, while Trina struggled, trying to loosen herself from her son's grasp. "Let me go, fool," she yelled over and over again.

"Ma, what did I do?" Antonyo asked incredulously.

Trina, not believing her own ears, was amazed that her child could stand before her and question her as if he were truly clueless as to why she had become enraged. In her shock, she limply dropped her arms to her sides and lowered her now hoarse voice to barely above a whisper.

"What do you mean, 'What did I do, Ma?' You have the nerve to stand there with your naked self and that naked heffa over there on my floor and ask me what you did? Boy, are you crazy? Get out of my house right now and take that tramp with you." Without another word or a backward glance, Trina stormed out of the bedroom.

After Antonyo and Bianca got dressed, he apologized to her, walked her to her car, and explained that he would call her later. He then went in search of his mother, finding her in her bedroom.

Trina was still so furious, the sight of Antonyo almost made her throw the television remote control at him. She refrained, however, not wanting to destroy her property. Trina, instead, opted to launch another verbal attack. "What are you still doing here? Didn't I tell you I wanted you out of my house?" she said in a heated but quiet tone.

"Yes, you did, Ma, but I don't understand why." Antonyo was still at a loss as to why his mother had thrown a hissy fit.

Again, the urge to hurl something at him came over her, and again she suppressed it. She realized this fool seriously had no clue about how he had caused her such fury.

"Antonyo, what makes you think you have the right to have female company spend the night with you in my house?" she asked.

"Because I pay rent and contribute to this household just like you do," he answered evenly.

No, he didn't, Trina thought. This boy actually thought he had the same rights and privileges in her home as she did. Heck, she had never even had a man spend the night with her in her home.

"You know what, Antonyo? All this sex with all these little girls has really caused you to lose your mind. It would not matter to me if we split the rent and all the bills evenly down the middle; you would still not be allowed to have your ignorant girlfriends laying up in *my* house. It was bad enough that I gave you money to abort a child, totally going against what I know to be right in the sight of God. I am not about to give you the okay to have premarital sex in my house. I am a Christian who is doing her very best to live right, and in this house, we will serve God. After this little stunt, it is very apparent that you have no plans to do that; therefore, you need your own house, where you make all the rules and do whatever you want to do."

"But, Ma—"

"But nothing, boy! I don't even want to hear it. I just want you to pack your things and get out. Today! Now! Leave!"

Antonyo thought about continuing to argue with his mother, but realized his urging would be futile. She was too angry right now. Instead, he left the room, packed a small bag, and headed to his aunt's house. He figured he would stay there a few days, giving his mother a chance to cool off.

When he arrived at his aunt's house, Treecie was waiting for him at the front door, knowing he would be coming after speaking with her sister.

"So, yo' mama done kicked you out, huh, playboy?" Treecie asked with humor.

"Man! She be bugging big time. I got to pay rent, but I can't have company. I got to contribute like a man, but I still got to follow her set of laws like I'm a child."

"That's the way of the world, young buck. As long as you live under somebody else's roof, you have to live under somebody else's rule. And the same thing goes here. Now, you know how I feel about you. I love you like you my own, but your mother is my only sister. I have to respect her wishes to some degree, you know. She doesn't want you here at all, but I'm not gon' just set you in the street, so you can stay here for two weeks; then you got to figure something else out. I suggest you start working on that now.

"By the way, don't be bringing them tramps up in my house thinking they gon' spend the night here either. That's what motel rooms are for."

Antonyo listened to his aunt in slight amazement. Knowing that Treecie would agree with his assessment that his mother was overreacting, he was somewhat caught off guard by her standing there reciting and telling him about respecting rules. When had she ever cared about rules? However, he knew she would always back her sister's play. Searching for a new place to lay his head concerned him only minimally, though. He was certain that after his mother cooled off, she would let him come back home.

Three days after leaving home, Antonyo went back to hopefully convince his mother to let him return, only to be sorely surprised when Trina stuck to her guns. She refused to let him move back in to her home. What Trina did do was give him her speech about responsibility, Christianity, and being man enough to take care of himself again.

"I'm sorry, son, but you cannot move back here. I have tried explaining to you that the measure of a true man is how well he takes care of his responsibilities and how much integrity he has. It has nothing whatsoever to do with how much booty he can get. God did not purpose you to sleep with and take advantage of these females the way that you do, but you choose not to listen to me. Now I've got to show and prove. It's time for some tough love and hard knocks lessons."

Okay! Wait a minute. What just happened here? Did his mother really say she was kicking him into the streets in an effort to teach him a lesson? What the heck was he supposed to learn from being homeless?

"Where am I supposed to live, Ma?" Antonyo asked in a whiny tone.

"I'm going to help you out one last time, Antonyo. I'm going to give you a couple of suggestions. Suggestion number one: get one of your girlfriends to let you stay at her house. Suggestion number two: ask one of your girlfriends to give you money to find your own place and pay your rent for you."

Trina was being sarcastic and Antonyo knew it. He also knew that she was serious about him not being allowed to come back home. Her tone gave every indication of being truly fed up with his ways.

He went to his room to pack all of what he could fit in his car and he left, not having a clue as to how he was going to find a place to live in the next ten days. While driving around thinking about a solution to his present dilemma, he found himself downtown at Belle Isle Park, one of his favorite spots to hang out and chill with the few male friends he had. This was often the place where he would initially meet a lot of the females he dealt with since leaving high school.

Finding today's weather quite pleasant, Antonyo sat on a bench in front of the water, contemplating what his mother had said. He had never lived on his own before. The two-hundred fifty dollars he paid his mom for room and board came easily, but he was certain having to pay full rent and utilities along with buying food and other necessities would be quite a bit more expensive. Would the women he dealt with, even collectively, be able to help him with such a huge task?

Antonyo had been sitting and thinking for a little while when someone approached and sat next to him on the bench. He remained uninterrupted in his musings until the squatter spoke.

"Excuse me, but you were sitting here so pensive, I thought I might come and try to see if I could be of some assistance. You are far too handsome a young man to have all that worry on your face. Are you hungry? I have half a sandwich that you are welcomed to."

Antonyo looked up and into the face of a beautiful woman holding out her sandwich to him. She dressed very professionally, wearing a navy blue pinstriped blazer and skirt accompanied by matching blue-and-white three-inch pumps. Her jet black hair was shiny and stylishly cut. The stranger's make-up was flawless, proficiently applied to her cinnamon brown skin, and her brown eyes twinkled as she smiled at him.

Wow! was all Antonyo could think. Not being the least bit hungry, Antonyo took the outstretched ham and cheese sandwich from the woman just so she would not leave.

"Thank you. My name is Antonyo Simms. What's yours?" Antonyo took a bite of what he assumed to be his companion's leftover lunch as he awaited her reply.

"I'm Regina Caffey."

Even her name sounded authoritative to him.

"I'm sorry you caught me looking so down. It's just that I'm having a little problem with my mom, and I need to figure some things out," he told her honestly, though that was not usually one of his best traits.

Antonyo's conversation caught Regina off guard. He sounded a lot younger than he looked. She then chided herself for jumping to conclusions. Perhaps the attorney skills in her blood read something into his brief dialogue that wasn't there.

"Antonyo . . ." The rest of her words hung in the air as he cut her off, preventing her from continuing.

"Only my mother calls me Antonyo. Please call me Tony."

Regina lifted an eyebrow at his statement. She figured if he wanted her to call him Tony, he should have said so when he introduced himself. She became surer now than before that he was indeed younger than he looked.

"How old are you?" she finally asked.

"I'm eighteen. How old are you?" he responded.

"Honey, it is not polite to ask a lady her age, especially not as soon as you meet her."

"Well, I'm only eighteen, so I don't know all the rules yet," he said sarcastically.

Regina shifted her position on the bench and stared Antonyo straight in his eyes, deciding she would like to get to know this young man. Not only was he fine, but seemingly intelligent and witty. He had the potential to be a very interesting molding specimen. However, before resolving to take him on as her own personal project, she needed a little more information.

"Tony, do you mind talking about the problem between you and your mother?"

Antonyo spent just as much time analyzing Regina as she

did him. He knew the moment he laid eyes on her that she was a professional career woman, but his internal mack-daddy instincts were beginning to see just a bit deeper. This woman exhibited an interest so that she could size him up, perhaps trying to figure out if she could construct him into some type of playmate for her.

He was so thankful for all the information he had received from his auntie. She had given him the extensive 411 on the older woman/younger man scenario. Regina needed to know his problem in hopes that she could solve it and become his hero. Maybe the answer to his troubles was becoming a little clearer already.

"The problems between my mom and me are typical. I'm a college student and she wants me to learn more responsibilities. She wants me to get a job. We've been going at it quite a bit, so to alleviate the stress on both of us, I moved out of her home and in with my aunt, my mother's twin sister." Antonyo figured he'd leave out the part about Treecie's moving deadline for right now, careful not to scare her off by giving too much information too fast.

"Well, I can understand what your mom is saying. Though I am not a parent yet, I recognize from my own parents that teaching your child about life and its realities is of the utmost importance."

Regina stopped talking for a moment to try and gauge Antonyo's reaction to what she'd said. She was interested to know if he would become defensive, or accepting of her input.

Antonyo had already anticipated Regina's typical response, so he played along with her game. The last thing he wanted to do was antagonize this woman of apparent means.

"Oh, I totally understand my mother's position, especially considering that my father was a deadbeat. She had to raise me all alone. It's just that I've been having a hard time finding suitable employment. I am an honor student in college, and I feel that a fast food gig is beneath me. I am looking for something that will challenge me intellectually and help me to grow into something more constructive than a fry cook."

Impressive, Regina thought. Here sat a young man with a little ambition. He sounded a lot like her when she was his age.

"I have an idea that could possibly help. Why don't you give me a call at my office tomorrow morning after ten? I may be able to find a position for you as an office assistant or something." Regina handed Antonyo her business card.

Just as he thought; she was a lawyer. The card read: RE-GINA LEWIS-CAFFEY, ATTORNEY AT LAW. The hyphenated name piqued his curiosity. Was she married, or did she carry the last name of both parents? That question, however, was best saved for another time. Right now he wanted to keep things on a platonic level. Rushing things with this woman would be a mistake.

"Oh, wow! I really appreciate this, Ms. Caffey. I will call you as soon as I'm done with my eight o'clock class," Antonyo replied enthusiastically.

"Call me Regina, Tony," she replied as she casually winked her eye. "I've got to get back to my office now. I look forward to hearing from you in the morning."

She stood and extended her hand to the handsome young man, but instead of shaking her limb, Antonyo stood with her and gave her a light peck on the cheek, followed by his lady-killer smile.

"Trust me when I say the pleasure will be all mine."

Regina was again impressed with his gesture. She gave him a huge smile in return and then left.

One week later, Antonyo began working part-time in the

law offices of Traylor, Goldwin, Kennell & Mark as an office assistant. He was assigned as an errand person for just about the entire office. Starting at eleven dollars an hour, Antonyo made almost twice the amount that most of his friends were making. He worked approximately twenty hours a week so as not to interfere with school.

During his second week of employment, Antonyo discovered the explanation behind the hyphen in Regina's name. He met senior law partner John Caffey when he was asked to deliver a package for him.

When given the assignment by his supervisor, Antonyo immediately recognized the name and assumed Mr. Caffey was Regina's husband. Surprise, however, came as he entered Mr. Caffey's office to find a much older white man and he instantly realized his mistake. This must Regina's father. Though she lacked the classic bi-racial features, he assumed she carried the name of both her African American mother and her father; either that or she was adopted. He introduced himself to the distinguished-looking gentleman.

"Hello, Mr. Caffey. I'm Tony Simms. I was sent here to pick up a package and instructions for delivery."

"Well, I finally have the privilege of meeting the young man my wife speaks so highly of. She was duly impressed with you on your initial meeting, son," Mr. Caffey replied. "I had no choice but to recommend you for an entry-level job after hearing all of the glowing things she said about your ambition. It's nice to finally meet you, Tony."

So, this is her husband. Wow, Antonyo thought. "It's nice to meet you, too, sir. Thank you for putting in the good word for me sight unseen."

"You can thank me by simply showing up every day and doing a good job." Mr. Caffey gave Antonyo a nice smile then handed him the package and told him the specifics about the delivery.

Upon his return from delivery duty, Antonyo ran into Regina. "Hey, you. How are you doing?" she asked excitedly.

Antonyo had only seen Regina in passing at the office for the past week. This was the first opportunity she'd taken to actually stop to talk to him. She looked even more beautiful today than she did the first time they'd met.

"I'm doing great, Regina. I met your husband today," he replied casually.

Regina appeared a little perturbed by his announcement, so he decided to play on her discomfort to see what came of it.

"Mr. Caffey seemed very nice. I guess you are quite proud of the fact he's a senior partner."

"My husband is nice. Why don't I take you to lunch? What time can you get away?"

Again, Antonyo noticed her mild agitation as she quickly changed subjects, seemingly wanting to avoid the topic of her husband. "Actually, I get off in about fifteen minutes. Can you leave then?"

"I'll meet you downstairs in the lobby."

Regina selected Sweet Georgia Brown as their lunch location, an upscale restaurant in downtown Detroit that featured live jazz and recipes that were flavorful and artistic in their presentation. Antonyo had never been to such a classy establishment and was somewhat taken aback by its extravagance. The prices were definitely out of the league of the ladies he usually dated; more evidence that Regina had money.

"These prices sure are expensive," he said after carefully looking over the menu.

"They're not that bad, actually. Besides, the food is worth it." Regina quickly surmised that perhaps Antonyo assumed that he was to pay for their lunch. His comment about the prices was probably his way of informing her that he could not afford to pay. *How sweet of him to even consider picking up the tab*, she thought.

"Oh, but don't worry about it. It's my treat," Regina told Antonyo as she patted his hand.

For sure! Antonyo thought, but instead he said, "Thank you."

"Did you ever fix things between you and your mother now that you have a decent job?"

Trina and Antonyo had talked since he started working. She told him that she was proud of him for finding employment, but that she was not going to let him move back home. Trina still had not found the will to forgive him for the way he disrespected her house. Her reasoning dictated that when a person is grown, he needs to be on his own. No need for Regina to know all that, though. Once he told Treecie about his job, she extended his stay an additional two weeks, giving him time to collect a paycheck and find himself an affordable place to live

"Yeah, we've talked and everything's cool. But since I've been out of her house, I've decided that I'm comfortable with it. I don't want to go back home."

Enough talk about him for now, Antonyo decided. He needed to steer the conversation back toward Regina and her husband. Just as he was about to do that, the waiter approached and asked for their order. Once that task was complete, the interrogation began.

"So, how long have you and Mr. Caffey been married?" Antonyo asked her.

"Two years," Regina replied uncomfortably. She took a sip of her water, choking slightly on the liquid as it slid down her throat.

Since the obstruction was a minor occurrence, Antonyo let it slide as if it had gone unnoticed, and continued with his interrogation. "How did you end up married to an older white man?" he asked bluntly.

"Excuse me, young man, but you are way out of line," Regina countered indignantly.

"*Young man*. That's funny considering . . ." Antonyo chuckled as he leaned back in his chair.

"Are you purposely trying to insult me, Antonyo?"

"Only my mother calls me Antonyo." He corrected her without too much attitude, knowing it was just her counter attack. Then he continued his assault. "And, no, I'm not trying to insult you. I'm just curious as to why a black woman as fine and as smart as you could end up married to some old white fogey."

Again Regina was caught off guard. Here sat this young man, paying her a wonderful compliment served as an appetizer to a backhanded slap. He was even more intelligent than she had given him credit for in the beginning.

"Tony, I appreciate you saying I'm beautiful; really, I do. But my marriage is none of your business."

"Okay. I'll step off, but only after I ask you one last question." Antonyo reached across the table and gently caressed Regina's hand. "Are you happy, Regina?"

Regina's eyes became blank as she stared off behind Antonyo for several seconds. She then looked down at her hand while he continued to tenderly massage her fingers. Her gaze eventually met his eyes, her silence answering his question loud and clear. Regina was finally able to look away when the waiter returned a few seconds later with their food.

They ate in a companionable hush for a while; then halfway through her meal, Regina started to speak. "John is not that much older than me; only seventeen years, actually. He will be forty-three on his next birthday. Not quite old enough to be my father."

Well, that cleared up the guessing game about her age. She was twenty-six. She was correct about the age difference not being as big as he assumed, yet the question remained as to why. Antonyo was pretty sure he knew the real answer, but he wanted it confirmed by Regina.

"Okay, he's not old enough to be your dad. He's still old and white. Tell me what made you fall in love with him."

"John is a very brilliant man. He sat in with a professor of mine at law school one day as a special guest. After observing one of my mock arguments, he told me I had the legal mind of the late Thurgood Marshall. John recruited me as an intern for the firm."

Regina took a few more bites of her food. Antonyo thought she was ending the conversation, but quite the contrary. She continued until she had given him a complete answer to his question.

"John and I started spending quite a bit of time together," she continued. "He became my mentor. He taught me so much about life, the law, racism's causes and effects, culture, everything. You name it; he seemed to know it and share it with me. We married two months after I received my Juris Doctor. I was hired by the firm as a law clerk and then as an attorney just after I passed the Michigan State Bar Exam.

"In the beginning, our union caused quite a bit of controversy within the office," she told Antonyo. "He was a senior partner and I an associate. But I set out to prove that I earned the right to be there on my own merits. It has been four years now, and I have made junior partner all on my own. The tongues have ceased to wag, and John and I share a companionable work ethic and peace."

"A companionable work ethic and peace? What about at home? Do you share a hot and sexy bedroom? I think not," he mocked.

Once again, Antonyo's insight surprised Regina, but the lawyer in her was not ready to concede to anything. She just wasn't ready to pour out her soul to a teenager, even one as fine as Antonyo. She ignored the question and instead weaved the conversation in another direction.

"It's Friday. How about you and I catch a movie tonight? John is always so busy. He hardly ever has time to go out with me. I'm sure he won't mind me hanging out with a friend this evening. What do you say?" she asked gleefully.

The words not spoken were again very loud and he heard them quite clearly. Regina was trapped in a bad marriage. Well, if she wanted to hang out with him tonight to get away from her husband, he would be more than happy to oblige the beautiful, rich attorney. He actually had plans with Bianca, but he was sure he could get out of those. Antonyo would make tonight a night Regina would not soon forget. "I say yes!"

Chapter 7

That evening, Regina had Antonyo meet her at her girl-friend's house, and they took off together from there. The night started with dinner at the Outback Steakhouse in Roseville, which was approximately thirty to forty-five minutes from the palatial estate Regina shared with her husband in West Bloomfield. They then proceeded to a movie theater that was another twenty minutes or so away. Their next destination was the place where they initially met for the very first time.

Antonyo realized the entire journey was so far out of the way because Regina did not want to take a chance of running into anyone she or her husband might know. This was typical behavior of someone in an adulterous relationship. Treecie had already put him up on what was going to happen before he left the house that evening.

The weather was quite a bit chillier down on the water at Belle Isle than it was the day they'd met, so they decided to sit in the car and talk for a while.

"So, Tony, tell me: what are you studying in school?"

"Right now I'm taking basic curriculum classes. I haven't quite decided what I want my major to be. Engineering used to be my primary focus, with law coming in second. However, since meeting you and coming to work at the firm, my perspective has changed a little. I am leaning a little more toward being an attorney."

Antonyo was definitely spitting game. Never before had he thought about being a lawyer, nor was he seriously considering it now. He knew he was going to be a software engineer. This was all just a spiel to impress Regina.

"If there is anything I can do to help, just let me know."

Well, since she was offering, he figured now was as good a time as any to let her know what it was she could really do for him. "Now it's your turn to tell me more about you. I want to know why you are still married to John Caffey when it is so obvious that you don't love him."

"Tony, please. Why don't you just let it go? My marriage is my business."

Antonyo undid his seatbelt and moved closer to Regina. He used his patented move of taking and caressing her hand and looking deep into her eyes before he continued in his pursuit of what he wanted—what he needed.

"Regina, I don't mean to offend or upset you. It's just as I said before. I think you are so beautiful and so smart. I am very attracted to you, but more importantly, I like you as a friend. If you are truly happy with your husband, then I'll ignore my fascination with your seemingly unfulfilling marriage. Otherwise, I have to say something."

Regina found herself truly enthralled with this perceptive young man. She had been from the first day they met. Antonyo was right; she was not happy with John.

"Tony, I married John because I was bored with being my parents' perfect little girl. They put such pressure on me to always be right. I had to do the right thing, go to the right school, and marry the right man. They were smothering me.

"When I met John and found that he was attracted to me, I saw him as my ticket out of the strangle hold my mother and father had on me. I decided to shake things up and marry an older white man. I rationalized that he was at least rich and could provide a good life for me, so marrying John would be a win-win situation. I would get the satisfaction of annoying my parents, and they could take comfort in knowing that their only child would not starve to death."

After revealing herself and her situation to Antonyo, Regina felt surprisingly good. He was the first person with whom she had honestly shared her feelings. Her girlfriends, family members, and eventually her parents figured she was lucky to have a man such as John in love with her. They all envied her, so giving any of them the truth about her feelings had become a non-issue.

"If you are not happy, why do you stay, Regina?" Antonyo knew the answer, but he wanted to keep playing the part of concerned friend.

"Tony, marriage is a lifetime commitment. Even though I'm not in love with John, I do like him. Besides, being married to him offers me incentives. I am a valued attorney at an impressive firm because he believed in me and admired my legal mind. He is rich, and I share in everything that he has. I love the esteem I receive from being married to a partner in such a prestigious law firm. The ups far outweigh the downs in my situation."

"The down being having sex with a man that you are not attracted to," Antonyo completed. Regina's information was nothing that Antonyo had not already expected to hear. Her admission to using John made him feel justified in his plan to use her.

Regina was again astounded by his astuteness. She scooted in her car seat in an effort to get as close to him as she could.

"Perhaps you could be of assistance in that area. I have played by the rules all my life. Now it is time for me to have some fun, and I need a playmate," she stated seductively.

Things were going just as he planned. Antonyo could not

have been more pleased. It was as if he had read this tale in a book and followed along with the storyline.

"I would love to play with you, Regina. You are such a gorgeous woman. I want you more than any other woman I have ever known; however, you are not the type of woman I want to sneak around with in sleazy motels. You are far too classy for that. We can't meet at my house because I stay with my aunt right now, and we definitely can't hang out at your crib."

Antonyo paused to see if his statements were having the desired effect. Regina had always been a sucker for his compliments. Looking into her smoldering eyes, he could see his flattering words still held the same power, so he continued.

"Listen, Regina. I'm not in a rush to start anything physical with you. I'm willing to wait for you as long as it takes. We can continue to hang out and spend time together, but before we talk about taking our relationship to that level, perhaps we should wait until I can save enough money to get my own place."

"Do you have any money saved as of yet, Tony?" she asked as she continued to caress his torso.

"No, not yet. With me working part time and helping my aunt pay the bills around her house, I only make enough to perhaps start saving toward the initial deposit. My plan was to wait until next semester so I can drop a class. I could then find a full-time job and be able to afford the deposit, the monthly rent, utilities, food, and general upkeep. But I think you are worth the wait, Regina."

After about one minute of silent cuddling and mind searching, Regina came up with a solution that would expedite her desire to have a fling with Antonyo.

"Tony, how about we find you a small studio apartment? I can pay the rent on it and help with the utilities. That way you can continue to work at the firm and stay on track in school.

You can provide your own groceries and a cellular phone. Do you think you can handle that?"

This game is getting way too easy, Antonyo thought. A lesser man would probably get the big head after assessing his own ability, but Antonyo remained humble and continued to play his role.

You reap what you sow, Antonyo. Trina's voice rang in his ear, but he ignored it.

"The question is can you handle that? Won't your husband get suspicious about the money?"

"Trust me. It will not be a problem. John never has to know anything about this."

"I really appreciate this, Regina. I look forward to every moment we get to spend together." No use pushing the game of concern too far.

Six days later, Antonyo moved into his very first apartment. The studio unit housed a living room and small kitchen in one area, and the bedroom and bathroom in another. Regina purchased a sofa, chair, dinette, and bedroom set, completely furnishing the entire apartment. It was small, but it was his. Finally he had the place his mother always talked about, the place where he could come and go as he pleased and do whatever he wanted to do.

For the first two weeks, Regina was the only woman Antonyo entertained at his new apartment. He hadn't completely stopped seeing other women, though. In fact, India, Ashley, and Bianca bought him sheets, towels, dishes, utensils, groceries, etc., etc., etc. He kept the young girls at bay by explaining that he wanted the apartment to be in tiptop shape before he invited them to visit.

Antonyo's stalling tactic did not extend to his mother. He was, in fact, anxious for his mother to see his new place. Wanting everything in its proper place, nothing missing, he extended an invitation for her to join him for dinner. His plan also included introducing Trina to Regina, hoping to score some respect in the eyes of his biggest critic. Antonyo assumed Trina would look at him differently once she learned of his involvement with a successful, rich attorney. The existence of her husband would remain as carefully a kept secret as the details of the JFK assassination.

When Antonyo invited Trina for dinner, he neglected to tell her that Regina would join them. He wanted the introduction of his exciting new friend to be a surprise.

When Trina arrived, she was indeed impressed with the décor and quaintness of her son's new apartment; however, even with his new job, she knew this was not something he accomplished all on his own. Any one, or more than likely all, of his female tribe had contributed to the acquisition of his new home. That fact diminished the accomplishment in her eyes.

When Trina got to the apartment, Regina was in the bathroom trying to make herself presentable. She was as nervous as a virgin bride on her wedding night, concerned about how Antonyo's mom would feel about the obvious age difference.

Regina made her appearance just as Antonyo walked his mother to the beautifully set dinette table. Regina had picked up takeout from one of the fancy restaurants she frequented. Antonyo made the introductions while both women were still standing.

"Ma, this is my friend, Regina Caffey. She and I work together at the law firm. Regina, this is my mother, LaTrina Simms."

Trina eyed Regina disdainfully. This woman looked to be nearly as old as she was. Regina could feel the uncomfortable heat from Trina's stare. She silently prayed that the floor would open up and swallow her whole. But her trained lawyer's demeanor allowed her to hold her face expressionless as she reached for Trina's hand.

"It's nice to meet you, Ms. Simms. Tony has told me so much about you," Regina said evenly.

"Unfortunately, I can't say the same. Antonyo has told me absolutely nothing about you. By the way, you can call me Trina, since you are probably closer to my age than you are my son's."

Regina's outer armor cracked just slightly. She was mildly irritated that Antonyo had never made mention of her to his mother, but more thoroughly flustered by Trina's jab about her age. Instead of replying, however, she simply took her seat at the table and began shuffling the food around so the plates could be prepared.

Antonyo, who sat between the two women, also became a little rattled by his mother's comments, but he figured as soon as Trina found out about Regina's career, she would change her sour disposition. Antonyo began talking as he made his mother a plate of food. "Mama, Regina is a junior partner at the huge law firm—"

Trina interrupted his praise for his new girlfriend and announced, "I think we should pray before we eat."

Both Regina and Antonyo stopped what they were doing. Trina held out her hands for each of them to join her in prayer.

"Heavenly Father, we come humbly before you this evening, asking you, Lord, to bless the food we are about to eat. Remove anything, Lord, that may be harmful to us, and let the meal be used to nourish us and feed our bodies, as well as our minds and spirits. This is our prayer in Jesus' name. Amen."

Regina and Antonyo murmured in unison, "Amen."

Just before Trina freed the hand she held during prayer, she realized Regina wore a ring on her third finger. When she released Regina's hand, she stared blatantly at the wedding set she wore.

Antonyo noticed the direction of his mother's stare and immediately set out to divert her attention. "Mama, where did you attend church this past Sunday?" he asked as he continued preparing Trina's plate.

Trina rolled her eyes away from Regina's hand long enough to answer her son's question. "I started attending Trinity Star Baptist Church with a co-worker about a month ago. I joined as a member last week. I decided it was time for me to give God complete control of running my life."

Regina found herself impressed by Trina's admission. Too much time had passed since she last visited her church home. In quick retrospect, she remembered that she had really enjoyed attending church when she was a faithful participant at Liberty Temple Baptist Church.

"Oh, wow! That's a great thing, Ms. Simms—I mean Trina. I used to attend church regularly with my parents. I even sang in the choir. It's been a while since I've been, though. I guess I'm a little ashamed to admit that I haven't been to church since I started at the law firm. I've been so busy. But you know what? I'm going to make it a point to find time to get back into service."

Regina smiled broadly after her declaration, feeling as though she had scored some brownie points with Antonyo's mother. She quickly learned differently.

"Are you planning on taking your husband with you?" Trina asked sarcastically.

The color drained from Regina's face and her eyes bulged a mile outside of her head. She was more humiliated than she had ever been in her entire life. How could she have been so stupid as to not remove her wedding ring?

Antonyo was as mortified as Regina. All the bragging about Regina being an attorney wouldn't amount to a hill of beans in his mother's eyes now. The only thing she would see is that he had snagged himself an older adulteress to take care of him this time.

The three of them sat there silently for several minutes, no one even bothering to play with the food on their plates, let alone eat it. The uncomfortable silence was finally broken when Regina decided that she should at least give some sort of an explanation for her predicament.

"Trina, I'm sure you don't approve of your son being involved with a married woman. I totally understand your feelings. But my marriage is far from being a happy one. I know that's not a good excuse for what I'm doing, but I truly get a lot of enjoyment out of spending time with Antonyo. He is very mature, well spoken, and intelligent. He makes me laugh, and he is such a good listener. He, in a way, makes up for what I'm missing at home."

Regina again wrongfully assessed that commenting on Antonyo's positive characteristics would impress upon his mother how well she felt he was raised.

"Regina, I did not raise my son to be a gigolo, someone you can use to get your jollies when you get bored at home. That's exactly the type of person you have just described to me. You simply left out the sexual aspect of your relationship with my son. But I'm not stupid."

"I don't think of Tony like that at all Tri—" Before she could finish her sentence, Trina interrupted her.

"Have you and your husband separated, or have either of you filed for a divorce?" Trina asked.

"No," Regina answered awkwardly.

"Then what you are doing is wrong. You are cheating."

Antonyo felt torn between pride about the statements Regina made about his character and shame behind his mother's interpretations of those same statements; however, he refused to be admonished or have his friend further humiliated in his home. His mother made the rules at her house, but this was his house.

"Mama, I feel what you are saying, but this is my life. You're trying to blame everything on Regina, and it's not her fault. I know what I'm doing. I'm grown."

Trina stood from the table and gathered her things. "I'm not hungry anymore. I really don't want to impose on any more of you and your girlfriend's private moments. I'm sure you only get a few, since she has more than one man to juggle."

"Mama, wait! You've always said that when I got my own place, I could make my own rules. Rule number one is you have to now respect me and my friends in my house. Mama, I'm grown," Antonyo reiterated.

"Being grown does not automatically mean that your decisions cannot be wrong. In fact, the letters that spell grown are the same letters that spell wrong! Regina, I pray that you follow through with your decision to start attending church service again. I will also pray for both you and your husband." Trina then walked to the door and left the house.

"Well, that went well," Regina said sarcastically.

Chapter 8

One week after the disastrous evening with his mother and Regina, Antonyo decided the time had come to host other small dinner parties for the other women in his life. Tonight his dining companion would be India. Tomorrow night, Ashley.

Antonyo knew he had been neglecting these two ladies since the arrival of Regina in his life. He also knew it was time to start showing them some attention before they became living proof of the old adage, out of sight, out of mind. Antonyo needed the continued support of these young women, both financially and sexually.

While he still enjoyed his "friendship" with Regina, he felt her becoming a little too clingy. Just yesterday she told him she believed she was falling in love with him—while at work, no less.

"Tony, can you come by my office when you get a chance?" Regina had asked as he passed her in the hall on his way to the mailroom. After completing his assignment, he made his way to her office. Once inside, she locked the door and handed him a beautifully wrapped package along with a greeting card.

"Thank you. I'll open these after work," he said and headed for the door.

"No. Open them now. You can't be seen leaving my office with presents."

Antonyo hadn't thought about that. He opened the gift

first and found a stunning Movado wristwatch. He immediately found himself impressed by both the style and detail of the watch and Regina's generosity.

"This is a great watch, Regina. Thank you so much!" he'd exclaimed as he placed the watch back in the box.

"Okay, now open the card," Regina demanded enthusiastically.

Antonyo eyed her cautiously, but did as she asked.

The card cover contained an African American couple in a very intimate embrace. The words LOVE IS LIKE A FLOWER were positioned above the picture. Antonyo was startled by the caption, and a little apprehensive about opening the card to read the inside.

"Read it, Tony!" Regina could barely contain her excitement.

Finally he opened the card to find these words: *Ours is just budding, still growing. I look forward to seeing it in full bloom.*

Antonyo looked up from the card to see Regina wearing a smile more bright than any he had ever seen. "I saw that card and felt it expressed perfectly how I feel about you."

Antonyo stood in the office feeling dumbfounded. Regina was a married woman and he was dating three other women. At no time had he ever given Regina any indication that they were in a monogamous relationship.

Antonyo looked at the card again and then back at Regina, who still held on to her brilliantly shining smile. He began to feel suffocated and needed to get out of the office.

"Thank you," Antonyo said in a monotone and left the office.

He avoided Regina the rest of the day at work and ignored her phone calls while at home.

Today was Friday, his day off, which afforded him the opportunity to dodge her again. He really did not feel like dealing with her. He was in no way, shape, or form, stupid enough to get into a monogamous relationship with a married woman, one of the many lessons he had learned from Treecie.

"Never make a female who is married your main woman, because you can never be her main man," his aunt had told him.

How could Regina actually believe that they could have an exclusive relationship when she had a husband at home, one that Antonyo saw practically every day? That was totally unfair. As soon as he prepared himself to deal with her **again,** he would tell her exactly that.

Tonight, however, he would concentrate solely on getting back to his usual way of doing things. Before now, he had been too involved with Regina. She would now, however, have to take her place as a co-inhabitant of his time and space, no longer the sole occupant.

India rang the doorbell at precisely 7:45 P.M., forty-five minutes later than he told her to be there. But what did he expect? Women were always late. He opened the door to greet his guest. To his surprise, however, not only did he find India looking as beautiful as a runway model, but also Regina, who looked angry enough to be India's mother, coming to confront the young man who had been sleeping with her underage daughter.

"Regina, what are you doing here?" Antonyo yelled.

"A better question would be what is she doing here?" Regina yelled back while thrusting her thumb in India's direction.

"She, who would be me, was invited," India retorted as she pointed her thumb mockingly at herself. "And since you're the one he's yelling at, I assume you were not."

Antonyo held the door open a little wider and allowed India to cross the threshold. When Regina tried to enter too, he blocked her path with his body. "Regina, you need to leave. As you can see I have company."

Regina took a step backward and planted a hand on her hip sister-girl style. Then her forefinger went to pointing and her neck went to rolling simultaneously. "How dare you tell *me* to leave, Tony? Did you forget I'm the one who pays the rent on this place?"

Antonyo stood with one hand on the door jamb. He pinched his nose with the fingers of his other in an effort to alleviate the frustrations building in his head. He suddenly chuckled to himself as a funny thought entered his head.

"My mama said there would be days like this," he said aloud. After several deep breaths, he addressed Regina. "Regina, you can't possibly believe that I'm not going to date other females. Why in the world would I commit to seeing just you when you are involved with someone else?"

Regina stood speechless for a moment with her arms now folded across her bosom, but the trained attorney would not remain that way for too long. "So, what are you saying, Tony? Are you asking me to leave my husband?"

Now it was Antonyo who stared speechlessly. Where in the world did that come from? That was the last thing he wanted, but before he could give voice to his thoughts, Regina started again.

"I love you, Tony," she stated softly as she caressed his cheek.

Antonyo gently rubbed the fingers that Regina held to his face for a few seconds. He then removed her hand and placed it back at her side. "Regina, I enjoy spending time with you. I really like the person that you are, but I'm not in love with you. I never let my heart get involved, because you belong to someone else. The last thing I want you to do is leave your husband."

Regina took two steps back and squared her shoulders. She stared wordlessly at Antonyo for several moments as one lone tear slid down her cheek.

"Fine, Antonyo! I expect you to move out of my apartment within thirty days. Otherwise I will be forced to take you to court and have you evicted. Leave all the furniture behind, seeing as how I paid for it all," she announced just before she turned to leave. She pivoted with a few additional words still clinging to her lips.

"Oh, and by the way, don't bother showing up for work on Monday. I'll simply tell everyone that you quit. I'll even give you a glowing reference should any potential employers call. But if you even set foot at the law firm again, I will make sure your name is mud."

Regina left the apartment, got into her car, and drove out of Antonyo's life forever.

Chapter 9

Antonyo ended up back at home with Trina after being formally evicted from the apartment Regina had paid for. It took a lot of begging, pleading, and promising on his part, but she finally relented and let her only child come back home. Trina still assessed him his monthly contribution of $250 (a far cry from the $650 Regina paid for the studio) and the same rules applied: No females were allowed to stay overnight. That was seven months and one birthday ago. Antonyo was now nineteen.

Regina held true to her word and gave him a good recommendation when the human resources representative from KLR Alarm Systems called her for a reference check. Antonyo began working with the company as a customer service representative six months ago.

Surprisingly, Antonyo had not been dating much since returning to his mother's home. He was now working full time and taking a couple of night classes in community college. He and his mother reconnected and were spending quality time together.

However, his little reversion was getting old. He began to feel like a recovering junkie on the verge of a relapse. The time had come for Antonyo to rebuild his harem.

On the job, one female in particular had piqued Antonyo's interest. Claire, his team supervisor, was not his usual cup of tea, but there was something relatively intriguing about her.

Claire stood approximately five feet and seven inches tall. She was a little on the heavier side, but she had beautiful green eyes and a very pretty face. Claire was also a lot older than Antonyo. He wasn't sure of her exact age, but he overheard her telling another customer service representative that she had a daughter that was a senior in high school. Antonyo guessed from that statement that Claire had to be around thirty-five or thirty-six. That would make their age difference more than double that of his and Regina's. Claire and Regina did have one thing in common, however: They were both married.

Claire was different from other supervisors at the company. She did not behave as a hardnosed, in-your-face dictator like the other team leaders. Those team leaders got their customer service representatives to work by issuing threats of reprimands and repercussions. Those representatives did their jobs out of fear.

Claire, however, was friendly, compassionate, and fair. She would write you up if she had to, but she always made you realize that she was doing it because it was what you deserved. She never made you feel like she got any pleasure out of it.

Claire never made her representatives feel like her job was more important than theirs either. They were all one big team working together. On occasions when the phone lines were jammed and a customer service representative or two were on break, most team leaders would interrupt someone's break before they would take a call themselves. Handling phone calls were too far beneath them. But Claire had no problem jumping in and helping on the phones. She was a very good leader. Her team responded to her out of genuine respect. Almost every representative at the company wanted to transfer to Claire's team.

Antonyo thought Claire to be amazing. Now he had to figure out a way to get next to her. This particular undertaking would require another heart to heart talk with Auntie Treecie.

Antonyo looked forward to seeing his aunt. While he loved his mother, he shared a special and unique relationship with Treecie. He always enjoyed the informational chats they shared. Treecie was a well of knowledge.

Treecie greeted Antonyo with enthusiasm as he arrived at her home. "Hey, boy! Where you been? Auntie ain't seen you in a minute."

"Hey, Auntie," Antonyo replied as he walked in, gave his aunt a kiss on the cheek, and sat next to her on the sofa.

Antonyo explained his desire to get with Claire and the potential roadblocks. He asked his aunt if there was any way that he could get around them.

"Let me tell you this first, nephew: If you're vibing this strongly over a female, it's usually because there is some mutual electricity between you two. A Negro can usually tell when a female ain't feeling him at all, especially after six months. What do you think? Has she shown you any special attention? 'Cause you know you are one fine piece of man. It would be hard for any woman not to be feeling you."

Antonyo thought about it for a minute and realized that Claire had been a little extra friendly with him. He shook his head in affirmation to his aunt's query and she continued.

"All righty then. Here's how you should start this: First, begin flirting with her, but make sure it's out of earshot of the other employees. You don't need nobody all up in your business. Now, she will probably not respond to you right away. Like you said, she's your boss, she's married, and she's older than you."

Antonyo stared at Treecie, hanging on her every word. Treecie noticed how intently her nephew listened to all that she had to say, and it filled her heart with pride. Most people would consider her ignorant and trifling because of her life-style, but her nephew never judged her. He always showed her respect. At times like these, she realized he even admired her.

"Auntie gon' make us a snack while we talk, 'cause I'm a little hungry. Come on in the kitchen. We can continue our conversation in there," Treecie announced, trying to get control of her emotions before she started crying.

Treecie truly loved her nephew like he was her own son. In her heart, she sincerely believed that the advice she gave benefited his life. Antonyo was very good-looking, so why shouldn't he use it to his advantage? He was also very intelligent, something she couldn't really say about her own son. Darnell was currently serving two years in prison for his role in an auto theft ring. She still had her girls, however, and thus far they were both doing okay.

Seventeen-year-old Taraija, who still lived with her dad, was an honor roll student in high school. Treecie was especially proud of her. When she was Taraija's age, she had already given birth to her first child, and high school had become a distant memory.

Fourteen-year-old Tianca wasn't quite as smart as Taraija. Her grades were average. But her baby girl was shaping up to be a fine female. Tianca was absolutely beautiful, outshining all of her little girlfriends. Her breasts, hips, and behind were envied by grown women. Yes, Tianca had it going on. Someday in the very near future, Treecie would begin schooling her just as she had her gorgeous nephew. Treecie knew from experience that beauty had a benefit all its own.

While Treecie prepared a light meal of fried catfish, grits, and scrambled eggs with cheese, she sent Antonyo to the store to pay a utility bill for her. He returned just as she completed cooking the meal. As soon as they were settled at the kitchen table, she continued educating Antonyo on how to score with his supervisor. They talked as they ate.

"Now, back to your boss lady," Treecie picked up between bites. "Once you start flirting with old girl, if her first brush-off does not include a statement about her being married, she's interested." Antonyo looked a little confused at Tree-cie's reasoning, so she broke it down further for him.

"Okay, listen. If she says something like 'Tony, I'm your boss, so we can't hook up' or 'Boy, I have a child at home your age,' then you should keep flirting. Her not mentioning hubby right out the gate means the relationship ain't that solid."

Antonyo chewed while pondering. In addition to mulling over the good advice she gave, he wondered where she'd acquired all of her knowledge. Then again, Treecie always managed to have a man in the house paying the bills and one in her hip pocket for backup, so he just assumed that her info came from direct experience, and he let it go. He continued listening to his professor lecture.

"Now, I know I ain't got to tell you what to say to get your mack on, do I?"

"No, Auntie. All I needed to know is how to get it started and what clues to look for. I'll keep you updated."

The following day when Antonyo returned to work, he waited for the perfect time to start in on Claire. Opportunity knocked during his thirty-minute lunch break.

Claire walked into the makeshift break room and flopped down as if totally exhausted. She sat at a table across from where Antonyo sat.

"What's up, Claire? Are they working you too hard out there?"

"I just got off the phone with a customer who requested a supervisor simply because he wanted to complain about his service being disconnected. When I tried to explain that his bill was more than ninety days delinquent, he called me everything but a child of God. Like it's my fault he neglected to pay for his alarm service."

Antonyo got up from his seat to join Claire at her table, making sure no one else was on their way into the room.

"Well, like my mama used to tell me, you've got to pay the cost to be the boss, and as one of the bosses around here, Ms. Lady, I guess your account has come due," he said as he sat down next to Claire.

"Some days, Tony, I wonder if it's worth it." She propped her arms on the table and put her head down on them.

Antonyo began lightly rubbing her exposed arm, careful not to put too much sensuality into his movement. "Hey! Come on now, boss. You are far too pretty to let these customers stress you out, adding worry lines to your perfect face."

Claire lifted her head slightly and looked at Antonyo. "Are you flirting with me, Antonyo Simms?" she asked seriously.

He started to correct her about the use of his name, but instead he said, "Maybe."

Claire sat upright and chuckled good-naturedly. "Boy, you know I'm old enough to be your mama. I've got a daughter at home just about your age."

Antonyo smiled at her reply, remembering his auntie's clues. Antonyo continued to rub Claire's arm, but he now used just two fingers instead of the palm of his hand, teasing and tickling her. "You know, having a daughter close to my age does not stop you from being beautiful to me."

Claire blushed all the way down to the bottom of her feet. She always did find Antonyo attractive, but he was her customer service representative, and nearly half her age. She was also married, but that relationship was strained at best.

She finally stopped squirming at the attention of this fine but young man and stood to go back to work. "You're sweet, Antonyo. I've got to get back to my team."

"Okay, Claire, but before you go, can I ask you to call me Tony? Only my mother calls me Antonyo."

"Sure, Tony. I'll see you back on the floor in about ten minutes." Claire left the room with a huge smile on her face.

For the next six days, Antonyo persistently but discreetly flirted with Claire, and he could tell that she enjoyed every word and gesture. On the sixth day, he anonymously sent her an inexpensive bouquet of flowers to the job. Everyone in the office assumed the flowers were from her husband, but Claire knew better. Leonard would never do something so thoughtful for her. The flowers were from Antonyo and she knew it.

Later that afternoon, just before Antonyo got ready to leave the office, Claire discreetly handed him a piece of paper. After Claire walked away, Antonyo read the note.

> **Tony,**
>
> **Thank you so much for the lovely flowers. No one has ever shown me as much kindness as you have this past week. It's hard to believe you are only nineteen years old. But if it's all right with you, then it's all right with me. Tomorrow is your scheduled day off. I am scheduled to get off at noon due to a dentist appointment that I set up a few weeks ago. However, I got a call earlier today from the receptionist informing me that they actually need to reschedule my appointment, so I have some free time tomorrow afternoon. Can we meet somewhere for lunch? Here is my cell phone number. Call me tomorrow around 10:00 a.m. and we can set something up.**

Antonyo and Claire met the following day for lunch, signifying their first date and the beginning of their secret relationship.

At work, the two had a ball sneaking around in an effort

to steal little kisses, hugs, and caresses. After business hours, they would steal away to a cheap motel, always at Claire's expense.

Their alone time was brief in the beginning. Claire, being a responsible mother with two teenage daughters, made sure her children knew nothing about their mother's duplicitous— albeit fulfilling—relationship with her young stud.

Claire had spent the last eighteen years in an unfulfilling marriage. The couple ceased having sex more than a year ago. Claire knew that Leonard was having an affair, and she couldn't care less. She used to just hope they could stay together until their youngest child graduated high school. Lately, however, Claire started thinking less and less about preserving her marriage and more and more about being with Antonyo all the time.

Part of Claire was beginning to feel guilty. Her guilt did not come because she felt bad about what she was doing to Leonard, her husband, but what she felt she was putting Antonyo through. Claire felt she belittled her relationship with Antonyo by sneaking around with him, keeping their affair a secret. While he never complained, she was sure he had to feel slighted on some level. He was available to her at all times, and her time for him was limited.

Claire then began to question her reason for staying in her loveless marriage. Yes, she always said it was for the sake of her daughters, but if she were totally honest with herself, she had to admit that she also stayed because she did not want to bear the stigma of being man-less. Sure, she could have found someone else eventually, but she had become content maintaining the facade of her seemingly comfortable life.

That was until two months ago, when Antonyo Simms awakened things in her heart she had not felt in more than eighteen years. Now, a seemingly comfortable facade no longer held the same appeal. Claire wanted more. Claire wanted better. Claire wanted Antonyo.

Claire knew it would be very difficult explaining things to her daughters. Her separating from their father would be hard enough on them. Couple that with the fact Antonyo was sixteen years younger than her, and she knew it would be the most difficult thing she would have to face with her girls.

But didn't Claire deserve some happiness? Mommy had been there for them their entire lives. Was it not her turn to do something exclusively for herself? *Most definitely*, Claire thought. Right then and there she had made up her mind. She was falling hard for Antonyo. She was going to tell Leonard she wanted a divorce.

Chapter 10

Antonyo and Claire's relationship had just entered the beginning of its third month, and Antonyo was well aware that the past two months had been sheer bliss for Claire. At every opportunity, Claire informed him how much she enjoyed being with him in every way. She also began to talk about how annoyed she had become by having to go home every day to a husband she felt nothing for anymore.

So, by Antonyo's estimation of his worth, the time had now come for her to start paying to play. And, no, the few bucks she shelled out for their dates and motel rooms were not going to be taken into consideration. It was time for Mrs. Claire Anderson to start anteing up and kicking in more.

Antonyo assessed his situation thusly: He was an adult male with a full-time job; therefore, he should no longer have to drive the same vehicle he had acquired while still in high school. The time had come for him to own a new or only slightly used car. Accomplishing this coup would require financing, a down payment, and a co-signer. The financing he could handle; the other two facets of this feat were what posed a challenged for him.

Approaching Claire about co-signing for a new car would have to be handled just right, though. The art of Antonyo getting a woman to take care of him hinged upon never making her *feel* like she was being used. He had to figure out how to make her want to do it for him.

***

Later that evening, Antonyo and Claire were together in one of their regular motel hangouts. Antonyo had just put in another spectacular performance, and Claire was floating on cloud nine. Her excitement stemmed from not only the fabulous lovemaking, but also her decision to ask Leonard for a divorce and planning to share the news with Antonyo. She lay in bed, wrapped in his arms, searching for the perfect words to tell him the good news.

Antonyo managed to impress even himself with his dance of the mattress mambo. He lay with Claire, figuring now was the best time to make his request known.

"I have something I want," they both began in unison.

"Ladies first," Antonyo said. Claire began.

"Tony, I haven't said this to you before, but I'm sure you know how much I care about you, how much I enjoy being with you. In all truth, Antonyo, I have fallen in love with you."

Claire paused for a moment to see what effect, if any, her words were having on Antonyo. When she saw his smile, she knew she was doing and saying the right thing. She sat upright in the bed and continued. "My marriage to Leonard has been dissatisfying for so many years. Meeting you and starting this relationship has made me realize that I can have so much more. That I deserve better. So, I've decided to ask Leonard for a divorce. I want to commit myself totally to us."

Claire had not rehearsed her speech. She simply spoke from the heart. Now that she had shared her thoughts and feelings with Antonyo, she swam in the satisfaction of the way she handled things.

Antonyo lay grinning like a Cheshire cat. He knew that Claire would assume it was because of her news, and that was exactly what he wanted her to think. The real truth of the matter, however, was that Claire's revelation simply made his desire to have her co-sign that much more of a reality.

The two sat in silence for a while, both happy in their own thoughts.

Claire finally broke the silence, remembering that Antonyo also had something he wanted to say. "Tony, what did you want to talk to me about?"

Antonyo thought about it for a minute, realizing that although Claire's confession of love went a long way toward getting what he wanted, the timing was not quite right. He did not want to spring it on her just yet.

"I was thinking along the same lines. I wanted you to know I'm really feeling you, but I was beginning to feel uncomfortable about our relationship because of your husband." Antonyo sat up and looked Claire in the eyes. "But now that you say you're leaving him, I feel so much better. I want to be with you too."

When Claire got home just after midnight, Leonard was sitting in the kitchen, eating a sandwich while watching the small sixteen-inch television that sat atop the counter. Claire figured now was as good a time as any to tell her husband her plans.

She sat down at the table across from Leonard and picked at the grapes in the fruit bowl. "Leonard, can we talk for a moment?"

"Sure, Claire. It's *only* midnight and I have to get up in the morning, but it's cool. I guess this would be your first opportunity to talk to me since you *just* got home."

Claire stared at Leonard, wondering where all the sarcasm came from. This was the most emotion he had shown in more than a year. Thinking about the sadness of that revelation, Claire realized how pitiful her marriage had become. The illuminating knowledge of this sadness forced Claire to forge ahead with her words.

"Leonard, I want a divorce. Neither of us is happy. I don't

see the point of staying together any longer. Before now, I figured it best to stay for the sake of the girls, but then I realized that I can't just live my life for them. I deserve some happiness too."

Leonard did not even bother looking up from his sandwich. He spoke to Claire as if this conversation meant no more to him than a discussion about an overdue phone bill.

"So, I guess you've met someone else," he stated more than asked.

Claire was a little surprised by his insightfulness, but not yet ready to admit to anything concrete. "Leonard, this is about you, me, and how dead our relationship is."

"You're right, Claire. Our marriage has been dead for quite some time. Our children have been my only reason for staying with you as well."

As strange as it sounded, Claire actually felt a connection with Leonard for the first time in a long time. But they still had a big problem to tackle: the emotional well-being of their daughters. It was obvious they both loved them equally. Their pending divorce would hurt the girls significantly.

"Look, Claire, this is definitely going to be difficult for our children, but as you said, we deserve some happiness too. We have always done what's best for them, so we shouldn't beat ourselves up too badly over this. Glendra and Yolanda are not babies. It's not like either of us are divorcing them."

"You're right, Leonard, but I'm scared for them. When do you want to sit them down to talk?" Claire asked.

"The sooner the better, I think. Why don't we do it tomorrow when you get home from work?"

Claire nodded in agreement.

"Leonard, thank you for not making this any worse than it has to be. I really appreciate this not turning into some ugly battle between us."

"Claire, we've shared eighteen years of friendship, if nothing else. We got two beautiful daughters out of the deal. Why should it be ugly?"

The two ended their conversation with a companionable hug. That night, Claire slept in the bedroom and Leonard slept on the sofa in the family room.

The following evening, the soon-to-be former couple sat down with their daughters and explained that they were splitting up. Each expressed how much they loved them and that the divorce was in no way caused by them. Leonard went on to convey that even though he was leaving the home, he would never leave their lives. He would always be there for his daughters, no matter what.

Despite what their parents said to console them, both girls were visibly distraught. Glendra and Yolanda cried and begged their parents not to separate.

The sight of her girls in pain shattered Claire's heart. The peace she shared after having her conversation with Leonard was nowhere to be found during her conversation with the girls. Glendra seemed more agitated than her younger sister.

"Mom, this is all your fault. I know it. You've been gone away from home more than ever. I know that's why Daddy is leaving," she yelled at Claire.

"That is not true, Glen. This is nobody's fault. Your mother and I just grew apart," Leonard said

"I don't believe you, Daddy. Mommy is cheating on you. I know it. That's why she stays out late at night. She never did that before."

"Enough, Glendra! I will not sit here and let you disrespect your mother," Leonard demanded.

Glendra sucked her teeth and rolled her eyes in her mother's direction, but she did not utter another word.

Claire sat in stunned silence. She really had not paid attention to how her actions were affecting her daughters. Had she been inadvertently sacrificing her children in exchange for Antonyo's time? Yolanda's question snapped Claire from her musing.

"Are either of you seeing someone else?" Yolanda asked.

Leonard looked to Claire to answer this question. Claire knew the truth about his new relationship, and he suspected her of having one as well, but Leonard was unsure if they should share these details with the girls just now. Claire answered for them.

"The issue between your father and me has nothing to do with anyone else. We simply are not happy being married to each other anymore." Leonard nodded, pleased with Claire's response.

Glendra was not as easily appeased. She continued to stare at Claire with hatred, silently blaming her mother for her heartbreak. Glendra was the epitome of a Daddy's girl, so she found it totally incomprehensible that her father could be responsible for hurting her like this.

Yolanda, although still quite upset, tried to be empathetic toward her parents. She loved them both equally, and did not want to cause either of them any more stress than the already horrible situation presented. "I'm really sorry that this is happening to our family, but I'll try to live with it. I don't want you to be unhappy anymore, Mommy and Daddy."

Claire smiled through her tears at the maturity of her baby girl. Her oldest child was not quite so willing to be as forgiving and understanding.

"Daddy, I want to go with you. I'm not staying here with her," Glendra announced.

Claire was devastated once again. Glendra could not have hurt her any more if she had stabbed her in the heart with a butcher knife.

"Glendra Diane Anderson," Leonard scolded. "This is the last time I am going to warn you about your disrespect. Your mother and I have already decided that you all will continue to live here. You don't need to add the stress of relocating to an already unpleasant situation."

"But, Daddy . . ."

"No buts, Glendra. We have made our decision."

Glendra jumped from her chair and stormed off to her bedroom. Leonard stood to go after her, but Claire stopped him.

"Let her go, Leonard. She has a right to be upset. And don't worry. I won't tolerate her disrespecting me after today," Claire stated.

Leonard moved out of the house four days later.

Chapter 11

Claire had not spent any time with Antonyo since announcing to her children that their parents were divorcing. She felt it necessary to give her girls her undivided attention during those difficult days of watching their father prepare to depart from their home. She even took an emergency one-week leave from work in an effort to be there for them totally. She explained all of this via several telephone conversations to Antonyo, and of course, he was very supportive.

A few days after Leonard left, the girls went to spend the weekend with him at his mother's house, where he lived for the time being. Since the girls would be away for the entire weekend, Claire figured this would be the perfect opportunity for her and Antonyo to reconnect. Antonyo thought it to be the perfect opportunity to ask Claire about co-signing for his new car.

Claire invited Antonyo to her home for the first time since they started seeing each other. She cooked a romantic dinner, set a beautiful dining room table, and lit the entire house with candles. She could not wait for her newly appointed one and only man to arrive. Though the dinner she prepared was delectable, her cravings were more for the touch of the love of her life than the food that would fill their bellies.

When he arrived at her home, Antonyo found himself very impressed with all that Claire had done to prepare for their evening. Many women had gone to great lengths to amaze him and make him happy, but in his still young age, Claire's efforts had proven the best thus far.

"Wow, Claire! This is all so fabulous. I can't believe you went through all of this trouble just for me," Antonyo complimented.

"Please, sweetie. Don't you know how much I love you?" This was exactly the kind of talk Antonyo wanted to hear.

"Aren't I lucky and happy that you do?"

After dinner, Antonyo reckoned it was the perfect time to bring up the car.

The couple had moved to the sofa in the living room, companionably sitting and enjoying the smooth jazz playing on the stereo.

"Do you know how much I missed you this week?" Antonyo asked as he played in Claire's hair while rubbing her scalp.

"No. Tell me," she cooed in reply.

"I missed you this much," Antonyo indicated by spreading his arms wide.

"You are so silly." Claire laughed, thoroughly enjoying her man's attention.

"I was bored silly, both at work and at home."

"Oh, I'm sorry, baby, but it couldn't be helped. My girls were really taking the breakup hard, especially Glendra," Claire said as she snuggled closer to Antonyo. "Okay, boo, let's talk. What did you do with yourself while we were apart?" Claire asked.

"Not too much of anything, honestly. An old friend of mine and I were going to go out one day, but we canceled our plans because my car wouldn't start," he lied.

"Oh, I'm sorry. What's wrong with your car?"

"It's old, tired, and it's time for a new one. I've been driving it since I was sixteen. It was old and busted when I bought it then."

"Well, I guess it is time for another one. Can't you afford a new one with what you make at KLR?"

"I could probably afford to pay a car note, but the problem would be getting financed and coming up with a decent down payment since I don't have any credit. The interest rate would make my payment more than I could afford if I tried to finance without a co-signer. I asked my mom to co-sign, but she says that she's too far extended. Her credit rating probably wouldn't help me."

Claire thought about Antonyo's predicament, and she really wanted to help him. Her credit was pretty decent since she and Leonard paid their bills on time. She could co-sign for Antonyo as long as he could afford to make the payments.

"Tony, I could probably co-sign for you as long as you bought a car that was reasonably priced and the payments are not too high." Claire's words played as music to Antonyo's ears, but his task was not quite complete.

"In order to get an affordable payment on a decent car, I will need to come up with a down payment. I've got a few dollars saved, but it could take a minute to save all that I need. I don't know if my car is going to last that long."

"Have you priced any vehicles?"

"Yes. I went to a dealership with my Aunt Treecie the other day. They have a great deal on a barely used Monte Carlo. To get it at a payment I could afford, I would need a co-signor and a couple grand on top of the grand I already have saved."

Claire's wheels started spinning again and she started smiling to herself. She was happy that she was in a position to help such a sweet man—the man that now belonged to her exclusively.

"Tony, I am embarrassed to ask you this. It's really something I should already know. When is your birthday?"

Antonyo thought that to be a strange response to his dilemma. It was just the beginning of July. He certainly did not want to wait two more months before he got his car; yet, he answered her question without sounding distressed.

"August twenty-ninth. I'll be twenty."

Claire cringed just a tad as Antonyo announced his age. Was the age difference really that great? She quickly got over it, however, as she thought about all of his redeeming qualities. She really needed to meet his mother. Ms. Simms raised an exceptional young man all by herself, and she sincerely needed to be commended.

"Well, consider my help an early birthday gift. We'll go over there after we get off work on Monday and get everything in order for you to pick up your new vehicle."

"You know you don't have to do this, Claire. I was simply telling you the story to make conversation. I wasn't asking you to help."

"I know, honey. It is my pleasure to help you. I love you." Normally it would have been Antonyo's turn to cringe after hearing those three loaded words, but he was too busy being elated over his good fortune.

"You are so incredible, Claire. Thank you. I am a very lucky man. You are my boo." Antonyo grabbed Claire in a big bear hug, squeezing her tightly.

Tuesday afternoon, Antonyo picked up his new car.

Another month passed and things between Antonyo and Claire were stronger than ever. Claire began behaving with a whole new abandon. She still had not introduced Antonyo to the girls, and for the sake of propriety, mum was still the word on their relationship at work. But Claire told her only sister, her mother, and her best friend all about her tender young lover.

Whenever the girls were spending time with Leonard, Claire spent hers with Antonyo. Since the girls were still on summer vacation from school, she allowed them to spend the majority of their days with Leonard.

Claire knew she should feel guilty about the time she was spending away from her girls, but she did not. She was a woman in love. She had spent half her life in a miserable marriage, being unhappy, trying to do what she thought best for her family. She, for once, wanted to do something for herself, something that made her happy.

On more than one occasion, she even toyed with the idea of giving Leonard physical custody of the girls once school resumed in September, so that she would be free to be with Antonyo all day at work and all evening at home. Claire was sprung.

One afternoon when Claire and Antonyo both had the day off, their time of blissful leisure came to a screeching halt.

The couple was upstairs in Claire's bedroom when all of a sudden Claire heard, "Mom, I was surprised to see your car in the driveway. What are you doing—Aaarrrghh!"

Claire did not hear Glendra's voice until she was at the top of the stairs outside her opened bedroom door. In that time, Claire only had time to cover herself and Antonyo before Glendra walked in.

"Glendra, what are you doing here? I thought you were at your grandmother's house!" Claire yelled at her daughter in exasperated embarrassment as she clung to the bed sheet, shielding her nudity.

"I was about to ask you the same thing, but I can see for myself exactly what you are doing," Glendra yelled back at the top of her lungs upon seeing a male in bed with her mother. She was furious.

"Glendra, give me a minute and I'll talk to you. Just close my door so we can get dressed," Claire pleaded patiently.

"That is so disgusting, Mom. Who is this? I knew you *were* cheating on my father all along."

Claire left the bed then. She tried to push Glendra toward the door out of the bedroom. "Glendra, leave now. I said I will talk to you later," Claire demanded.

"Mom, this guy looks to be my age. How can you leave Daddy for him? You are such a slut. I hate you!" Glendra violently snatched from her mother's grasp and ran from the house.

Claire was furious with her child for her blatant disrespect, furious with herself for the hurt and anger that she caused Glendra, and furious with Antonyo for being so addictive that she had been careless and reckless in her own home. She sank to her bed with her face in her hands and cried.

By this time, Antonyo had managed to put on his pants. He walked over to the bed and sat next to Claire, placing his arms around her shoulders. He sat there trying to comfort her, but his mind stayed on Glendra and how attractive the young woman was.

Claire told Antonyo to leave soon after Glendra did. She needed some time alone to recuperate. Later that evening, she received a phone call from Leonard regarding the episode witnessed by Glendra. Surprisingly, Leonard did not berate her for the incident. He instead came across as very understanding.

"Claire, your fight with Glendra was just an unfortunate accident. You have every right to be happy and involved with a man." Leonard lightened his mood and continued. "Though I hear the word *man* would be a stretch for this person."

"Forget you, Leonard," she playfully responded. "He makes me happy." Claire was glad that she and her soon-to-be ex could communicate like this. Obviously they were meant to be friends, not life partners, but together they still had to deal with the unpleasantness at hand.

"Well, what should I do about Glendra?" Claire asked.

"We will just have to sit her down and explain the truth about your new relationship. She's not a baby. She is going to have to get used to the fact that life is not always going to go the way she wants it to."

"The sooner the better, I think. Can you all come over for dinner when I get off work tomorrow?" Claire asked.

"We'll see you then."

Claire felt much better about her unpleasant encounter after talking with Leonard. It was good to know she had an ally in handling this. Now she needed to talk to her man. She really wanted to see him. Claire dialed his number.

"Hey, you," Antonyo answered upon recognizing the phone number.

"Can you come back over now? I need to see you. I want you to hold me and help me alleviate the stress of what happened when we were interrupted earlier."

Claire's mention of the episode immediately brought images of the sexy Glendra to his mind. His body responded instantly. "I'm on the way."

Claire hung up the phone, smiling brightly at the thought of being with her lover in just a little while. Her love for Antonyo overflowed, making her want to spend every waking moment with him.

Then it hit her. After she and Leonard talked with the girls and explained their new relationships, she would ask Antonyo to move into her home. Claire figured this would be the best way for the girls to get to know him and get used to him being around.

Claire ordered pizza and salad and had already set the dining room table for dinner when Leonard arrived with Glendra and Yolanda the following evening. The family only used the dining room for special occasions and important family talks. Claire felt tonight's discussion would be appropriate for its use.

Claire hugged Yolanda with relative ease, happy to know that at least one of her children still loved her. She approached Glendra a little more cautiously, hoping not to get another fight started. She wrapped her arms around her daughter.

Glendra respectfully but stiffly returned her mother's embrace. Claire could feel the tension. She could only hope that by the end of the evening things could be rectified between her and her daughter.

Everyone sat down at the table and all began digging into the food but Glendra.

"Honey, have something to eat. I made sure that I ordered your favorite pizza," Claire said.

"I'm not hungry," Glendra replied.

Leonard and Claire eyed each other, both with the same thought running through their heads: *This is going to be as difficult as we anticipated.*

Leonard began first while they ate. "Girls, your mother and I have gotten together to discuss something with you. Specifically, we want to talk to you regarding our personal lives."

Glendra rolled her eyes hard and sucked her teeth so loudly that Claire was sure the neighbors could hear her. Leonard shot her a look of warning before continuing his speech.

"We understand that our split is hard on you two girls. We both apologize to you for that. We have simply grown apart and we no longer make each other happy. But we feel it is unfair of us to stay together just to make you two happy."

Claire figured she should jump in now. She didn't want

Leonard to have to do this by himself. "Both your father and I have moved on with our lives. I, in particular, have started seeing someone else seriously. Leonard and I understand that this may be difficult for you to accept right away, but we don't think we should sneak around behind your backs and be deceitful." Claire looked directly at Glendra when she finished talking. She was rewarded with a glare of pure contempt.

The room fell silent for several moments, everyone stewing in their own thoughts. The only face completely readable was Glendra's. She held so much hatred in her heart for her mother.

Yolanda spoke first. "I don't know if I will ever get used to seeing you with someone else, Mom, but if you're both cool with it, then what can I say? I just don't want to have to call anyone else Dad."

Glendra decided to hold her anger in check and pretend that she felt the same way as her baby sister. "Me too," she lied.

Leonard and Claire eyed each other again, thinking the same thought: *This was not so bad after all.*

"Well, is there anything else that either of you want to say?" Claire asked.

"I'm cool," Yolanda stated.

"I'll have some pizza now," Glendra answered.

Chapter 12

Antonyo jumped at Claire's proposal to move in with her. Her offer stated that for the first six months, she would handle all the household bills while he began building himself a little nest egg. After that, he would begin paying one-third of the bills, which included the mortgage, the utilities, and the car insurance. One half seemed unfair to Claire, since her daughters were her responsibility. Besides, she made quite a bit more money than he did.

Antonyo had no intention of ever paying Claire a dime. His plan included being gone right as the six months came to a close. As a matter of fact, he was going to try to work on getting her to pay a couple of his car notes while he stacked his cash until moving day.

When Antonyo informed Trina of his plan to move in with Claire, he was prepared to hear a sermon about the perils of his wayward lifestyle, and he was, unfortunately, not disappointed.

"When, Antonyo, are you going to stop with this craziness? Did you not learn anything from the last time you got involved with someone else's wife? Do you remember how that woman tossed you out on your ear, leaving you with your pitiful self standing at my doorstep?"

"Ma, Claire and her husband are getting a divorce," Antonyo stated as if it really made everything A-okay. Trina's eyes rolled so far in the top of her head, Antonyo doubted he'd see anything but the whites of them ever again.

"So, do you plan on marrying Claire when her divorce is final? Are you going to spend the rest of your life with a woman who is twice your age and has two almost grown daughters, one of whom is only two years younger than you?"

It was now Antonyo's turn to show her the whites of his eyes. An actual answer was not necessary because they were both aware that marriage was nowhere in his life plan.

"Antonyo, don't you see this is a dead-end lifestyle? You flitting from woman to woman, leaving a string of broken hearts in your wake is not what God has purposed for your life. Each of us was created to glorify God, Antonyo. The Bible says so. One of my favorite scriptures says, 'For I know the plans I have for you, declares the Lord, plans to prosper you and not to harm you, plans to give you hope and a future.' You were created to be so much more, sweetheart."

"Ma, I appreciate your concern. I understand that you love me and you worry about me, but you do that based on your own moral compass. I'm cool with my life. I'm not dissing God or anything like that. I'm just not ready to become a monk."

"This woman obviously has deep feelings for you, Antonyo. How can you just use her until you're tired of her, and then break her heart? Don't you have any remorse for how you treat these women? Or did I actually raise you to be a complete sociopath?"

"Ma, none of this has anything to do with you. I am an adult and I am responsible for my own actions. God may not be pleased with me, but I'm sure you and He are cool. Let me worry about the consequences of my actions."

"Trust me, Antonyo; there will be consequences," LaTrina stated as she left him to his packing.

The day before Antonyo moved in, Claire called a meeting between herself, Antonyo, and the girls. She intentionally waited until the last minute in order to give the girls no more than one night to voice their displeasure with the situation. She explained to Glendra and Yolanda that Antonyo was the new man in her life. They were in love, and he would be living with them.

Antonyo expected a negative reaction from both girls, but to his surprise, only Yolanda became slightly irate. Glendra reacted as if she were perfectly fine with the situation, even happy that her mother had found someone to love.

"Mom, I'm all for you having a new man, but why does this young guy have to move in here with us? I think that's too much!" Yolanda exclaimed.

Claire opened her mouth to rebut, but Glendra came to her mother's rescue. "Yolanda, you are not being fair. We cannot dictate who Mom falls in love with. We need to be supportive of both our parents now. We don't get to make the rules and we shouldn't complain. We should be happy that our parents are friends with each other and not dragging us through some ugly custody battle. We should also appreciate the fact that Mommy is willing to be open and honest with us about her new relationships. Both Mom and Dad deserve our cooperation."

Claire was stunned, but happy. She really wanted the girls to get along with Antonyo, and having Glendra's cooperation would go a long way toward accomplishing that goal. Her daughter's change of heart thrilled Claire immensely.

Antonyo was shocked out of his socks. The trained schemer in him detected a set-up, though he was not quite sure yet what the beauty had in mind. Manipulation was his claim to fame, so he could smell Glendra's brand of crap from a mile away. Game recognized game.

Two weeks later, they were all living as one big happy family. Yolanda maintained a polite and respectable distance, but Glendra behaved as if she and Antonyo were best friends. Oftentimes she would approach the couple, prompting them to engage in board or card games. Antonyo would always decline, feigning tiredness, on which occasions Yolanda, Glendra, and Claire would play; or he would say that he just wanted to spend time alone with Claire. Because of his attraction to Glendra, he knew being around her too often, even in Claire's presence, could prove dangerous for him.

During the initial weeks of cohabitation, there were two occasions where Claire and Antonyo found themselves faced with conflicting schedules, leaving Antonyo with the day off while Claire was scheduled to be at work. Antonyo spent those days at his mother's or his aunt's until Claire came home from work; however, on the third time around, his dodge game came to an end.

Glendra had a dentist's appointment scheduled after school the following evening, and Leonard was supposed to take her. He called Claire to inform her that an emergency came up at work. He asked Claire to reschedule the appointment if she was unavailable to take Glendra.

After hanging up from Leonard, Claire remembered that Antonyo had the day off, so she volunteered his services. She explained to Antonyo that it was just a routine cleaning; therefore, no parental signature would be required. He just needed to get Glendra there and back home.

"Claire, are you sure the dentist will allow me to sign her in? I'm not a relative," Antonyo pleaded, trying to get out of doing the favor.

"Glendra is almost eighteen years old. She can sign herself in for a regular check-up. She just needs a ride." Claire walked away as if the simple matter were decided.

Antonyo didn't want to protest too much for fear he might raise Claire's suspicions, so he let the issue drop; but he was very uncomfortable with the whole idea of being alone with Glendra.

Glendra had been plotting in her mind a way to get back at her mother for breaking up their family since the day her parents told them about their separation. She was standing there as the exchange went down between Antonyo and her mother. A sly smile crept upon her face as she grasped the impact of their conversation. Tomorrow would be the first time she would be able to put her plan of "operation get even" into motion.

Antonyo saw Glendra's smirk just as Claire turned to leave the room. *Yep. This fine young woman has something up her sleeve,* he thought to himself.

"Come on, Tony. It's just a doctor's appointment. It's not like Mom is asking you to take me to the prom or anything." Glendra laughed out loud at her little joke as she followed in the direction of her mother.

The following day, when Antonyo arrived at Glendra's school, she and another young lady were waiting out front for him. Both girls approached the car. Glendra opened the door, letting the seat up for her friend to get in the back.

"Tony, this is my girl, Tamara. We usually walk together, but since I'm not going home, can you drop her off at her house? She lives right around the block from us," Glendra explained as she settled herself in the front seat, assuming the matter to be settled. Antonyo guessed she got that trait from her mother.

Antonyo turned to look at Tamara. She was an average-looking girl, nothing special about her; quite a contrast to the beauty occupying his front seat. "Sure. I'll drop her off," Antonyo replied nonchalantly.

Tamara scooted forward in her seat so she could whisper *loudly* in Glendra's ear. "Girl, he is foine as fish whiskers."

"I told you he was," Glendra whispered back, sending both girls into a fit of giggles. The two continued to talk amongst themselves in their secretive girl talk the remainder of the ride to Tamara's house.

When the car stopped in front of Tamara's house, Glendra stepped out to allow Tamara to exit the back seat. She grabbed her friend and spoke directly into her ear. This time Antonyo could not hear a word. When they parted, the giggles started again.

"Girl, you are crazy. Call me when you get back from the doctor's office," Tamara told her.

When Glendra returned to her seat in the car, Antonyo asked, "What was the joke? I want to laugh too."

"It's just silly girl talk. Nothing that you would find amusing, I'm sure," Glendra said, and chuckled again. After several minutes of silence between the two, Glendra struck up a conversation. "Tony, can I ask you something?"

Antonyo became slightly unnerved because he knew Glendra had some deviousness planned, but he answered affirmatively. "Sure, what is it?"

"Do you think I'm pretty?"

Antonyo's inner cautionary red flag went up again. He decided to tread lightly in answering her question. "Yes. I think you are very pretty. Why?"

"Well, there's this guy that I'm into. I mean, he is fine as frog hair. Problem is he's seeing someone else. I'm not necessarily trying to steal him away from her. I just want a little bit of his time for right now. What do you think I should do?"

So, this was her little scheme. *Very clever*, Antonyo thought. Glendra was trying to seduce him. The idea appealed to Antonyo greatly because of his attraction to her, but he wondered how she believed they could pull it off without Claire ever finding out. It was time for him to ask a few questions of his own.

"Well, how cool are you and the girl he's seeing?"

"What difference does that make?"

"I mean, is she someone whose feelings you care about, or is she just another female to you?"

Glendra thought about that for a moment. How did she really feel about her mother? She thought about the hurt her mother caused her and her sister when she decided to choose her young lover over their father. She thought about how selfish her mother was for splitting up their family, and she thought about her own horror the day she caught her mother and Antonyo in the bedroom together. Then she answered Antonyo carefully. "Let's just say we're cordial. If she found out I was kicking it with her man, she would truly be angry with me, but my plans are to keep it all on the hush-hush. She ain't really got to know nothing, if you know what I mean."

He knew exactly what she meant, and her answer was like sweet music to his ears. "Well then, I think you should go for it. Just be sure you're careful. A harmless fling can turn into a dangerous situation if things don't go well. The best thing to do is to be very discreet. This is something you shouldn't tell anyone, not even your best girlfriend. The more people that know about it, the more chances there are for you to get caught, and the last thing you want is to have your friends start talking behind your back. They may begin to distrust you, thinking that if you are willing to creep with one woman's man, you might just creep with their man too."

Antonyo couldn't really care less about what Glendra's friends thought about her. He just wanted to make sure there was no chance of him getting caught.

They completed the rest of the ride to the doctor's office in stone silence, each of them stewing in their own thoughts of what to do and say next.

After the appointment, on their way back home, Glendra announced, "You know what, Tony? I'm going to go for it."

She placed her hand on his upper thigh and began softly massaging it, as she looked him directly in the eyes.

From that moment forward, it was on and poppin' for the two of them. Whenever the two of them schemed to be together, Tamara was always Glendra's alibi, and Aunt Treecie was Antonyo's.

One month had passed since Glendra and Antonyo began their scandalous and unscrupulous affair. Each night, Glendra wrote in her diary, recording their tawdriness in permanent ink. The only people the two ever discussed their affair aloud with were Tamara and Aunt Treecie.

Tamara also knew that the initial motivation behind Glendra starting the affair was revenge; however, things had taken an unexpected turn for Glendra. She found herself falling for Antonyo and getting extremely jealous of the nights he spent in her mother's bed. She not only wanted to hurt her mother with their affair; she now wanted Antonyo all to herself.

Claire noticed a change in her daughter's behavior toward her over the past few weeks. Her assumption led her to believe that Glendra was once again upset about her and Antonyo's relationship. At times when they were all together, she would catch Glendra rolling her eyes at the two of them. Claire remembered how well Glendra and Antonyo seemed to be getting along initially and how their budding friendship had thrilled her. Now she was at a loss as to what to do to make her daughter feel better. Claire decided she would try talking to her after dinner one night.

Claire approached Glendra in the kitchen while Glendra loaded the dishwasher. Antonyo was away visiting his aunt, and Yolanda was upstairs doing homework.

"Glendra, sweetie, are you having problems because of my relationship with Tony?" Claire asked.

Glendra almost dropped the glass she held in her hand, totally caught off guard by her mother's question. Before her mother approached, she stood there thinking of a way to let her mother know about her and Antonyo so she could have him all to herself; but upon hearing Claire's voice, she realized she was not prepared to spring the news on her mother just yet.

"No, *Mother*. Why do you ask that?" Glendra answered with attitude.

"Well, you've been a little short with me, and you seem very distant toward Antonyo."

"Look, Mom, the real reason I have been acting a little funny is because I have my own relationship and my own relationship troubles to deal with." That was as close to the truth as Glendra could get.

"A relationship with whom? And why is this the first I'm hearing about it?"

"Perhaps you've been too busy with your own *boy*friend," Glendra snapped.

Clair was real sick and tired of her oldest child's disrespectful mouth. Breaking a piece of her foot off in Glendra's tail felt like an exceptional idea right now, but she struggled to maintain cool and chalk it up to her daughter having relationship drama.

Pointing a stern finger in her daughter face, Claire said, "Glendra, that's all I'm going to take from you in the manner of disrespect. I realize you are going through something with this friend of yours, but nobody in this family has anything to do with that, so nobody in this family is going to put up with your sour disposition."

Glendra just stared at her mother. She dared not open her mouth for fear that the real truth might tumble from her lips.

"How long have you been seeing this young man anyway?" Claire asked her daughter.

"About a month," Glendra answered, still disgruntled.

"Well, I want to meet him. Soon! Set something up." Claire left the kitchen.

Oh! You will find out who he is soon enough, Glendra thought.

Two weeks passed and Claire saw no improvement in Glendra's behavior or demeanor. As a matter of fact, she seemed to somehow get worse. And she still had not made it her business to produce and introduce this so-called boyfriend. On her drive home from work, Claire decided it was time for another talk.

As she walked into the house through the garage door, she thought she heard raised voices. Upon coming further into the kitchen, she found Antonyo and Glendra arguing in the family room.

"Girl, are you crazy? I'm not about to do that," she heard Antonyo say.

"Why not?" Glendra yelled.

"Because you said this was just a fling. So why are you tripping now?"

Claire stepped into the family room just then, interrupting their verbal battle. "What is going on in here?" she demanded.

Neither Antonyo nor Glendra noticed Claire's entrance into the room. They both jumped at the sound of her voice.

Claire stood there looking between the two of them. They stood there looking bug-eyed and scared out of their minds. Neither of them said a word. Claire took what she heard from their conversation and drew her own conclusion. "Glendra, are you bothering Tony with your boyfriend troubles? What do you expect him to do?"

Antonyo realized that Claire had not heard much of their argument. His face and body showed visible signs of relief as he sagged and dropped onto the sofa.

Glendra stood, still stunned at her mother's appearance. She was torn, however, between relief that Claire had not figured out why they were really arguing, and anger because Claire immediately assumed that she was causing Antonyo grief.

"Whatever, Ma!" she snapped as she found her footing and ran up the back stairs.

Claire snapped at that moment as well and went up after Glendra. More than enough disrespect had been hurled at her by her oldest daughter. She reached Glendra's bedroom door just as it slammed in her face.

Clair pushed the door open and went straight to Glendra's desk, where she sat preparing to write something in her diary. "Listen here, heffa. I have told you more than once that I am tired of your crap," Claire yelled, pointing her finger in Glendra's face. "Now, since you can't control that funky little attitude of yours, your behind is grounded for the next two weeks. No phone, no television, no leaving this house other than going to and from school. Oh, and no seeing that boyfriend of yours either."

Glendra stood from her desk, replying, "That's what you think!"

Claire slapped Glendra's face with all of her might.

Glendra grabbed her stinging cheek and glared at her mother, tempted to crush her right then and there. Not physically, of course, because she would never strike her mother, but she knew she held the power to demolish her emotionally by telling her they were seeing the same man. There was still some small something in her, however, that just would not allow her to admit to the affair she'd been having with Antonyo for more than six weeks. She left the room, running again, heading downstairs as tears flowed freely from her eyes.

Claire sat in the seat vacated by Glendra, emotionally drained by the episode with her daughter. She closed her eyes and held her temples as a full-blown headache loomed in the midst. When she reopened her eyes, Claire spotted Glendra's diary sitting on the desk. Perhaps the answers to Glendra's man problems were in there.

Claire felt only a mild sense of guilt for invading her daughter's privacy, but she felt it important to find out what was making her baby so crazy. She opened the diary and scanned the pages, determined to look no further than five or six weeks back. She only wanted to know about this boyfriend.

The first entry she read made her heart leap painfully into her throat. She felt as if she were going to choke to death right there on the spot.

> *I can't believe we actually did it. We actually had sex. I mean . . . it was cool and all, but now I don't know how I feel about it. Part of me is happy and another part of me feels guilty. But what the heck. I'm on a mission.*

Oh my God! They are having sex, Glendra thought. She was mortified. The last thing any mother wants is to slip and find information that says her baby is sexually active. But she read on to see what else had been happening.

This is getting crazy. Tony and I are having a ball. . . .

Wow, what a coincidence. Glendra's boyfriend was named Tony, too, Claire thought.

> *I knew he was gorgeous the moment I first laid eyes on him, but somehow he gets more and more handsome.*

Again the hair on Claire's arms stood up. What in the world was she going to do or say to her child? Right now, the only rational thought she could muster involved hoping Glendra used protection. The two entries she read thus far gave no clue as to why Glendra had been so uptight. These words said everything was cool between her and this young man. She went forward a few entries to find out where the problems started.

This entry was dated three weeks later than the others:

I can't believe I have fallen in love with my mother's man . . . .

Instantly, Claire's chest heaved and her stomach flipped. She threw up all over Glendra's desk and diary. The entire contents of her stomach came up all in one lurch. Her head was spinning. Her palms were sweating, and her temples were throbbing out of control. She tried to stand and fell straight to the floor with vomit dripping on her from the desktop. Claire saw her entire relationship with Antonyo flash before her eyes. Certainly death would snatch her from her own puddle of puke right then and there.

Suddenly, she let out a loud, continuous wail, unable to stop herself from screaming. She lay in the floor literally losing her mind.

Antonyo, Glendra, and Yolanda all appeared in the doorway simultaneously. The sight of Claire lying there screaming at the top of her lungs made them all very nervous. Antonyo was the first to approach her.

"Claire, baby, what's wrong?" he asked gently as he bent down to take her hand and try to help her up.

Claire finally stopped screaming long enough to growl. "Get away from me, you trifling bastard." Claire's eyes bulged from their sockets and she literally foamed at the mouth. Her reaction to his offer of help coupled with the smell of the vomit made Antonyo back away quickly.

"Mama, what's wrong? What happened?" Yolanda pleaded from a few feet away.

She didn't answer her youngest child. She just started screaming and crying again at the sound of her soft, concerned voice. The next voice made her lose it again.

"Mom, you're scaring us. What is wrong with you? Are you sick?" Glendra asked.

"Shut up talking to me, you tramp."

Everyone in the room visibly winced at the comment. Antonyo and Glendra knew that somehow she had found out the truth. Glendra then spied her diary on the floor next to her mother and figured out how. Her hand flew to her mouth. Now she too wanted to scream.

Antonyo stood frozen in his spot, sweat beads popping up on his forehead. What in the heck was he supposed to do now? He suddenly turned and tried to leave the room, but Claire noticed his hasty retreat and stopped him cold.

"Wait one flippin' minute, you raggedy piece of crap." She leapt from the floor like a tigress and bound to where Antonyo stood in two steps. Once in striking distance, she balled her fist and punched him in the jaw. "Now get out of my house! Don't you even stop to get your stuff! If you are not out of here in two minutes, I swear on Yolanda's life that I will shoot you straight in your pitiful manhood."

Antonyo held his jaw and backed out of the bedroom. He knew from the look in Claire's eyes that she meant what she said. Figuring it was worth losing the possessions he had at her home in an effort to save his life, he bolted from the room, the house, and Claire's life.

Glendra watched the horrible exchange between her mother and Antonyo. She was torn between leaving with the man she loved and staying with a mother who probably hated her. Overwhelmed with guilt, she began crying uncontrollably. She finally made up her mind to follow Antonyo.

"Don't you dare leave this room," Claire hissed. Glendra stopped dead in her tracks, knowing her mother would hurt her if she continued to move.

Yolanda stood totally confused. She still had not figured out what was going on, why everybody in her house seemed to go crazy all at once.

"Mama! Glendra! Please! Somebody tell me what's happening here," Yolanda begged.

Neither of Antonyo's lovers uttered a word. They just glared at each other. Yolanda started crying, and the two women simultaneously went to comfort her. As they both embraced Yolanda, their hands accidentally touched. The contact seemed strange initially, each caught up in the same jumbled, confusing emotions.

Both Claire and Glendra were in love with Antonyo; both hurt by betrayal. They were both also experiencing feelings of guilt and turmoil over how they treated each other. Each had placed their affections for him over the family bond they had built for more than seventeen years.

"I'm so sorry, Mommy!" Glendra cried while they still held on to Yolanda.

"I'm sorry too, baby," Claire responded. Mother and daughter forgave each other immediately, and the healing began that moment.

Antonyo ended up back on his mother's doorstep in need of a place to stay.

Chapter 13

Trina woke one morning to find Antonyo outside, cutting the lawn at her new house, a chore he'd done of his own volition.

Trina stood proudly at the window of the small three-bedroom ranch-style home she'd purchased about a month ago, nestled in the beautiful working-class neighborhood near Wyoming and Oakman Boulevard.

Trina received a blessing in the job market about two years ago when she met a man at church looking for a receptionist. Having never worked in corporate America before, she knew this opportunity had to be none other than the hand of God working in her life, and Mr. Davis, her employer, was truly a servant of God. Mr. Jordan Davis hired Trina and gave her a chance to prove that she could be trained to be the best receptionist his company had ever seen.

Soon after going to work for Mr. Davis and learning her job, Trina decided that she wanted to be more than a receptionist. She soon grew bored with the menial and mundane requirements of her position, knowing she was capable of doing so much more. So, Trina enrolled herself at the Detroit Business Institute and took night school classes. Eight months later, she received her certificate in office administration. One month following her graduation, Trina received a promotion to the position of administrative assistant. Three months ago, she was again promoted, this time into the position of executive assistant to Michael Stanford, the owner of the company.

Thirty days ago, she closed on her lovely new home. Not bad, Trina thought, for a woman who had gotten herself pregnant at fifteen and dropped out of high school. Joining the church and turning her life over to God had been the best thing that Trina had ever done for herself. Now she stood looking from the picture window in her living room watching her only child, wishing she could convince him to do the same.

Antonyo was now twenty-one years old and showed no signs of changing the behavior he began exhibiting at age thirteen. There were so many females calling the house for him that Trina had long ago stopped trying to keep track of them all. She simply called them all "baby girl" and took their messages.

While continuing to live under her roof, Antonyo still had to abide by the house rule of no overnight guests, and his monthly contribution to the household increased to $350 per month. Trina could only hope, pray, and talk to Antonyo about his womanizing, believing that God would someday change his conduct. He'd completely quit attending school. She could at least be proud that he had amassed some seniority at his job with KLR and now worked as a junior team leader at the company.

When Antonyo moved back with his mother last year, he was stalked relentlessly for three months by Glendra. Trina, having no idea that Antonyo had also become involved with the young woman while living with her mother, became concerned for Antonyo's life as a result of the continued harassment.

In an attempt to put an end to the stalking, Trina went to visit Claire. She left the home of Glendra and her mother totally ashamed after learning the truth about her son's ugly, disrespectful, duplicitous, demeaning, and destructive involvement with both mother and daughter simultaneously. Claire gave Trina all the ugly details about the triangular affair and the devastating affects it had on her family. Claire was so distraught as a result of the drama that she resigned from her job at KLR in an effort to never lay eyes on Antonyo again.

After hearing her mother replay the tawdry details of her and Antonyo's betrayal to Trina, Glendra's shame and embarrassment forced her to see that Antonyo was not worthy of her efforts and her mother did indeed deserve her loyalty. That was the last that Trina saw or heard from either woman.

While Trina stood in her window watching Antonyo mow the lawn, for the first time in a long time, she began to think about Sheldon, Antonyo's father. Her musings led her to think that if Sheldon had played a bigger role in Antonyo's life, perhaps her son would have turned out differently, having more respect for a woman's value. Trina firmly believed that Antonyo's activities were a result of his witness to how Sheldon had treated both her and Antonyo.

Neither Antonyo nor Trina had heard a peep from Sheldon since the day of Antonyo's senior prom. Trina knew that God wanted her to hate no one, but when she reflected on things like this, it was hard for her to have love for Antonyo's sperm donor.

Antonyo came in the house and interrupted her musings. "Hey, Ma. What you over there thinking so hard about?"

"Antonyo, do you ever think about Sheldon?" Trina asked, trying to honestly answer his question.

"Is that what you're over there staring out the window, concentrating so hard on? Why?"

"I just feel that if maybe he had been a better father, perhaps you wouldn't be so hard on these women you deal with."

Antonyo could not believe that she used thoughts of his punk father to dredge up this same old argument. Sheldon had no influence on his life one way or the other, good or bad.

"Forget Sheldon, Ma. I have," he said unemotionally as he walked from the living room back to the bathroom to wash his hands just as the phone rang in the kitchen.

Trina decided to drop the conversation for now. She refused to upset her son after he cut the lawn without having been asked to do it. She just went on and answered the telephone on its third ring. "Hello."

"Hello, Ms. Trina. May I please speak with Tony?"

"Who should I say is calling?" Trina asked dryly.

"It's me, Ms. Trina. Clarke! You don't know my voice by now?" the young lady asked sweetly.

If only you knew how much I didn't, Trina thought to herself, but instead said, "Just a minute, baby girl. I'll get him for you." She removed the receiver away from her face. "Antonyo, Clarke is on the phone," Trina called.

Clarke ranked number one on Antonyo's list of women. At eighteen, she stood out as the youngest, the prettiest, and the smartest. Clarke had graduated from high school at age sixteen and now attended Wayne State University as a sophomore. Her status as number one also resulted from the fact that Clarke started out as the only virgin in his current stable, so the need for protection from disease had been a burden he did not have to worry about when the two became sexually active. Her intellect and pursuit of excellence insured that she would handle the precautions against pregnancy.

"Hey, Clarke!" Antonyo answered.

"Hey, boo! Just thought I would give you a holler to see what you were up to on this beautiful, sunny Saturday afternoon."

"I do have plans later this evening, but I'm free until about eight o'clock. What do you have in mind?"

There were no problems between Antonyo and the women that he currently dated. In other words, no one expected monogamy.

"I was thinking we could catch an early movie and perhaps have lunch. I haven't seen you since last Friday night." Just as Clarke finished her sentence, the phone beeped, indicating there was a call waiting to be answered on the other line.

"Hold on, Clarke." He activated the call-waiting button and answered. "Hello."

"Heeeeey, boo! Whatcha doing?" The caller was obviously another of his female friends, but he could not quite make out the voice.

"Who is this?" Antonyo asked directly

"I can't believe you never know who I am when I call you, Antonyo. This is Lynn."

"What's up, Lynn? I'm going to have to call you back because I'm on the other line."

"Who you talking to, and why can't they call you back?" Lynn asked with attitude.

"Lynn, you know the rules. Ask no questions, you get no lies. Now, you can either hang up politely and I'll call you back, or I'm going to hang up on you and not deal with you and your attitude anymore."

"You better make sure you call me back, Tony. Bye."

Antonyo hoped their conversation ended that way, because he had learned to never make a threat he was not prepared to carry out; therefore, he would never appear to be weak. Lynn spent money on Antonyo like money had little more value than tap water. He would hate to have to kick her to the curb. He reconnected the call with Clarke. "Sorry, Clarke."

"It's cool. So, can we hook up today?"

"Sure. Give me a chance to shower and change and I'll pick you up in about an hour." They both agreed to the time and disconnected the call.

Antonyo liked Clarke Tyler even though she did not have the financial wherewithal to do things for him. Somehow, there always managed to be one in his stable that he cared for. Clarke was a struggling student attending school on full academic scholarship. She was the oldest of six children, all born to a single mom. Clarke worked part time as a cashier in the neighborhood grocery store to help her mother make ends meet.

Lynne Trevelle, on the other hand, was the spoiled rotten twenty-two-year-old daughter of a white mother employed as an obstetrician, and a black father who was a high school principal. She graduated college with a pre-law degree, but was not doing anything at the current time toward going on to law school. As she put it, she was taking time out for herself. Lynn was bossy and controlling with most people; however, Antonyo refused to take nonsense from her, and this is what she liked most about him.

Lynn's personality traits included being high strung, overly emotional, frantic, and paranoid: in short, a drama queen. Clarke was mild mannered, soft spoken, fun-loving and stable. Lynn was rich. Clarke was broke. The character of the other three women he dealt with fell somewhere between these two.

The other women in his crew included Katrina, a twenty-one-year-old administrative assistant, Charleyna (Shar-lay-na), a twenty-three-year-old department store manager and part-time student, and Timber, a twenty-year-old cashier who worked for the same department store chain as Charleyna, but at a different location.

Antonyo had amassed a respectable savings nest egg as a result of his salary and the money he saved from having the women in his life pay his car note, insurance, and the rent his mother assessed him. There were also many extra perks, such as clothes, jewelry, and extravagant nights on the town that the lovely damsels in his life provided.

Antonyo dressed and left the house to pick up Clarke. On the drive to her house, he began to think about his mother and why she resolved to waste good brain power meditating about Sheldon today. Years had passed since he last thought about his father, and never had he considered Sheldon responsible for his having no desire to settle down with any one woman.

Sheldon was a punk when Antonyo was a child. Sheldon had been a punk since Antonyo had become an adult, and more than likely, Sheldon was going to be a punk for the rest of both of their lives. Sheldon could teach him nothing about being a man, other than how to do it differently than Sheldon had done it.

Antonyo concluded long ago that if Sheldon cared so little as to never try to contact him, then forget him. He was better off living his life without his dad. His mother had given his father far more credit than he deserved. Antonyo lived the way Antonyo lived because Antonyo was happy living this way. Period!

Antonyo felt that Trina had been bugging a lot lately. Today, talking about this Sheldon crap, and before then and at every given opportunity, she seemed to be telling him about how his life lacked a true and intimate relationship with God. She'd been talking about how God had changed her life for a few years now.

Sure, he believed in God just as much as any of the other folks he knew. Antonyo understood creation, thanks to Trina, and gave God His due for it. He recognized that God was all powerful and able to do all things. God could heal the sick, feed the hungry, and take care of the poor. What he did not understand were all the rules God had that seemed to eradicate the possibility of having any fun. As a young man, Antonyo assumed he had plenty of time before he had to slow down and allow God to have His way in his life. But for now, he was going to live his life the way a young man should be able to—carefree.

Antonyo arrived at Clarke's, and the two spent the afternoon just as planned. Their day together was perfect, as had been all other dates the couple shared. Well, almost perfect anyway. The only exception came as a result of Lynn constantly ringing Antonyo's cell phone. He went from answering the first time and informing her he would contact her later, to putting the phone on vibrate during the second, third, and fourth call, to turning it off altogether. The girl's relentlessness had defied Antonyo's understanding. This was unusual behavior, even for Lynn's demanding demeanor.

Clarke never let on that the nuisance bothered her one bit. No matter what happened, she was simply content to be in Antonyo's presence. Clarke understood he dated other females, and though she was less than thrilled, she appreciated his honesty, accepted his standards, and rolled with the situation. Clarke could only hope that one day he would come to feel about her the way she felt about him and then realize she was all the woman he needed.

After Antonyo dropped Clarke at home, he returned Lynn's call, anxious to know the urgency behind her blowing up his cell phone. The four voice mail messages were all uninformative.

"Lynn, what is your problem today? Why were you calling me like a maniac this afternoon and then not bother leaving me a decent message?" he yelled.

"Oh, calm down, boo. I missed you, that's all. Nothing more. Nothing less," she replied nonchalantly.

This girl is truly nuts, Antonyo thought to himself. He also contemplated that perhaps the potential headaches connected with continuing to date this whacky chick would far outweigh the financial benefits associated with an ongoing involvement. Lynn was a spoiled rotten brat, and Antonyo was truly tiring of having to deal with her childish and psychotic behavior.

"So, what you doing now, stud man?" Lynn asked playfully.

"Nothing that has anything to do with you, crazy woman. Look, Lynn, I am going out tonight, and I do not want to hear from you. If you can refrain from ringing my phone, I will call you tomorrow when I get off work. If you call me even once, I promise you will never see my face again."

"Tomorrow is Sunday, Tony. You have to work on a Sunday?" Lynn asked humbly.

"I am a supervisor, Lynn, and the company is open seven days a week; therefore, I have to work some weekends."

"Okay. I'll be good. I'll talk to you tomorrow," she replied in a sing-song voice then hung up.

Antonyo shook his head as he hung up the phone and drove home to prepare for his evening date. He intended on forgetting about crazy Lynn and concentrating on having a nice, peaceful evening with Timber; however, peace was not to be found immediately. The moment he walked into the house, Trina was on the attack.

"Antonyo, some crazy girl named Lynn called my house seven times since you left. Seven times. Do you hear me? I have told you I am not going to deal with these stupid girlfriends of yours disrupting my peace. Now, before you leave this house tonight, you will call the phone company and make an appointment to have your own phone line installed, and you will pay to have my phone number changed so I never have to hear from those tramps again." Trina stomped away from Antonyo and headed toward her bedroom, never bothering to give him a chance to respond.

After his mother's verbal berating, Antonyo again considered getting rid of Lynn for good. Were the perks really worth
the hassles? He thought about his car note, insurance, rent,
and fully stocked closest. His answer was an affirmative yes!

Chapter 14

In the passing months, Clarke's unwavering infatuation grew to full-blown love. She and Antonyo spent an average of three to four days a week together, and with each short-lived moment, Clarke allowed her heart to be totally opened to a man she knew belonged to her only when he was in her presence. Antonyo vowed himself to no one woman, including her—at least not yet.

The indifference Clarke used to feel about Antonyo's other lovers had now transformed and manifested itself into pain and jealousy. In the beginning, she had little trouble grinning and bearing what she knew to be so; however, lately, the past month or so in particular, Clarke found herself irritable and very unhappy at the mere thought of Antonyo in the company of the other witches in his life. And those, too, had changed since the two started dating. At the start, he was involved with females named Timber, Lynn, Charleyna, and Katrina. Of that original brood, only Lynn and Timber remained, as far as Clarke's minor investigating revealed.

One evening, Clarke decided to snoop through his cell phone while he showered in the motel bathroom they were in. By each of the women's names in his cell phone's address book, Antonyo listed his relationship to the female. Of all the names there, Timber, Lynn, and herself were the only ones listed as "a boo," and by each of their acronyms were stars: one by Timber's name, two by Lynn's, and three by her own.

Clarke was ecstatic over the fact that she had starred higher than the other two women, and hoped the trophy marks were indicative of his feelings and not just sexual performance. She decided that she would take a chance and find out by writing down Lynn and Timber's phone numbers and giving each lady a call.

The following day, Clarke called Timber first. After spending about ten minutes on the phone with her, she assessed that Timber seemed content to stay in the background and play stable mate. Their conversation revealed that Timber was not a one-man type of woman. Antonyo was only one of a few guys she dated. When their talk time concluded, Clarke felt absolutely no threat from this woman, which made the goal of getting her out of the picture for good quite achievable.

Lynn Trevelle, however, proved to pose a far greater threat to having Clarke's mission of being Antonyo's one and only executed. During the phone conversation these two women shared, Lynn's vocal demeanor revealed a demanding, controlling, spoiled and possessed woman, while not necessarily expressing the characteristics of a woman in love. Yet, Clarke still knew that getting her out of Antonyo's life would be far more difficult because Lynn was used to getting her way. Losing at anything was not an option for a woman like Lynn.

"Hello, may I please speak with Lynn?"

"Who is this?" Lynn responded with attitude.

"My name is Clarke. I'm a friend of Tony's."

"So! Why are you calling me?"

"My purpose for calling, for lack of a better reason I guess, would be curiosity. I just want to know the true nature of your relationship with Tony."

Clarke felt silly asking questions she knew she had no right to ask, but for her, the situation had reached a critical point. She loved Antonyo, and she needed to know, for one thing, what her chances were of getting him all to herself; and two, what she had to do to improve her odds. Giving Antonyo up was not an option she would even remotely consider.

"What do you mean by 'the true nature of our relationship?' Are you writing his biography or something?" Lynn questioned.

Clarke's youth, inexperience in love, and perpetually smooth conversation with Timber left her unprepared to handle the smug, nasty disposition of Lynn. Yet she was even less prepared to let go of Antonyo, so she bit the bullet and pressed on.

"I'm sorry if I seem intrusive, Lynn. I don't mean to come across as aggressive or confrontational. It's just that I have been seeing Tony for four months. I would really like the opportunity at an exclusive, monogamous relationship with him. "

"You have got some nerve, little Ms. Clarke. Tony has spoken about you, so don't think that you informing me about your involvement in his life is going to upset me enough to stop seeing him. If one of us has got to go, trust me when I say it is you he will bid a fond farewell to. Tony is like my puppet, Clarke. I pull strings and he dances. I am beautiful. I am educated. I am mature. I've got plenty of money, and I don't mind sharing it with my boo, so recognize your place, little girl, and stay in it." Lynn ended the call with a departing laugh filled with scorn.

Clarke replayed her conversation with Lynn and became concerned, but not despondent. Her resolve to make a life with Antonyo remained strong. There had to be options available that would cause either Antonyo to dump Lynn or vice-versa. Clarke was intelligent, crafty even, and resilient where Antonyo was concerned.

Since realizing she had fallen in love with him, she suffered the heartache over and over of watching him leave her arms, her bed even, to crawl into those of other women; yet somehow, she had remained steadfast and calm, never once letting her emotions get the best of her or her predicament.

Patience and planning were her strategies to win the fight. Soon enough her weapons of warfare would reveal themselves.

Antonyo sat quietly, nursing a headache as he listened to Trina preach to him about the glory of the Lord and the benefits of establishing a relationship with Jesus.

"Antonyo, I know all of this sounds foreign and boring to you. I am doing my best to put this in layman's or sinner's terms for you. The easiest way to make you understand is to tell you what a change in my own life having a relationship with God has made. A testimony, if you will.

"I never before thought I could own my own home, until I started attending church. I had relegated myself to the simple belief that I was the daughter of a woman who had no value for her own life. Therefore, my life had no value, no real joy. Before I met God on His terms, Antonyo, I merely existed. I was raising you, loving you and my sister, but my life had no real purpose. All I am asking you to do is to just come to church with me a few times. See if you hear something, see something, or feel something that makes you want to give God a try. God already knows you, Antonyo, and He loves you right where you are, just as you are."

Antonyo was definitely not anti-God. He even noticed the positive differences in his mom's life. His problem with her was her belief that he was unhappy and merely existing, when nothing could be further from the truth. Antonyo's life held much satisfaction for him. Why fix something that wasn't broken?

"Ma, I hear you and I am so happy for you. I will even agree to go to church with you sometime soon. It's not that I don't believe in God or that I am running from Him. I am just currently cool with my own life. So, if nothing else, I can go to church with you to thank Him for that."

Trina started to protest further, but quickly decided against it. She chose to revel in the victory of at least getting her only child to agree to attend church with her eventually.

"I'm holding you to that, Antonyo," she said as she smiled and left him to himself.

Trina's leaving came at the perfect time, too, because just as she made her exit, his phone rang. His caller ID revealed that Lynn was on the line. He did not need to hear his mom's mouth or see her roll her eyes as he spoke on the phone with one of his women.

"What's up, girrrll?" Antonyo answered.

"What's up? What's up? I will most certainly tell you what's up, Tony. What's up is I don't appreciate you giving my phone number to your hoochie girlfriends. That is exactly what's up!" Lynn yelled.

Forever the drama queen, Antonyo thought. "What are you ranting about now, Lynn?"

"That little wench Clarke called me today, talking all out the side of her neck. What was that about, Tony? Why did you give her my phone number?"

"Whoa, Lynn! Stop accusing me of giving her your phone number, because I did no such thing. I don't know how Clarke got your phone number, if she even called you at all."

"Well, whoa back at you, Tony! Are you calling me a liar? I know you ain't calling me a liar, because I have no reason to lie to you, Tony; especially not about one of your skanky, low-class females. That wench called just like I said."

Antonyo found himself becoming irritated by the harsh

adjectives Lynn used to describe Clarke. Surprised by his desire to lash out at Lynn and defend Clarke, Antonyo relaxed his grip on the phone and calmed himself, remembering that while he was quite fond of Clarke, Lynn was the main caboose car on his gravy train. Clarke was a broke passenger, hitching a complimentary ride. He only continued to hang out with Clarke because she was very smart and very pretty. She worked harder than both Timber and Lynn to make him feel good on a level that had little to do with sex and absolutely nothing to do with monetary benefits.

"Okay, Lynn. What did Clarke say?" Antonyo asked with a calm that totally betrayed his actual feelings.

"Like I said, she came all out of pocket. She was rude and aggressive, and the gist of the conversation was that I should leave you alone because you are her man. The youngster did everything but threaten me," Lynn yelled.

Antonyo knew Lynn exaggerated her version of Clarke's call at the very least. After hearing Lynn give her account, Antonyo again began to doubt if Clarke even made the call; however, he determined that he definitely needed to get to the bottom of the situation.

"Look, Lynn. If Clarke called you—"

"What! Are you still saying you don't believe me, Tony?"

"Let me finish, Lynn!" Antonyo now raised his own voice, frustrated by Lynn's annoying persistence. "If Clarke made the call, I will definitely deal with her and make sure it never happens again. On the other hand, if she tells me she never phoned you, I am through with you, Lynn. I am tired of dealing with your drama. Do you understand?"

"Oh! So if she called me she will simply be reprimanded, but if I lied about her calling me, I'm going to get kicked to the curb, correct? Don't even bother answering that question, Antonyo, because I'm not worried. I am not lying. And that witch better not tell you otherwise," Lynn screamed. Then she slammed the phone in Antonyo's ear.

Of all the crazy stunts Lynn had pulled while they dated, Antonyo could not remember her ever blatantly lying. She was constantly animated; definitely dramatic and on a few occasions even borderline psychotic. But all of these characteristics were exhibited during Lynn's routine behavior; nothing out of the ordinary for her. Lying would be a new character flaw for this loony female.

Just as Antonyo came to the conclusion that Lynn was more than likely telling the truth, Timber rang his phone and put away any lingering hope that perhaps Lynn had been less than honest.

"Hey, Tone. Just wanted to give you a heads up. Some chick named Clarke called me today wanting to know about the seriousness of our relationship. She wasn't hostile or anything; said she was simply asking from a standpoint of curiosity."

"Thanks for letting me know, Tim. I'll make sure she never calls you again." Antonyo ended the call. Now he had to face the inevitable. He had to confront Clarke and get to the bottom of her intrusive inquisition into his other relationships. He added to his conversation agenda the fact that he must give Clarke an ultimatum. Either she never called any of his friends again, or she never saw him again.

Clarke fumbled around her bedroom, stumbling around her younger sister and all of her crap, trying to release the pent-up nervous energy that had surrounded her since she received Antonyo's phone call. She went from sitting cross-legged on the floor to popping up a minute and a half later and lying across the bed, staring at the ceiling, to flopping onto her belly after just a few seconds.

Nikia, one of Clarke's five siblings, became annoyed and voiced her displeasure. "I wish you would sit your butt still, girl. What in the heck is wrong with you anyway? You are flitting around this room and kicking over my stuff like you have lost your mind."

"No, not my mind, Niki, but maybe my man," Clarke replied absently.

"What! What do you mean, you might have lost your man? I never realized that Tony was your man, Clarke. I thought you said the two of you were in a casual relationship, free to see other people."

Clarke and Niki were very close, best friends even, and Clarke shared just about everything with this sister since they were closest in age. While she had told Niki about her informal relationship and all of the juicy details, she had yet to tell her sister about the current state of affairs. Until Clarke had secured her position as Antonyo's one and only, she felt it safer to keep that information to herself.

"I don't mean my man in the true sense of the word. I just mean . . . it's really nothing, Niki. Antonyo called and said he needed to speak with me ASAP. So I'm just a little nervous about what he has to say, that's all," Clarke lied.

Antonyo had called, telling her he needed to speak with her in person about something serious, informing her then that he would be over to pick her up in about an hour. While he gave no absolute reason for the need for this spur of the moment conversation, Clarke was sure it had everything to do with her conversations with Lynn and Timber, and she was more than a little nervous.

That was forty-five minutes ago. Clarke finally settled on the bed, trying to think of a reasonable explanation, other than the truth, to give Antonyo for calling Lynn and Timber. However, nothing that came to mind made any logical sense.

Clarke, you are an intelligent young woman. The best thing for you to do is simply play this conversation by ear. No need for any pre-conceived lies or manipulations. Answer the questions as he asks them, speaking clearly and confidently. What is the worst that can happen? "He'll decide to stop seeing you, that's what!" Clarke had not realized she voiced her last thought aloud until she heard her sister question her comment.

"What are you babbling about now, Clarke?" Niki asked.

"Huh? Uh . . . nothing, Niki. Just ignore me." Before Niki could question her any further, Clarke heard her mother calling, announcing Antonyo's arrival.

Clarke descended the stairs with trepidation, feeling her knees go weak as she spotted Antonyo sitting on the sofa. His face looked pensive. She could tell he knew of her phone calls to Timber and Lynn and he was less than happy about it.

"Hello, Tony," Clarke said, trying to make her voice sound normal, contradictory to her jumpy emotions.

"Hey, Clarke. Can you take a drive with me right now?"

"Uh . . . sure, Tony. Give me a minute to grab my purse and let my mother know I'm leaving."

"Okay. I will wait for you in the car," Tony said as he stood and left the living room.

Clarke went back up the stairs as fearfully as she had come down them to go and retrieve her purse from the bedroom. She still had not come up with even a half-decent excuse to give for making the phone calls, and now the moment of truth loomed upon her. After grabbing her small handbag, Clarke sought her mother, finding her standing in the kitchen about to prepare dinner.

"Mama, I'm going to go out with Tony for a little while, if that's okay with you." She almost hoped her mother would forbid her from going just so she would not have to face the music with Tony.

"Sure, honey. It's fine. Just remember I have to work tonight, so I need you home before six." Clarke's mom kissed her cheek and noticed the trembling in her daughter's body. "Are you all right, Clarke? You're shaking, sweetheart."

Clarke felt like telling her mother of the dilemma she faced with Tony. Perhaps she could offer some sort of sound advice on what she should say to him; but shame prevented her from spilling her guts. She did not want her mom to know how foolishly she had been behaving over a man who was supposed to be no more than a casual acquaintance.

"I'm fine, Mama. I'm just excited to see Antonyo. I'm really beginning to like him a lot," Clarke confessed as honestly as possible.

"Well, just be careful, Clarke. You make sure you keep your head on straight and keep your priorities on your studies. Don't you let no man get you sidetracked and have you give up on your brilliant future. You hear me?"

"Yes, ma'am." Clarke kissed her mom and left the kitchen before she broke down and cried in front of her. She had a paper due in English in three days, and she had yet to begin working on it. Yes, she was beginning to let her class work slip, and that, too, made her ashamed. She had to get this relationship with Antonyo under control, and fast, before she really started messing up.

Clarke approached Antonyo as he sat on the hood of the car waiting for her. She stepped up to him, kissed him gently on the forehead, and then walked to the passenger's side of the car. Antonyo followed and opened the door for her to get in. Neither of them said a word during this interchange. Once Antonyo finally settled in the driver's seat, he drove away from Clarke's house, heading toward Belle Isle.

Antonyo always went to Belle Isle to think, chill, and relax; and relaxation was just what he needed in order to confront

Clarke regarding her intrusiveness and scheming. He would have expected something like this from Lynn, but from Clarke it was a severe slap in the face. He trusted her; he believed her to be mature and level-headed. Now he found himself distrusting his own instincts. He needed clarity, and he would settle for nothing less once he and Clarke began talking about what he regarded as a complete betrayal of his trust in her.

Clarke sat nervously in her seat, feeling quite double-minded. While she wished Antonyo would say something to her, she dreaded hearing what would come out of his mouth. When she could no longer stand the pregnant silence, she aborted its existence.

"So, what has been up with you, Tony? How has your day been so far?" Clarke asked with as much normalcy as she could muster.

"Clarke, I would really rather we not talk until we get downtown. I have a lot on my mind and I would really like to use the drive to Belle Isle as an opportunity to think things through," Antonyo replied pensively.

Clarke's breath nearly stilled in her chest. She could hear Antonyo's anger and feel his disappointment in her, suffocating her within the few cubic feet of the automobile. She nearly began crying, but she fought the urge because she did not want Antonyo to witness her distress. She still had not decided how she would handle this situation. Breaking into tears at this moment would declare her guilty before the interrogation even began.

Antonyo parked in the area where he normally did when he visited Belle Isle, the historical and beautiful landmark of Detroit. He shut off the engine and took a deep breath, inhaling the spring air drifting in off the Detroit River. Just being there helped to alleviate some of the stress he felt over his predicament with Clarke.

For several moments the couple sat in the car silently. While the quiet gave Antonyo an opportunity to think and process his thoughts, it threatened to drive Clarke insane. To keep herself from screaming, if for no other reason than to simply end the horrible silence inside the car, she decided to start the dialogue with Antonyo. She figured she would begin in a position of offense versus defense, hoping to somehow gain a leg up on the crazy situation she created.

"Tony, I think I know what this is all about. I called Lynn and Timber earlier today. I did this without really thinking about it, just kind of curious about your overall relationship with them. I know it was nosy and intrusive, and I apologize from the bottom of my heart."

Antonyo turned to look in Clarke's direction for the first time since parking the car. He stared at her, realizing her strategy, and somewhat marveling at her initiative. Antonyo had always been impressed with Clarke's intellect.

"Clarke, what you did was wrong. It was immature and disrespectful. It was also embarrassing, hopefully as much for you as for everyone else involved. From the beginning of our relationship, you were informed I would be seeing other people. You were also free to do the same. You said you were cool with that. Now all of a sudden you decide to start sneaking around like a private eye, investigating me and what I do with my other female friends. I don't understand it. You're going to have to give me a better reason than sheer nosiness."

Clarke raised her eyes from her lap, where they had remained focused while Tony chastised her. She looked at him to find him glaring intently at her, waiting impatiently for her to answer his question. Clarke stared sheepishly at the love of her life, wondering if she should be honest with him, or use her book smarts to devise a crafty response.

"Listen, Tony. I want to again apologize for calling Lynn

and Timber. Like you said, it was silly and immature; but I was sincere when I said I was curious about the status of your relationship with each of them. I know we are not in a committed relationship, but I guess I just wanted to see if I could find out if you liked either of them more than you liked me. Call it pride or ego or whatever. As I think about it right now, I realize I just did not want to be the low man, or perhaps I should say low woman, on the totem pole."

After speaking, Clarke felt satisfied with her partially truthful response. She sat silently and prayed that Antonyo did as well, because she now knew for sure she was not yet ready to divulge the level of her feelings for him.

As Antonyo sat and listened to Clarke's response, he found himself just as confused as he was when he initially heard about the phone calls to Lynn and Timber. He knew that Clarke was smart, but he could not determine if she was also deliberately being cunning at this moment. In the beginning Antonyo would have bet money that Clarke was not a schemer, but he would have also bet that she would not have pulled the stunts of sneaking through his phone to find numbers and calling his other friends either. He was sure that the blank look he now had plastered all over his face gave Clarke indication of his cluelessness.

In an effort to remain in control of the situation, Antonyo decided that he would give Clarke the benefit of the doubt and believe her story of temporary insecurity. No need in her sitting here assessing and detecting his own uncertainty and later using it against him at some point. One of the keys to his being able to maintain his current player status was making his women feel like he always knew what they were up to. Antonyo resolved to simply keeping a closer watch on Clarke, her actions and her attitudes.

"Clarke, I believe you, and I assure you that you are not

the low woman on the totem pole. In fact, because of your intelligence, you are probably the one I like spending time with the most. But, I am still a long way from being ready to settle down and have a monogamous relationship with you or anyone else, so now that you have heard it from the horse's mouth, can you please stop with the spy games so we can get back to being good friends and lovers?"

"I'll be good from here on out, Tony. I promise. I will never do anything that silly again. I want you to always be able to trust me," Clarke replied wholeheartedly with her mouth; however, she began plotting and scheming on her next move to make Antonyo all hers in her heart and mind.

Chapter 15

After months of relentless persuasion, Antonyo had finally consented to attend church with his mother. As he changed from the outfit he'd worn to service this morning and prepared for his date with Clarke, he reflected on the words of the sermon. Today's message was delivered by the youth and young adult minister, which was one of the reasons Trina completely insisted and practically demanded that Antonyo attend church with her that day. Trina kept reiterating that today's message would be something he could more than likely relate to because of the messenger.

Being that the messenger was a beautiful young female named Keisha Hearn, who could not have been more than a couple years older than himself, Antonyo was amazed that he was able to actually hear and concentrate on anything she said. Minister Keisha spoke about how important it was to capture and hold the attention of the youth, being that they were the future of the church. Antonyo remembered specifically the four Rs she used in her sermon to inspire the younger generation: Real, Relevant, Relational and Rousing. Minister Keisha was all of that, in addition to being *really* sexy. At some point during the morning, Antonyo stopped noticing how pretty she was and started paying more attention to what she was saying. He even remembered one of the key scriptures she used, I Timothy 4:12: *Don't let anyone think less of you because you are young. Be an example to all believers in what you teach, in the way you live, in your love, your faith and your purity. As well as 5:1-2: Never speak harshly to an older man, but appeal to him respectfully as though he were your own father. Talk to the younger men as you would do your own brothers. Treat the older women as you would your mother, and treat the younger women with all purity as your own sisters.*

Minister Keisha explained that Timothy was a young minister being schooled by an older man named Paul, who gave Timothy life lessons as well as spiritual messages to share with those he would preach to. After hearing and reading in his mom's Bible that scripture about how to treat women, Antonyo jokingly wondered if Timothy was once a playboy like himself.

In an afterthought, he also pondered on the scripture about respecting older men as if they were your father. Antonyo was sure that God did not want him to have the same amount of respect for all older men as he had for his own pathetic dad. Only every blue moon would he even entertain a thought about his father, and the things he thought about were far from anything that could be considered respectable. Since his mother had become saved, she would often quote scriptures to him about forgetting the past and forgiving those who had hurt him, including his father, Sheldon. Antonyo always insisted that while he wanted nothing to do with the counterpart in his conception, he held no ill will for the man. Sheldon was simply a dead issue to him.

Now it seemed as if the two things his mom spoke to him most often about were also being reiterated to him in church by the beautiful minister. Was God really trying to tell him something? Of that he was not sure, but he did tell his mother after the service that he would attend again on Youth Sunday.

***

"No, Clarke! Please tell me you are kidding. This cannot be happening. This cannot be real," Antonyo roared after hearing Clarke's revealing news.

"Antonyo, I'm sorry, but it's true. I am seven and a half weeks pregnant. Here is the pregnancy verification they gave me at the clinic today. The expected date of delivery is two days before your twenty-third birthday. It is all written right here in black and white, Tony." Clarke attempted to hand the paper to her infuriated lover, but Antonyo simply glared at her, never even bothering to look at the paper she held.

"It doesn't even matter what that paper says, Clarke, because you are going to have to get rid of it. You are going to have to have an abortion," Antonyo stated plainly, as if the matter had already been decided for both of them.

"No, Tony. I am not having an abortion." Clarke was just as plain in her denial of his demand.

"What do you mean, no? Clarke, I'm only twenty-two years old, I live at home in my mother's house, and I'm not even really your man. You are only nineteen and you still have a year to go before you finish college. Neither of us is in the position to parent a child."

Clarke calmly listened to Tony rant, already knowing ahead of time that he would try to talk her out of keeping their child. She was prepared for his anger, his opinions, and even his denial, if it should come to that. But Clarke was adamant about keeping the baby she had been planning to conceive for the past few months, ever since he had confronted and forgiven her for calling Lynn and Timber. Since then, another female, Cocoa, had been added to his collection, but Clarke fretted not. She knew in her heart of hearts that Antonyo would one day be all hers, and the child she now carried would seal the deal.

"Tony, I hear and understand all of your opposing viewpoints, but you can't honestly believe that they are enough to warrant us getting rid of our child. Your mother raised you after giving birth to you at age fifteen and without a high school education. My mother had me when she was just seventeen and has since had five more children and we are all surviving. Both of our parents were single mothers. Tony, we have more going for us than either of our parents did when they started having babies, so I know we can do this too, especially if we do it together. You have a good job, and having this baby will not keep me from getting my degree on time. Tony, we can do this."

Antonyo could not believe his ears. He could barely believe that it was Clarke who stood before him uttering this nonsense. He always thought her to be so intelligent.

"It's obvious that you don't get it, Clarke. I'm not trying to do this. I don't want to do this. I am not going to do this." With those as his final words, Antonyo turned and headed toward his car, leaving Clarke sitting on her mother's porch, staring after his retreating back. Once he got in his car he sped off, leaving burning tire trails in front of Clarke's home.

Clarke had grown to know Antonyo very well in the more than one year they had been dating. She knew his reaction to her news would be harsh initially. She also knew that he would come around eventually and the two of them would finally be the type of couple she had been dreaming about: exclusive, with eyes and love only for each other. Clarke did not fret Antonyo's callous handling of their situation. She opted to remain calm and to be patient. She understood that she was now a mother-to-be and that her own health and mental well-being were paramount to the health and development of her and Antonyo's baby.

***

Clarke is crazy, nuttier than a fruitcake, weird as a wino, Antonyo thought as he drove recklessly through the neighborhood away from Clarke's house. "How could she do this to me? How could she trap me like this?" he mused aloud to himself. Antonyo was now certain that this was a deliberate ambush by Clarke to get him into a serious relationship with her. Clarke's intellect made her too smart to accidently get pregnant.

He then started questioning his own brain power and function. Back when he found out about the phone calls to Timber and Lynn, he knew in his bones that he could no longer trust Clarke with the same abandon as he had in the beginning; yet he did nothing about his revelation. He continued on in the same manner of having unprotected sex with her because he had become somewhat addicted to the feeling of being with her that way. Now look at what his compulsion had cost him.

Antonyo knew that he could scream and threaten all he wanted to. He knew in his heart that he would never be able to convince Clarke to have an abortion. As much as he hated to think about it, Antonyo knew he needed to talk to his mother about his current predicament. He hoped that she would pray and ask God to make Clarke change her mind.

Once he arrived home, Antonyo found his mother sitting in the small formal dining room of their house with a male companion. Apparently she had prepared dinner for her company, because it looked as if the two of them had just finished their meal. This was a new sight for Antonyo. For as far back as he could remember, he could not recall a time when he had seen his mother entertaining a gentleman caller at their house. The picture painted by the dining couple disturbed him quite a bit.

"Ma, who this?" Antonyo asked rudely as he walked farther into the dining room.

"Excuse me, young man! Is that how you greet a guest in my home?" Trina was well aware that Antonyo was not accustomed to seeing her with a man, but she would not tolerate his rudeness, surprised or not.

Antonyo could not tell if his mother expected an apology, but one would not be forthcoming, at least not in front of this stranger. Mother and son eyed each other menacingly as the tension built and floated through the room in small waves. While Trina did not appreciate Antonyo's rudeness, she could understand his shock. And while Antonyo realized this was his mother's home and that she was an adult, he could not easily accept that his mother needed or wanted male companionship. Trina eventually gave in to her son's discomfort, and then turned to address her guest.

"William, I am so glad you came by for dinner. I hope you enjoyed your food," Trina stated as she rose from her seat at the table.

William Rucker was a handsome executive who worked for Blue Cross Blue Shield of Michigan and belonged to the same church as Trina. He'd been trying to get her to go out with him for months, and she finally relented two weeks ago, agreeing then to join him after church for dinner at a small soul food restaurant in Southfield. Trina found the food to be bland and anything but soulful, and expressed her displeasure about their meal to William. He then challenged her to do better, which resulted in this, their second date. No need in explaining all of that to him now, however.

"The food was delicious, Trina. You're right; you are a much better cook than the people at that restaurant we went to, whose name I won't mention." William followed Trina's lead and stood.

Antonyo immediately caught on to what Trina's guest said and began to wonder how long his mother had been seeing this chump. Trina, too, caught William's faux pas, wincing a little at his compliment.

William then turned and addressed Antonyo. "You must be Trina's son. I have heard a lot about you, young man. It is nice to finally meet you in person," William said as he extended his hand in Antonyo's direction. Antonyo simply stared at the outstretched hand, never bothering to reciprocate the gesture.

This time, Trina was embarrassed and fed up with her son's rudeness. She stepped toward him with her finger pointed in the direction of his face. Before things could get heated, however, William moved between mother and child to intervene.

"Trina, I need to get going. How about you walk me to the door? Antonyo, it was nice to meet you." William gently placed his hand on Trina's arm, guiding her toward the front door.

Trina let the matter drop for the time being and led her guest to the front door, all the while giving Antonyo the evil eye, letting him know this matter was far from being over. Once William had left the home, Trina reappeared in the living and found Antonyo standing rooted in the same spot, his body vibrating with attitude.

"Ma, who was that clown you had all up in our house?" he snapped.

"Young man, you better quickly check your tone and remember who you are talking to, because despite what you think, this is my house and I am allowed to have whomever I please here. Now, I suggest you calm yourself, then explain your rude behavior," Trina stated, giving back to him as much attitude as she had gotten.

It was then Antonyo remembered the real reason behind

his foul mood. Yes, it was unnerving to find his mother with a man in their home; however, he was sure his strong reaction had more to do with his predicament with Clarke than anything else.

"Ma, I have a serious problem and I need your help. In all honesty, I'm not sure what you can actually do to assist, but I'm hoping you can at least come up with some good advice."

Trina looked intently at her son to find a distressing expression to go along with the tense words, and she instantly became very worried. She sat in the chair closest to her, awaiting her son's next words with bated breath.

Antonyo sat in the chair nearest his mom and began to pour out to her his dilemma with Clarke. "Mom, Clarke is pregnant." Trina raised an eyebrow, but did not interrupt. "I tried talking her into having an abortion, but she is not listening to me. She insists on having this baby, in my opinion, simply to hold on to me.

"Ma, I'm not ready to be tied down like that. I like my freedom. I'm still young, and I do not want to be financially responsible for a baby right now. Tell me, Ma, what can I do to get out of this mess?"

Trina closed her eyes and shook her head slightly from side to side, preparing herself mentally and spiritually to deal with her only child. She silently prayed for God to give her the words and wisdom to express to her son what he needed to hear.

"Man up, Antonyo! Stop making excuses about being immature and irresponsible. Those two facts are a given; otherwise you wouldn't be in this mess. But you are in it, and in it deep. I'm not about to sit here and tell you 'how to get out of it,' as you so eloquently put it. And I'm not about to counsel you or support your decision on asking that girl to have an abortion, as I did the first time you landed in this same boat.

That is no longer where I am spiritually. God would not approve. So, man up and prepare yourself to lie in the bed you made."

Antonyo stared at his mother with confused irritation. He could not believe she sat there, making it sound as if the solution were really as simple as just doing it. Did she think she was in a Nike commercial?

"Ma, you make it sound as if I have no other choice other than to accept Clarke's decision to keep this baby and be a father to it. What about my rights? What about what I want? Don't I have any say-so?"

"You have had your say-so, Antonyo, and you already made your choices. You *said* that you were going to engage in premarital sex with this young lady, and you *chose* to do so without using protection. Now what you have to do is accept responsibility for your irresponsibility and deal with the consequences of your actions.

"I have talked to you over and over again about how you have dealt with all these females, but you chose to chart your own course and sail your own waters. Now this is where all your cruising has landed you. Aye, aye, Captain."

Antonyo dropped his head and buried his face in his hands in complete frustration. First Clarke decided to try to slash open his life with her drama, and now his mother was pouring vinegar all up and through the wound. These women were crazy.

Suddenly he came up with a sobering revelation. "Ma, Clarke can't make me take care of a baby that I don't want. She made this decision without me, so she can't just decide all by herself to make me a father. The most she can do is take me to court to pay child support. If she does that, no big deal. They can only take money from my paycheck. They can't touch what my other friends give me or the money I have in my bank account. The only thing Clarke can make me do is be a financial donor to this child, and she can only do that once we have a paternity test done to prove the baby is even mine."

Antonyo stood up from his chair feeling refreshed and once again in control. He figured the money the state took from his paycheck could easily be replaced by adding another woman to his "special friends" list after he dumped Clarke. This time he would look for someone who had money, somebody who could add something to his life, not drain him or cause him drama. Clarke would be the last time he deviated from the usual type of women he messed around with.

Trina watched her son pacing the dining room floor, looking like the proverbial peacock, strutting around like he had said something impressive. She silently prayed for the Holy Spirit to give her patience and just the right words to say to Antonyo, because if she spoke from her flesh, her house would be set ablaze from the fire that would spew from her tongue.

"So, in other words, what you are saying is you are choosing to become a Sheldon wannabe? Perhaps you may be a little better, only because you are at least willing to pay child support. But when it comes to the emotional and spiritual needs of your son or daughter, your own flesh and blood, you are stating that you are going to be M.I.A.?"

Antonyo stared at his mother intently, looking at her as if she had just thrown ice-cold water on what he thought to be a very hot idea. He watched his mother for several moments in silence, with a baffled expression on his now solemn face.

"I didn't ask for this baby, Mama. Why should I be forced to be a father?"

"I didn't ask for you either, Antonyo. Neither did Sheldon, for that matter. I was fifteen years old when you were born, and your father was only two years older, yet we wanted to do grown folks' things, and we ended up with grown folks' responsibilities; however, only one of us handled our responsibilities like an adult. Sheldon chose to treat you as if you were a toy that he could play with only when he felt like it, and now you have the nerve to stand here in my face, practically announcing that you want to be just like your father," Trina stated, once again becoming angry at her child's lack of accountability.

"Antonyo Ian Demonté Simms, you stand here at twenty-two years old, acting as if you have no clue where babies come from. At least I can say I had the ignorance of childhood youth and inexperience as my excuse when I became pregnant with you. But you are a full-grown man who has been having sex since the age of thirteen, if I calculate correctly, so you know much better than to stand there and speak about someone *forcing* you into becoming a father." Trina, in frustration and haste, stood from her seat at the dining room table and stormed from the room, leaving Antonyo to again stare after her in utter confusion.

Antonyo resented his mother's accusation and her comparison of him to his deadbeat father. He did not think himself to be anything like Sheldon, nor would he ever be like him. Sheldon was a punk who, like his mother said, treated him like a dollar store toy. His father had walked in and out of his life up until his eighteenth birthday. Then, as if he had done his job of raising Antonyo to adulthood, Sheldon finally walked away for good. Antonyo had not heard a peep from his dad since the day of his senior prom.

Antonyo's rationale dictated that his situation and Sheldon's situation were completely different. Antonyo felt that Sheldon had played games with his emotions by being a sometime dad. He would not do that to Clarke's child. He reasoned that staying out of the child's life altogether would alleviate the confusion that he felt as a child. No child should have to deal with the feelings of rejection and abandonment that he'd felt growing up. In his mind, Clarke's child would even be ahead of the game because he or she would at least have some financial support to replace the emotional support it may be lacking. Antonyo had found out early in life that money was a great substitution for love.

Once again pleased with decision, Antonyo proceeded to his room to dress for his date with Lynn. He would discuss his decision with Clarke tomorrow.

After another exhaustive yet pleasant evening with the ever annoying but very generous Lynn, Antonyo found himself more than ready for bed when he returned home later that evening. Once he'd showered and changed into a fresh pair of silk pajama bottoms, Antonyo settled into his comfortable bed for a cozy and peaceful sleep.

But peaceful was the absolute last adjective that could be used to describe the fitful sleep he found in his bed that night. Antonyo tossed and turned in an effort to shake loose the unsettling images that plagued his slumber. Horrible scenes played on the vivid screen of his mind.

Antonyo's dream took place at Belle Isle, where he sat chilling with a new female about whom he could remember nothing in particular. Suddenly, a destitute Clarke, holding the hand of a faceless, genderless, hungry child appeared. Clarke and her child approached him and his date at the bench they occupied. She begged him for his help and begged him to love her child. Antonyo tried calmly asking her to take her child and leave him alone, but she fell to her knees, grabbing his legs and wailing loudly for him to be a father to their child. Antonyo's nondescript date stared bug-eyed at the scene she witnessed. Then suddenly, without warning, she slapped him mercilessly, asking how he could treat this woman and his own child this way.

Antonyo closed his eyes in shock after being hit. Upon re-opening them, he found Sheldon sitting in the space previously occupied by his date. His father smiled and grinned at him, patted him on his back and said, "Way to go, son. You're a chip off the old block. Your mother should have named you Sheldon Jr." It was this last scene that caused him to awaken startled, sweaty, and perplexed.

When his eyes popped open, he examined the clock on his nightstand to find that he had only been asleep about an hour; however, the torturous dream seemed to have held him captive for much longer than that. Obviously the dream had started the moment he closed his eyes, because it seemed to have gone on forever.

The dream had disturbed Antonyo to his core. Certain that he would be unable to fall back to sleep, he got up from his bed and paced around his bedroom for several minutes. Antonyo had made up his mind about how he wanted to handle the situation with Clarke and her child. He was comfortable with his decision, so why now did this dream shake him like this? Then he remembered the conversation he'd had with his mother just before he left for his date. That is when she made the comparison between him and his father. Convinced that Trina was responsible for his interrupted rest, he decided to wake her to confront her. Why should he be the only one losing sleep over what she imparted into his subconscious?

Antonyo left his room and headed toward his mother's room. When he reached the door, he knocked a little more forcefully than he intended, fueled by his anger at what she started, as well as his lack of sleep.

Trina yelled from the other side of the door, "What do you want, boy?"

"Ma, I need to talk to you. Can I come in?"

"This better be more important that what we talked about earlier, Antonyo."

Antonyo entered the bedroom, headed straight to his mother's bed, and sat right on the edge on the same side where she lay. Trina adjusted her position so she was sitting, in an effort to avoid her son crushing her with his weight. Even before his mother could make herself comfortable, Antonyo forged ahead with his complaining.

"Ma, it was wrong for you to say what you said earlier about me being like Sheldon. I'm nothing like Sheldon. I don't appreciate you saying otherwise."

Trina stared at her only child as if he had grown an additional head. She could not believe that this fool would have the nerve to come into her room spouting off about the same crap that she just told him she did not want to discuss.

"Get out, Antonyo. I'm going back to sleep." Trina attempted to move her son from her bed by gently nudging him with her foot so she could get comfortable again. She decided instantly she would not have this discussion with him again, especially at three A.M.

"Ma, come on. I really need to talk about this with you," Antonyo said as he stood from the bed after his mother's foot gesture. "I just had a horrible nightmare with Clarke begging and crying and Sheldon acting like the proud papa while he insinuated that I was just like him."

Trina immediately returned to her seated position on the bed, watching Antonyo as he paced from one end of her bedroom to the next. Once he finally stopped and stood still at the bottom of the bed, he looked over to find a big ole cheese-eating grin on his mother's face.

"Ma, how can you possibly find anything funny or amusing about this?" Trina once again nestled herself under the beautiful gold-colored comforter that lay atop her queen-sized cherry wood sleigh bed before responding with her final words to her child.

"Antonyo, I am not the person with whom you need to have this conversation. I suggest you go back to your room and talk to God. Sounds to me like He is trying to tell you something. Now get out. I'm going back to sleep."

Chapter 16

Clarke sat up in the hospital bed, staring into the beautiful sleeping face of the daughter she had just given birth to not more than six hours ago. She could not believe the overwhelming joy she felt in her heart for this precious child, who only a short while ago had her screaming in overpowering agony. She also had just as hard a time believing that the father of her child had missed the entire labor and birthing process.

Seven and a half months ago when Clarke broke the news to Antonyo about her pregnancy, he was furious at her for "getting herself pregnant." Those were not his exact words, but they may as well have been. He stomped around her front yard, screaming and yelling, acting in a way she had never seen him before. Clarke was pretty much prepared for his anger, considering the fact that she had actually tried to trap him by intentionally getting pregnant; however, by the time Antonyo stomped away from her house that day, she would not have been the least bit surprised if she never saw him again.

But to her total surprise, he arrived on the doorstep of her home early the next morning, retracting all of the venom he had spat at her not twenty-four hours previously. Antonyo had stated to her that he'd given things some serious thought and decided that he did want to be a father to his child. That news alone caused Clarke to shiver with joy, but what he said next accounted for her near fainting spell on her front porch.

"Clarke, not only do I want to be a father to my son or

daughter, but I would also like to try and make a real relationship work between us. I know I said some hateful things yesterday. If you never want to speak to me again because of my immaturity and stupidity, I will understand. But I'm just asking you to take a few days and think about it."

Without a second's hesitation, Clarke hurled herself into Antonyo's arms, kissing his face hysterically. Her plan was coming together much quicker than she ever imagined it would. She could not have been happier. Whatever happened to change his mind did not concern her in the least. Clarke only cared that his mind had changed. She would now hold the privilege of being the only woman in his life.

Thirty days later, the newly crowned couple moved into their own small but cozy two-bedroom apartment. The money Antonyo had saved as a result of having his former harem support him enabled him to pay the first year's lease and security deposit in its entirety at signing. Clarke continued to work her part-time job, while Antonyo maintained his supervisor's position at KLR. Within a month, their love nest had been completely furnished, including a fully stocked nursery for the baby.

During those initial two months together, Clarke could not have been happier. Antonyo had been attentive, generous, and seemingly excited about their pending bundle of joy. Clarke knew, of course, Antonyo had not yet fallen in love with her. She held no illusions regarding that area of their relationship; however, with the way things had been progressing, she was certain his complete devotion would eventually be hers. Until that time came, she remained content in lavishing him with the love she knew that she would always have only for him.

When Clarke had entered her second trimester, things within the couple's cocoon of well-being had taken a dramatic shift. Clarke began to notice restlessness in Antonyo. Little by little, week by week, the fragile peace the two had built began to disintegrate. Clarke tried remaining positive, believing that her man's antsy behavior was the result of her expanding figure and not his previous inability to sustain a monogamous relationship.

Over the past several weeks, evidence, mostly circumstantial, had begun surfacing, indicating that Antonyo had gone back to his playboy ways. He began staying away from home more often, returning later in the evenings as time went by. Antonyo explained his absences and extended late nights by simply stating he was hanging out with his cousin, Darnell, who had recently been released from prison for the second time. Clarke had met Antonyo's delinquent relative on just one occasion. Even after such a brief acquaintance, she found herself almost as uncomfortable with her man hanging out with Darnell as she did with the possibility of him seeing other women.

Then an old name resurfaced—Lynn. The same Lynn who caused a big stink when Antonyo informed her he would no longer be seeing her once he decided to make a commitment to Clarke and their child. In the beginning, Lynn called Antonyo's cell phone up to forty-five times per day for more than a month and a half. One of those times, Clarke answered his ringing phone while he was in the bathroom. The ensuing conversation was none too pleasant:

"Why are you answering Tony's phone?" Lynn asked indignantly.

"Why are you constantly calling Tony's phone?" Clarke had replied.

"Why shouldn't I call him? Since I want to talk to him, it makes perfect sense that I would call him, right?"

"You need to leave him alone. He is with me now. We have

a child on the way. We are trying to build a life together. Why don't you just go away, Lynn?" Clarke stated as politely as she could. Under the circumstances, she thought she did a great job, but Lynn would not be deterred by pleasantness.

"Ha," Lynn replied mockingly. "You are such a naïve little child. Antonyo will never be the man you want him to be to you. It is not in his nature. This little spell you have cast by using the oldest trick in the book to trap him will eventually wear off, so I will do everything but go away, because I want him to know as soon as he comes to his senses, I will be right here waiting for him."

Antonyo entered the living area of their apartment at that moment. He took the phone from Clarke, already knowing who held the other end.

"Lynn, I'm changing my phone number today. I don't know what else to do to make it clear to you that we are finished. Clarke is my woman now, and you will stop this blatant disrespect of her, our home, and my time." Antonyo left the apartment right away, returning less than forty-five minutes later with a new cell phone number, leaving no room for Clarke to doubt his intentions toward her at that time.

Then a week later, Clarke saw the name Lynn on Antonyo's call list. Clarke had taken to checking his phone as frequently as his absent-mindedness would allow him to leave it in her vicinity when he left the room for extended periods of time. Her snooping netted her information indicating that a call had been placed to his phone from Lynn around eleven-thirty P.M.

Of course this wasn't the first time she had seen female names on his phone, but it was the first time she had seen or heard of Lynn since he changed his cell phone number. She chose to handle finding the name on the phone as she had all the others. She said nothing, believing that once the baby was born, Antonyo would recognize the lifetime bond they created and shared. Clarke trusted that Antonyo would fall in love with her completely the moment he saw her give birth to his seed. Clarke's entire existence as his woman and the mother of his child rested on this being true. So, she put up with all the suspicious behavior because she was unwilling to walk away from the possibility of him allowing their child to totally change his life.

Both Clarke and Antonyo had attended church with Ms. Trina on several occasions. Clarke had also joined her in the women's Bible study from time to time. Clarke still felt quite unsure about becoming saved and living in accordance to the ways of the Bible. After all, she was unwed, pregnant, and living with the father of her child. Yet and still, Clarke found herself actually praying, asking God to keep her and Antonyo together. The changes in their relationship were beginning to take a toll on her, and in light of her mounting desperation to hold onto him, she found herself unconsciously speaking aloud to God more and more often. She even began compromising with God, stating that if He would have Antonyo ask her to marry him once the baby was born, she would become saved and give her and her child's life to Christ.

Today, however, during her eight-hour labor, Clarke had become pretty sure God had decided her sins had been too many to want anything to do with her. She was certain that a God who loved her, a God who wanted a relationship with her would not have allowed her to face such excruciating pain, physically and emotionally, all alone.

Clarke had begun calling Antonyo right after her water broke at three o'clock that morning. She rang his cell phone every five to ten minutes, praying each time as she listened to the annoying song playing as his ringtone, that she would hear his voice. Finally, after sixty-five minutes of calling without success, Clarke decided to call an ambulance to take her to the hospital. She contemplated calling Ms. Trina, as well as her own mother, but she was too embarrassed to tell either of them that Antonyo was missing in action at such a late hour.

By the time the ambulance arrived, she had scribbled a note for Antonyo, letting him know she would be at the hospital preparing to deliver his child, in the hope he would arrive in time to witness the birth of their baby.

The sound of the chair at the foot of her bed scraping against the tiled floor of her hospital room brought Clarke back to the present moment. She took a moment to look away from her beautiful daughter to notice a sleeping Antonyo trying to wrestle himself into a comfortable position. Clarke stared after him in amazement, aggravated that he dared be so tired. He had made it to the hospital less than thirty minutes ago, more than fourteen hours after she began trying to get in touch with him to let him know her labor had begun. Antonyo waltzed into the hospital room five and a half hours too late to behold the birth of his beautiful daughter.

Antonyo squirmed in the uncomfortable, ugly, floral-covered chair, doing his best to find a suitable position to resume his disquieted slumber. Suddenly, the hair on the back of his neck stood at attention, jolting him perfectly upright in his seat. Blinking rapidly, he tried to bring his surroundings into focus. He smelled the disinfectant, saw the pristine white walls, and heard the voices that startled him awake on the loudspeaker overhead. Then he remembered Clarke.

He turned to look in her direction and found her staring at him with what appeared to be loathing in her eyes. He quickly shifted his eyes and noticed the swaddled bundle she lovingly held in her arms. The disjointed contrast unnerved his agitated soul even further.

Antonyo gradually began to recollect recent events, concluding that he was at the hospital with Clarke and his newborn daughter. He stood and timidly walked the short four-step distance from the chair to the edge of the hospital bed where Clark still tenderly held his child. He chanced another glance at Clarke, still finding the same disdain. He decided against saying anything to her right away, choosing instead to gently pull the receiving blanket away from the face of his daughter. He hoped not to see the same hate in her face as he saw in her mother's.

The child, his child, was beautiful. Only a few hours old and already she was stealing his heart. Antonyo reached hesitantly for the baby, half expecting Clarke to refuse to hand her over to him. Surprisingly, however, she released her hold on the infant. Antonyo carefully walked the short distance back to the chair and sat cradling the baby as if she were fragile porcelain.

Wow! The magnitude of feelings that came over him nearly suffocated him. He became overwhelmed at how, in such a short span of time, he could fall so completely in love with another human being. The only other people he had felt this deeply for were his mother, Aunt Treecie, and his cousins. But even what he felt for them paled in comparison to what this little person had quickly stirred in him. He moved the blanket farther away from her face and examined her features closely. It was not because he was checking to make sure she resembled him. His heart and soul told him she was irrevocably his. He simply wanted to know more about her. Yes, he missed her entry into this world, but as he held his daughter, Antonyo vowed to never miss another major event in her life. After the way he'd been behaving over the past few months, he was unsure of how things would turn out between him and Clarke, but that would not be a concern one way or the other.

No matter what happened, he would forever be a father to his daughter.

Antonyo reasoned he had to run the risk of Clarke's wrath by asking her to talk to him. She had not uttered a syllable to him since his arrival. Her only acknowledgement of him had been the viciously creative frown she gave him when he initially entered her hospital room. Right now, however, he needed her to answer a very important question.

"Clarke, have you decided on a name for my daughter yet?"

Before answering his question, Clarke shot Antonyo the horrific glance once more, offended that he had the nerve to refer to their child as simply his own, as if he had been the one to bring her into this world all by himself. How dare he exhibit such bravado after not even caring enough to be there to witness her birth? Her love for him, as always, overrode her anger, and she acquiesced by answering him.

"I have played around with a couple of choices, but I figured you should *at least* be in on the final decision of what to name *our* daughter," Clarke answered.

Antonyo did not miss the snide emphasis of Clarke's statement, sarcastically referencing his absence at the time of the baby's birth; however, the reference of dual ownership of the child went right over his head. Antonyo could only relate to the precious little girl as his and his alone—so much so that he had actually already decided in the last few moments exactly what he would call his daughter. In politeness, though, he figured he should at least hear what Clarke had to say about it.

"What names have you played with and thought about?" he asked.

"I like Nahla, like in the *Lion King*, or Tahlia, both accompanied by the middle name Ann," Clarke announced, proud of her choices.

"Those names are cool, I guess, but they don't really have

any significance. They don't reflect either of us or who she really is," Antonyo said as he stared deeply in the sleeping face of his baby girl.

"Well, we don't exactly know who she is yet, Antonyo. She is only six hours old. She doesn't have a personality yet." Clarke seemed irritated by Antonyo's dismissal of the names she liked, but he was not going to be deterred by her opinion. His mind had been made up shortly after holding the baby in his arms.

"What do you think of this: LaToya Diamond Simms?" he asked out of politeness, not really caring what she thought one way or the other. Then he went on to explain his choice. "LaToya after my mother, Trina, and my aunt, LaTreece. Those are the two most significant females in my life. Diamond because she is absolutely the most precious little gem in this world."

The barb about his mother and his aunt being the most important women in his life cut into Clarke's heart just a little. This was no surprise to her, but having just given birth to this child he claimed was so precious to him, she would have thought perhaps an upgrade in her favor was due. Nonetheless, this was not the conversation to discuss the subject of his feelings for her. This had to do with the lifelong moniker for her daughter.

As she thought about it briefly, she rationalized the name would help her develop a better relationship with his mother, and a possible relationship with his aunt. She did attend church and Bible study with Trina, but she felt the older woman simply tolerated her in an effort to get her saved.

Clarke had met Aunt LaTreece only twice. The woman, on both occasions, seemed bothered with her. Clarke assumed it was because she had been the one who finally succeeded in having her protégé nephew settle into a monogamous relationship. Even with all that in mind, she thought the baby should at least have her last name.

"How about we give her my last name, Tyler, since we aren't married? Or perhaps we could hyphenate it, using both our last names?" Clarke questioned. In the back of her mind, she hoped to hear Antonyo disagree just a bit, because he would profess to her that it was his plan to marry her soon.

"LaToya Diamond Tyler-Simms. It actually sounds kind of nice that way when you say it out loud. I don't know if I have ever told you, but I've got four names too. But instead of having two last names, I've got two middle names. Yeah, I like it a lot. What do you think, Clarke?"

"The name sounds fine to me, Antonyo. I hope your mother and aunt appreciate the honor you are awarding them," Clarke stated sincerely, but she did feel the sting of disappointment as no mention of marriage came forth.

Antonyo smiled broadly as the subject of the name for his princess had been settled with no issues. Too bad everything with Clarke wasn't as easy. In all honesty, Antonyo realized the problems in their relationship were completely a result of his uneasiness with monogamy; yet he had truly given it the old college try, as the saying went, up until about four or five months ago.

Antonyo had woken up one morning, looked over at the expanding mid-section of Clarke, who slept beside him, and was almost certain that her morning sickness had become contagious. He became so sick to his stomach at the sight that lay next to him that he nearly threw up onto the bedroom floor. It had been three months, and Antonyo had gotten no more comfortable with his current relationship status and pending fatherhood than he had been the day Clarke initially told him she was pregnant.

The startling real dreams he experienced on the night of

her news made him certain that his decision to be with Clarke had been the right one to make at the time. His father, patting him on his back, assuring him he would be just like him one day seemed so real. Antonyo determined in his mind during the wee hours of the morning just after the dream that he was a better man than his father would ever be.

Trina suggested it was God talking to Antonyo through his dreams, insisting his initial decision to stay out of the lives of both Clarke and the baby was wrong. Antonyo, having no solid relationship with God, was unsure if it was Him or not. He only knew the dream shook him to his core and rocked loose his previously solid notion of simply cutting out on Clarke and the baby. Perhaps it was God. It seemed to Antonyo that God did have an odd way of getting his attention. For instance, the way He used the absolutely lovely Minister Keisha Hearn to get him to hear the things his own mother could not.

While he would never admit this to Trina, he had started attending church services with his mother more often over the past few months because he was sure this was the one place he would run into Keisha. Coincidentally, Antonyo saw Minister Keisha for the first time on the same day Clarke announced her pregnancy to him. He wondered now, as he thought back, if God had anything to do with the way that worked out.

During his time in Sunday services, Antonyo would scope out Minister Keisha within the sanctuary and spend a majority of his time focusing on her rather than on Pastor Mitchell's message—although it became obvious after service that he had actually heard more of the lesson than he realized. During the ride home with his mother and sometimes Clarke, he was able to hold up his end of the discussion regarding the sermon.

Antonyo often fantasized about being with Keisha, then

found himself feeling guilty—condemned, if you will—for having such thoughts about a woman of God. Antonyo did not attend church every Sunday like his mother did, but he made it his business to be there every second Sunday, which was Youth and Young Adult Sunday, just so he could hear Keisha either preach or be in charge of the services in some way. On the Sundays she did actually give the message, Antonyo always felt as if the Word she delivered had been written especially for him.

One message in particular, where she preached about presenting one body as a holy, living sacrifice to God and making reference to treating one's body like a temple, especially pricked his soul. On this Sunday, Keisha quoted one biblical scripture after another about sexual immorality and God's view on the like. Antonyo sat in his seat that morning feeling pretty unaffected by the moral lecture, yet still unusually fascinated. He wanted to believe Minister Keisha knew his character and had designed her message to let him know she had been paying special attention to who he was and what he was about. The two had been introduced by his mother at the previous week's service.

For the first time in all the years since he had become a self-proclaimed player, Antonyo found himself doubtful as to whether he could actually woo and win the attentions of a female. Keisha Hearn was strong, intelligent, and clearly saintly, the latter quality being the major cause of his skepticism. Minister Keisha Hearn was the first female Antonyo had met that he actually considered out of his league. Antonyo believed Keisha to be very dedicated to the work she did for God, leaving very little space for a sinner such as himself. Until he gave himself to the Lord and changed his lifestyle, as his mom had so eloquently put it over and over again, he could forget about getting next to the beautiful minister on any level. He had decided to be content with simply ogling her from his seat in the sanctuary.

But just because he could not get next to that one woman didn't mean his desire for women other than the mother of his child had waned. As his time spent living with Clarke had increased, so did his longing to leave. Too afraid, however, to be looked at as a clone of his irresponsible father, Antonyo continued to cohabitate with Clarke. That soon became as far as his commitment to her would go.

During the wee hours of the morning when Antonyo finally made it to the bed he shared with Clarke, an overwhelming guilt consumed him. He slept fitfully and his dreams were initially filled with visions of Sheldon grinning, giving him the thumbs-up sign, and singing, "That-a-boy, my son." Then suddenly, those dreams were replaced by the calming voice and beautiful face of Minister Keisha saying, "God will forgive you and give you peace if only you just ask Him."

Antonyo awakened that morning feeling thoroughly conflicted and confused. On the one hand, he wanted so desperately to be out of this commitment he had made to Clarke. On the other hand, he never, ever wanted to be anything like Sheldon. And then there was God. On what hand was he supposed to put Him? Antonyo thought about seeking the advice of Minister Keisha on a purely spiritual level, but only for a moment. He quickly rejected the idea because he knew before long into any counseling session they may have, he would be flirting with her. Astonishingly, even to him, Antonyo had too much respect for Minister Keisha to disrespect her in that manner. It was another first for him to be attributed to the attractive woman of God. To himself, though, he pondered about God and what it was He expected from the likes of him, until he finally fell back asleep.

For a few weeks after *this* dream, Antonyo again tried to

remain on the straight and narrow. He went to work, came home and gave Clarke his undivided attention. The attention may not have been devoted, but undivided nonetheless. Then a ghost from his recent past resurfaced, enticing him with both her beauty and her material goodies.

Antonyo, needing some time away from his self-suffocating commitment, decided to take a drive to his favorite relaxation spot, Belle Isle. He parked his car away from the busy strip where he would usually go to flirt and meet women, and instead chose a spot of serenity facing the river and an absolutely beautiful view of Canada.

After he had been sitting for about an hour, someone knocked on the car window. He was so deep in deliberation about his current state of discontent that he didn't even notice the interruption. The second knock startled him from his muddled thoughts. The familiar face framed by the glass, smiling broadly, brought about a frightened reaction. He reflexively recoiled.

"Lynn! What the—? Are you stalking me?" Antonyo asked after he rolled down the driver's side window.

"Man, ain't nobody thinking about you like that. I just happened to see your car parked over here while me and my girls were on our way over to the strip," Lynn said as she gestured toward her Mercedes filled with three additional attractive women. "I figured it would be rude to not stop and at least say hello."

While Antonyo could never accuse Lynn of being a flat-out liar, she definitely held the heavyweight title in the scheming manipulator category. Because of this, he could not be sure if this intrusion was chance or planned.

"Sure. Whatever you say, Lynn. What do you want?"

"Ugh. What a nasty attitude you have this afternoon. What's wrong? Trouble at home with the little lady? Or perhaps I should say big lady, since she is with child." Lynn was so multi-faceted. One moment she could be "ackin' skrate ghetto," and in the very next moment, she could become the picture-perfect image of class and sophistication. Then there were the times like now, when she could combine both worlds.

Antonyo rolled his eyes at his former lover's comments, wishing she were not so dead on point. "Lynn, just go away. It looks as if your girls are over there anxiously awaiting the opportunity to hit the strip so they can get their ho on," he said as he gestured with his head toward the car full of women.

"Ugh again. My girls are not hoes, Tony." Lynn then did what Lynn did best; she became assertive. She boldly walked around the car, opened the passenger's side door, and flopped her tail into the front seat of Antonyo's car. "Look, Tony, I know we are no longer hanging out or kicking it like we used to, but I would like to think we are still friends. Or at least we could be. So tell me what has you so down that you are hanging out by yourself at Belle Isle over here instead of over at the strip, chasing tail like you normally do."

"Lynn, I am not hanging out on the strip because I am no longer interested in chasing tail. You may act a little slow, but I'm sure you remember that I have a woman now." His sullen tone said more to Lynn than his words conveyed.

Suddenly, she hopped from his passenger's seat, announcing quickly, "I'll be right back. Don't move." Lynn raced to her car, spoke a few words to her girls, then raced back to Antonyo's car as one of her friends hopped from the passenger's side into the driver's seat of her Mercedes and drove away.

When she got back into his car, Antonyo asked, "Why did you send your girls away without you? You should have left with them, Lynn, because I am really not in the mood to deal with you right now."

"Poor, pitiful Tony. See, I told you when you made that

whack declaration of monogamy you would end up miserable without me."

Antonyo wanted badly to refute Lynn's statement, but he could not. He truly was miserable. If he were totally honest with himself, he would have to admit that, in part, Lynn was correct in stating that he missed her. Antonyo knew that devilish temptation fueled what he now thought, but did Lynn actually look more beautiful than the last time he'd seen her?

"Lynn, you are right about my missing you." He would not concede to being miserable, but in order to get back in her good graces, he figured he should at least throw her a bone.

Lynn smiled as if Antonyo had just crowned her Miss Black America. "I miss you too, boo, and I'm available any time you need me to help wipe that sorrowful look from your beautiful face."

Man, Antonyo thought. He still had the magic. Jumping right back in the proverbial saddle, and also Lynn's bed, would be a lot easier than he could have imagined. Though feeling a slight pain of guilt and hearing Minister Keisha's voice of warning in his head, Antonyo decided to follow his own mind and jump right back in to a full-fledged affair with Lynn.

From that moment until just a few hours ago, he would be with Lynn and help her spend her plethora of loot while doing fun-filled and exciting activities together. She was also generous enough to spend quite a bit of dough on his then pending and now newborn daughter, LaToya. Nearly every time he came near Lynn, she presented him with something new and wonderful for his child. Antonyo had, of course, passed the beautiful gifts off to Clarke as things he had purchased himself.

But now, as he stared at LaToya, the gorgeous little mini replica of both him and Clarke, his heart broke. His soul ached because his baby would never know the security found in a two-parent household. Antonyo would never fall in love with Clarke, and he knew it beyond a shadow of a doubt. In fact, he doubted he would ever fall in love with any one woman. So, in fairness to himself, and heck, he rationalized, even to Clarke, he would have to walk away from the commitment he had made. It just would not be right to go on living with Clarke simply for the sake of baby LaToya, while cheating on Clarke the entire time. Now was as good a time as any to tell Clarke, he figured.

"Clarke, I want to thank you from the bottom of my heart for my precious angel of a daughter. She has instantly become the love of my life," he began as he continued to gaze upon his child.

Clarke smiled broadly at Antonyo's admission. She felt her heart open to receive the love she knew he would establish for her once their daughter was born. Clarke had put up with the pain of knowing that Antonyo never truly loved her in the beginning only because she knew this moment would eventually happen. She braced herself in her bed, anxiously anticipating the words she had longed for since meeting Antonyo.

Antonyo looked in Clarke's eyes. The pure joy he saw there made him hesitate. Did he really have it in him to destroy the woman who had just given him the greatest gift he had ever received? Maybe, just maybe, he could hang in there for a little while longer, perhaps until his daughter at least turned a year old. He mulled the possibility over in his head for a few brief moments. He looked down at his daughter and then said, "Clarke, I want out of this relationship. I have tried to do the right thing by you by being in this commitment with you and living with you, but it has just been too much for me, for who I am as a person. I am simply not ready to be in a monogamous relationship."

The pain of Antonyo's words severed Clarke's heart in two. The force of the blow he delivered rendered her unable to speak. She sat silently in the hospital bed, grateful that she was not holding her daughter. She was completely shaken by Antonyo's admission. Still, there was more for her to hear.

"I feel I need to be honest with you in fairness to us both. I have not been faithful to our relationship. There have been a couple of times that I have been with other women, and for a while now, I have been hanging out with Lynn."

This latter part of Antonyo's disclosure did not surprise or even further devastate Clarke. This she suspected. This is how it started out for them. This she was used to. But what had happened in the short span of time between his initial holding of his daughter and just a few seconds ago? Clarke had been two-hundred percent sure that when Antonyo thanked her for his child he had also opened his heart to her. Obviously, she had mistaken his outpouring of gratitude for a non-existent seal of his love for her. Now she felt utterly foolish. The proof of her stupidity began flowing from her eyes.

Antonyo had never felt this bad for a female in his life, not even Claire, and he had slept with both her and her daughter. Clarke, however, was the mother of his own daughter. He wondered if this new emotion this woman evoked in him could be equated with love. *No way*, he realized quickly. What he felt was an overwhelming sense of guilt. Plain and simple!

"Clarke, I apologize. I do. I hate seeing you cry like this, but if I stayed, I would only cause more pain for both of us. I'm not happy, and I can't make you happy. You deserve better than what I can offer you. I hope you won't let this affect my building a relationship with my daughter, because I love her more than anything. I know I have a lot of nerve asking for anything from you right now, but please don't do that to her or to me."

Clarke's pain provoked in her a strong desire to retaliate against Antonyo. She saw how much he loved his child, and that provided an easy avenue for her to be vindictive. Maliciousness had never been her style, but then again, neither had gullibility—until she met Antonyo. She warred internally between what she wanted to do and what she knew she should do; between who she was, who she had become, and who she wanted to be.

Never bothering to check the raw pain that flowed from her eyes, Clarke gestured for Antonyo to hand her the baby. She stared at her daughter, the child whom she thought could seal happiness for her, and realized that she would be a horrible parent for stealing any happiness from her. Clarke loved Antonyo, but she was an intelligent, goal-oriented woman before she met him. With or without him, she recognized, she could be that again. LaToya represented in her something that had changed her forever. No matter where her daughter lived, no matter what her daughter did, no matter if her daughter loved her or not; even if her daughter died, Clarke would now and forever be a mother.

"All right, Tony. I get it. It's over between us," Clarke stated while still crying audibly. "As you can see, it hurts to accept it, but I do. I have my daughter to buffer my pain. I have to move on and learn to be okay because I owe her my best. I believe that God has given her to me for just this reason."

Antonyo bristled at the mention of God. He was certain of two things more consciously at this moment than at any other in his life: one, he loved his daughter and would do all in his power to be a better father than Sheldon, and two, God was not pleased with him right now. He also harbored a little confusion in the awkwardness he felt. When had Clarke become so tuned in to God?

His concerns remained unvoiced. Clarke continued to

speak. "It is also obvious that being a father has sparked a positive change in you, so I won't stand in the way of you having a relationship with our daughter. It is probably better that she start her life with the routine of our co-parenting in separate households than you walking away from us after she has gotten used to us being together as a family."

Antonyo was elated with Clarke's decision. He was prepared to fight her tooth and nail to have a relationship with his daughter if he had to, but at least for now, that would not be necessary. Gratefulness covered his features. "Thank you, Clarke."

"Thank you too, Tony." Her tears had lessened, making it easier for her to continue in their conversation. "Tony, I want LaToya to spend a lot of time with your mother. I want her to grow up learning about God and building a relationship with Him from her earliest understanding. I don't want her to be deprived for as long as I have because she didn't know any better."

"I'm sure my mother would love to spend time teaching her granddaughter all about God," Antonyo said as he reached for the baby to hold while he spent just a few more minutes in Clarke's hospital room.

"Clarke, you can keep the apartment. The lease is paid for the next five months. I'm sure you can find a job by then to cover the rent, or you can move out if you want and find a different place. I will help you financially with LaToya, so I know you will be able to manage." He handed the baby back to her mother just as the nurse walked in, needing to check on Clarke. "I'm going to go now and get some stuff to take back to my mom's, but I want to come back later to see her. Hopefully I will get a chance to feed her. I'll also be here to drive you both home when they release you."

"That should be tomorrow morning, sir, as long as mother and baby continue to do well," the nurse interjected.

"Okay, cool. I'll see you both later." Antonyo left the hospital room feeling lighter and freer than he had in months. Guilt still hung around just a bit because he knew he had caused Clarke a great heartache. It had, however, released its suffocating hold on him, choosing instead to just squeeze his hand every now and then.

Clarke watched him leave, knowing that, while she still felt an incredible pain, she, too, was somehow lighter and freer as well.

Chapter 17

LaToya ran from the front porch of her grandmother's house to meet her father as he approached. Her tiny body moved as fast as her little three-year-old legs would carry her. Oh, how she loved her daddy, and her daddy loved her equally. Antonyo's heart nearly jumped out of his chest whenever he would see her.

"Hey, baby girl," he sang as he scooped her up in his arms when she reached the end of the walkway. "Did you have a good time with your grandma today?"

"Hi, Daddy. I had fun with Grandma, but I'm glad you came to get me. Are you taking me home to my mommy and Greg, or are we going over to my other house with you again?"

Antonyo smiled broadly at his daughter, happily announcing, "You get to stay with Daddy this weekend. Mommy and Greg will be back on Sunday night, just in time to get you off to your first day of preschool on Monday."

"Yeaaaahhh!" LaToya squealed.

"Yeaaaahhh!" Antonyo joined in.

Clarke had gotten married a week ago to one of her former professors at Wayne State University, and they were currently away on their honeymoon. Greg Martin was a straight-laced brain who graduated from high school at aged fifteen, received a bachelor's degree by age eighteen and his master's at twenty-one. Though he was once Clarke's professor, only one year separated them. The two of them were perfect for each other. They were very smart, good-looking, and ambitious. Clarke was now in her second year of medical school. In addition, they were also now members of Trina's church, where they were married. Antonyo respected Greg. He was great with his daughter, and LaToya loved him.

For Antonyo, life had pretty much remained the same. Aside from having become a wonderful father, he kept up his practice of being playa-playa. Antonyo and Clarke agreed that he would have custody of LaToya every other weekend and every Wednesday, or on the Thursdays that preceded his weekends.

With LaToya, he acted completely responsible. He read to his daughter, and along with her mother and new stepfather, he taught her to how to count, how to recite her alphabet, how to spell all of her names, her address, and so on. On very rare occasions—thank goodness for the rarity—he even administered necessary discipline, which he hated as much as he loved LaToya.

Together, they attended church with his mother on his weekends. This might have been the only time he "misbehaved" while in his child's presence. During these times, he flirted shamelessly with the still single Minster Keisha. Antonyo was determined to one day at least take the beautiful clergywoman out to dinner. This would accomplish two feats: first, getting her to agree to go out with him, and second, him paying for dinner. Antonyo still rarely ever paid for anything with his own money.

In his personal life, when away from his daughter, however, he was just a bit more reckless. Antonyo currently found himself involved with three different women. Claudia was a bored, married housewife with a set of twin sons the same age as LaToya. Her husband played professional basketball as a third-string power forward for the Detroit Pistons. Jessica, also married, worked as an accountant at a firm in the same building where Antonyo still worked for KLR. Jessica's husband was a gym teacher at a Detroit public high school. Then there was the ever-present, always annoying, yet forever spending Lynn.

He would see none of these women before Monday. He never mixed his time with LaToya with the women in his life. Not even Lynn had met his child.

Antonyo carried LaToya back into the house so that he could visit with his mother for a little while.

Life for Trina had changed almost as much as it had for Clarke. Trina Simms was engaged to be married to William Rucker, the man from her church she had begun seeing four years ago. Their private wedding ceremony was due to take place on New Year's Eve, just before the beginning of the Watch Night service at the church.

Antonyo guessed he liked William all right. He seemed to really care about his mother and he always treated her like a lady. William opened doors, never let Trina do heavy tasks or lifting, and he never spent the night.

Although he had accepted him, Antonyo still had not become accustomed to seeing his mom with a man. It was a good thing Trina or Toya would never have to worry about getting used to the same thing with him, he thought to himself as he entered the house and called for his mother.

"Hey, Antonyo," she responded as she appeared from the back bedroom, where her grandbaby slept when she visited. "Your daughter is sweet, smart, lovable, adorable, and I love her so much, but she is messy." Trina walked to the garbage and dropped in the armful of junk food wrappers that she pulled from the bedroom. "I'm so glad you are still here, Toy-Toy. Grandma needs you to go into your bedroom and put away all the toys you left scattered on the floor."

Antonyo put his daughter down and she scampered off to do as she was told.

"She had me sitting here at this kitchen table pretending to play Uno, knowing she was really just wanting to watch the window and wait for you to get here. Sometimes I think that little girl is just too smart for her age—a result of good genes and environment, I guess." Trina smiled at her son.

She still totally disapproved of his womanizing lifestyle, but she was completely proud of him as a father. His only example of fatherhood had been a lot less than shining. Sheldon had not been in contact with his son in eight years. The lowlife pig did not even know he had a beautiful granddaughter. Trina had forgiven Sheldon for his treatment of her and her son a few years ago, letting go of the pain. Having the opportunity to watch her baby be a good dad and do right by his child despite the circumstances was such a blessing for her.

"Ma, what is that grin all about? Are you sitting over there thinking about your boo?"

"Yes and no. I'm thinking about my baby all right, just not the one you're referring to. I'm thinking about you, Antonyo; thinking about how, aside from the way you treat the females in this world, you turned out to be a great man. More specifically, how great a father you are, even though Sheldon has never really been there for you."

"Ma, why is it that every blue moon you bring up that bum? You have a great guy of your own in your life right now, so I know you are not still pining away for that fool."

Trina made the face imitating a gagging motion. "Antonyo, please. I have not pined for your father in more than twenty-five years. I just wanted to pay you a compliment. Yuck!"

Antonyo laughed as his mother made the face again, this time pretending she was choking on her closed fist. "In actuality, though, Ma, Sheldon did play a role in how I parent my daughter. The way he treated me made me determined to do it different, better. I remember when Clarke was pregnant with LaToya. I used to dream that Sheldon was taunting me, telling me I would be a chip off the old block and things like that. Those nightmares helped shape me into the father I am today."

Trina smiled again then added, "Too bad he never took you around the hoards of other women he mistreated right along with me. Perhaps you would have determined to be different from him in that regard as well."

Antonyo decided not to engage in this dialogue with his mom. "On that note, I'm going to get my daughter and go home. What do you have planned for the evening? You and William getting together and hanging out on this fine Friday night?"

"No. I am actually going to hang out with my sister tonight. We are going to have dinner at Red Lobster, then catch the new Tyler Perry movie."

While it seemed that everyone else had made forward progress with their lives, LaTreece Simms had remained exactly the same. No better. No worse. She even still lived just two blocks from her twin sister. Aunt Treecie now rented a modest little house in the same neighborhood where Trina bought her home. She continued to play a variety of men, using them to pay her rent, car note, insurance and the like. It mattered not if these men were married or single, cute or ugly, black or white, gainfully employed or day to day hustling. As long as they had cash they were willing to share, Treecie was willing to spend time with them. She was still Antonyo's hero, and he hers.

Her children had managed, however, to make moderate to major improvements in their lives, depending on which child you were talking about. Darnell had not returned to jail since his last stint for his role in the car theft ring. He worked a blue collar job, but barely managed to make ends meet because he had three children with three different women. All of them "ganked" him for a percentage of his paycheck to pay child support. Whenever he wasn't living with one woman or another, he crashed at Antonyo's house because he could never manage to keep the rent paid on a living spot of his own.

Taraija had earned a bachelor's degree in marketing and worked in public relations for the top local news station in Detroit. She married her college sweetheart, who was an attorney. The couple was expecting their first child in three months.

Tianca had recently decided to go to college and earn a degree in early childhood education. Her classes would start the next coming semester. The turnaround in her life came after giving birth to two children in less than two years, just after finishing high school. Her ex-boyfriend, the father of both her children, was currently serving five to ten years in the state penitentiary for armed robbery of several neighborhood pizza parlors.

"Sounds like an entertaining evening, Ma. I hope you two have fun," Antonyo stated.

LaToya returned to the kitchen after surely only half-cleaning the bedroom and announced, "I'm all done. Are we leaving now, Daddy?" She was probably looking to escape before her grandmother discovered her sloppy work.

"Yes, precious. We can go now." Antonyo reached for LaToya's outstretched hand. "Thanks for picking her up from daycare and keeping her this week while I worked, Ma." He reached into his pants pocket with his free hand, pulled out a designated wad of bills, and handed them to his mother. "Here is a small token of my appreciation— and reimbursement for gas money. I know you would have preferred to come home and rest once you got off work."

Trina accepted the money, stating, "I love spending time with my granddaughter. You know that. But I will accept your token for gas reimbursement. I also love assisting you in being and doing the responsible thing for your child. Thank you, Antonyo. Now I can treat my sister to a night out instead of us going Dutch as previously planned."

Antonyo kissed his mother's cheek, smiling, filled with pride.

He hugged and kissed his daughter as he put on her sweater. Clarke stood there in the living room watching the exchange between father and daughter. She had always loved watching the two of them interact. When they initially broke up, Clarke often toyed with the idea of using Antonyo's feelings for his daughter to blackmail him into coming back to her. She loved him so much and suffered with a broken heart for quite a while when they separated. But seeing the way LaToya responded to her dad, even in the beginning of her life, made Clarke know that she would hurt her child as much, if not more than she would hurt Antonyo by playing games.

Once Clarke returned to school, she had become so busy with studies and being a mother that there was less and less time for crying over losing the then love of her life. Then she met Greg, and before she knew it, all traces of romantic feelings for the father of her child had disappeared. Clarke attributed Greg's entrance into her life as an answered prayer. She'd been working on and improving her relationship with God since the birth of LaToya.

"Okay, you two. Enough of the lovey-dovey," Clarke announced. "We have to go so I can get the little one into a tub and ready for bed, so she is refreshed and ready for her first day of school tomorrow."

"Mommy is right. After two more kisses, I have to let you go. But I promise I will be at the school in the morning to meet your teacher." Antonyo kissed his daughter twice, buttoned her sweater, and kissed her once more before picking her up and delivering her into her mother's arms.

"I missed you and Greg, Mommy," LaToya said.

"We missed you too, little dove. Greg can't wait until I get you home." Clarke hugged her daughter as she exited Antonyo's house with him right behind her.

"I'll walk you all out to the car so I can strap my princess securely in her car seat. I want to see her face until the very last second before you drive away with her," Antonyo stated.

Antonyo worked at putting his daughter snugly in her car seat while Clarke locked her suitcase in the trunk of her Ford Focus. Just as he closed the rear door of the vehicle, he lifted his head to find Lynn pulling her Lexus SUV into his driveway. Clarke had not yet gotten into her car, so she, too, saw the truck pull up, but was not totally sure of its driver. She soon would find out, however.

Lynn bounced out of her truck and over to the parental unit as if she were a welcomed visitor, paying little attention to the scowling glare on Antonyo's face. Clarke's features were none too pleasant either. Both were giving Lynn dirty looks for different reasons. Antonyo's anger came as a result of Lynn showing up forty-five minutes early for their scheduled date. She knew he did not allow women at his home while his daughter was there. Clarke stared angrily because she still held animosity toward Lynn for the drama she caused her while she and Antonyo were still in a relationship. She was a growing Christian. Forgiveness, especially toward this sneaky serpent, was still an area she had to work on.

"Heeeey, boo. What's the matter? You look angry. Did Clarke do something to piss you off?"

Before Antonyo could speak, Clarke went on the defensive. "Look, tramp—" Clarke started.

"No, Clarke. Don't go there with her. Remember our daughter is in the car," Antonyo reminded her.

Clarke took some deep breaths to calm herself, suddenly feeling very glad Antonyo intervened before she clowned in front of her baby. Lynn had the absolute worst effect on her. She realized, after coming close to having her daughter see her in a very ugly situation, she needed to pray down the hatred she had so deeply embedded in her soul for Lynn.

"Antonyo, your daughter and I are out. We will see you at the school in the morning." Clarke got in the car and made ready to leave. As an afterthought, she added out of the window, "You have a blessed evening, Lynn." Then, she drove off without waiting for Lynn's saucy reply.

"What in the world are you doing here now? You were not due at my crib for another forty-five minutes. You knew I would be here with my daughter, and you know I don't want you anywhere near her." Antonyo was yelling at the top of his lungs. He was furious with Lynn for her immature intrusion. He stomped away from her, heading toward his house, intent on leaving her outside.

"I'm sorry, boo. I just happened to be over this way already and decided we could get our party started early. I totally forgot that your daughter would be here," Lynn offered as she jogged behind a quickly moving Antonyo, who was doing his best to get away from her.

Suddenly, he stopped, causing Lynn to run into his back, just before he turned to face her.

"You are such a conniving liar. You make me sick, Lynn. Get away from my house. You have crossed the line for the final time. Leave!" He turned again and continued his hasty trek to his house.

Lynn stood stunned for a moment, feeling like perhaps Antonyo finally meant it this time. He had always been adamant about keeping his kid away from her and the other women he dated. Maybe, just maybe, this time she had gone too far with her games. Then she remembered her ace in the hole: the thing she had in her purse that made her feel confident enough to show up unannounced while his ex and his daughter were still at his house. Yes, Lynn knew Antonyo loved LaToya, but he also loved the trinkets she always used to woo him and/or make up with him. Lynn removed the beautifully wrapped gift box from her purse just before Antonyo crossed the threshold of his home.

"Tony, wait. Don't leave without this," Lynn announced aloud as she silently hoped he would react as she wanted him to.

Antonyo stopped just before closing the door. He stared at both Lynn and the box. At that very moment, he hated the materialistic creature he had become. In his right mind, he knew it would be best to slam the door in Lynn's face, but his head screamed for him to take the box he knew contained fabulousness. He believed that Minister Keisha described this as his spirit being at war with his flesh. Wow! What an awkward moment for him to think about the one woman who could probably settle him. Wait! Where the heck did that come from? Okay, back to the matter at hand.

"Lynn, you play too many games. Whatever you have in that box is not worth you breaking the rules when it comes to my daughter. You cannot buy my trust or my forgiveness this time. I want you out of my life. Go!" Antonyo walked in the house and slammed the door behind him. It took everything in him not to turn around and ask Lynn to give him the gift. He knew it was the Rolex watch they had seen when they were at the mall together last week. He really wanted that watch.

But, like he said, no matter how much he wanted the watch, getting rid of Lynn and her devious antics was more important to him right now.

Lynn stood outside of Antonyo's door for more than five minutes, confused and stupefied. He had never, ever, ever, ever turned down a gift. She loved Antonyo, had loved him for the past five years. She wanted his love in return, and believed that eventually, after all the time and money she invested in him, she would one day receive it; but now she was scared. Perhaps she would now, after all her games and manipulations, have to face losing him for good.

Lynn began reasoning with herself, trying to figure the best way to handle her current predicament. In order to keep up with his change in behavior, she realized she too had to do something different. She was a brilliant attorney, for goodness' sake. Surely she could out-think a working-class stiff, even if he was a charismatic, devastatingly gorgeous working-class stiff.

Then it hit her. Lynn ran back to her car to fetch a piece of writing paper. She jotted Antonyo a brief note.

> *Tony, again I apologize for my unwelcomed intrusion. After all these years, I'm sure you know me well. And as such, you know that I would never do anything to intentionally hurt you. It is my sincerest wish that you forgive my indiscretion today. Your friendship means the world to me. Please accept this gift as a token of my heartfelt admission of guilt.*
>
> *Lynn*

She folded the note and slipped it, along with the wrapped package, into his mailbox. As she mentioned in the letter, the two of them knew each other pretty well. Lynn was therefore positive that she would be hearing from her future husband real soon.

***

Antonyo admired the watch as it gleamed brightly on his wrist. Lynn had really outdone herself this time. She had been generous throughout the run of their relationship, but this watch was the icing on the cake.

Antonyo had not thought much else about Lynn after he slammed the door in her face yesterday evening. In fact, he took his mind completely off her antics by inviting Jessica over. The way Jessica would lie to get away from her husband whenever Antonyo called was a turn-on in itself. The girl could work miracles to get out of the house to come and get with him. Antonyo had, of course, been with married women before. Most of them at some point had been willing to leave their husbands if he had given them the word that he wanted an exclusive relationship with them. Since Claire, thought, he had not met a woman as eager to get away from her marriage as Jessica.

The thing about it was Jessica didn't necessarily want to be with Antonyo permanently. She just wanted to not be with Jason. She never talked about her husband in a negative manner; she actually didn't talk about him at all. So, Antonyo had no idea why Jessica resented her husband as much as she did. The fact that she didn't talk his ear off about it intrigued him. But what the heck? As long as he benefitted from her broken relationship, who cared why it was broken?

Antonyo had woken up this morning, washed away last night's indiscretion in the shower, and prepared himself to meet Clarke, LaToya, and possibly Greg, at LaToya's preschool. As he walked out of his front door, he had noticed his mailbox slightly ajar. At further inspection, he'd found Lynn's note and the beautifully wrapped watch he now gazed lovingly upon. Lynn was a headache, a nuisance, a prima donna, a spoiled brat, a jerk, but she sure gave great presents. The watch had been the best thus far.

After gazing at the diamonds on the wristwatch for several minutes, Antonyo pushed forward with his day, heading to the preschool to meet LaToya's teachers and to take plenty of pictures. Eventually, he would forgive Lynn. He always did. He would simply make her suffer a little longer than usual as punishment for the severity of her actions. The rules set regarding his child were non-negotiable. Lynn being silly and reckless in this regard was a serious breech of their friend-ship, definitely warranting the ending of their association. The watch, however, went a long way in assuaging his anger.

Antonyo continued on his trek to get to his daughter's pre-school, beaming brightly as he drove the streets to get to his baby girl. When he arrived, he spotted LaToya and crew, then immediately made his way over to the classroom, where they stood outside speaking with an older, white-haired black woman. She looked as motherly and as nurturing as anyone Antonyo would have hand-picked himself. This day thus far was working out great.

"Hey, gang," Antonyo spoke as he approached the group as they chatted with the teacher.

"Daaaaaddyyyyyy," LaToya screamed and leaped into her father's arms.

"Girl, you are so dramatic when it comes to your daddy," Clarke said to LaToya then turned to her daughter's teacher. "Please excuse her, Mrs. Collins. My daughter is a certified Daddy's girl." Clarke laughed at her ex and her child as they loved all over each other.

Antonyo took a moment off from kissing and squeezing LaToya to acknowledge her stepfather. "What's up, Greg? How was your honeymoon?" Antonyo approached Greg while still holding LaToya in his arms. He shifted his daughter in order to shake Greg's hand.

Greg felt a little awkward talking to his wife's ex-boyfriend about the beautiful time he had on his honeymoon, but in keeping with the history of this entire relationship, he decided to keep in line with the status quo. The three of them usually got along pretty well. Greg didn't want to begin rocking the boat. "The honeymoon was absolutely fabulous." For emphasis, he cuddled up next to his wife and gently kissed her cheek.

Antonyo watched the exchange, wondering if Greg was attempting to make him jealous. If that were the case, it was a wasted effort. Antonyo couldn't care less who or what Clarke did. As long as the two of them never tried to keep him from seeing his baby or hurt her in any way, he was cool with whatever.

"I'm sorry. Mrs. Collins, is it?" Antonyo asked.

"Yes, Mr. Simms. I'm Mrs. Collins," LaToya's teacher replied.

"I apologize, Mrs. Collins, for our rude behavior. I assume we are keeping you from starting your class."

"This is quite a cute scene, but you're right. I do need to get things started. Since it's the first day, you all are welcomed to sit in for the first twenty minutes or so, but then I need you to leave. I need the kids to get used to being in class without Mommy and Daddy . . . and Stepdaddy." Mrs. Collins smiled at the unconventional family and then walked into her classroom.

The clan of parents belonging to LaToya made their way into the classroom, joining the other parents. The presence of Clarke, Greg, and Antonyo as LaToya's parents was probably an oddity. She then realized how very blessed both she and her daughter were. She was married to a man secure enough to handle being around the only other man she had ever genuinely loved. God had taken what started out as a crazy situation and turned it into a wonderful family for her innocent baby.

Once parent time had nearly ended, both Antonyo and Clarke became a little anxious, each worrying if LaToya would be okay with them leaving her in the classroom without them. Greg glanced at his wife as he felt the tension begin to ooze from her body. With a quick look at Antonyo, he realized the biological unit wore twin expressions. It was during times like these that Greg felt like such an outsider. He loved Clarke; he loved LaToya; he even liked Antonyo. Usually he was quite comfortable with their irregular situation; however, there were times like this when he had to pray for control over his see-sawing emotions and insecurities. Greg knew Clarke loved him and him only, but his wife shared a bond with another man that he could not compete with. For the hundredth time, he wished for two things: that LaToya was his daughter, and that he and Clarke had a daughter or son of their own.

"Okay, mommies and daddies, it's time to say good-bye so the children can get back to learning," Mrs. Collins announced to the parents as discreetly as she could. She did not want to alarm the children.

Antonyo stood and walked toward LaToya, who played contently with colored alphabet blocks along with another little girl. "Hey, Toy."

"Hi, Daddy. Hi, Mommy," she added as Clarke trailed behind Antonyo, Greg a few feet away.

"We all have to leave now. So I want you—"

"No, Daddy. I'm not ready to leave. I want to stay here with Stacey and play."

"Well, sweetheart. You don't have to leave," Clarke jumped in, "but Daddy, Greg, and I have to go. This is your school now, remember, so you will come here every day and one of us will come and pick you up. Do you remember how I explained that to you?" Clarke said to her daughter.

"Okay. I'm glad I don't have to leave right now. I'll be ready to go when you come back to get me," LaToya announced confidently.

The trio of parents stared at each other, all visibly relieved there would not be a scene about them leaving LaToya with her teacher and classmates on her first day. Again, Clarke inwardly praised God for blessing them with such a special child. Each adult took turns kissing the baby, then all filed out of the school.

Once outside, Antonyo said his good-byes to Clarke and Greg. "This seems like a good school. LaToya is comfortable; Mrs. Collins is cool. All is well."

"This is a nice school, and I am so happy our daughter is happy." Clarke smiled broadly at her ex.

Greg, again, became aware of that small tinge of jealousy. In order to not feel so left out, he added his two cents to the conversation. "Yeah, it seems as if preschool is going to work out well for our little LaToya."

Clarke absorbed her husband's discomfort and decided to get him out of there. Never before had she noticed Greg being uneasy around Antonyo. For some reason, today he appeared bothered by the relationship the four of them had established. Once they were in their car, she would question him about it, hopefully finding out she was completely off base.

"Tony, thanks for coming by this morning. LaToya loved having her daddy here. Why don't you call me—or us tonight so we can work out a pick-up schedule? As far as drop-off, we'll drop her off on the days we have her. You can drop her off on the Wednesdays you have her. Cool?"

Antonyo felt the tension and realized it was the reason behind Clarke's rambling. "All right, I'll call later. I'm gone. Talk to you later." Antonyo headed to his car, turning once to glance at the couple walking awkwardly toward their own vehicle. That type of drama was one of the reasons he had tried his best to avoid monogamous entanglements. He was at least glad that his one attempt had been with someone as special and as sweet as Clarke. He thanked God she was LaToya's mother. He also hoped things worked out between her and Greg.

When he got to his car, Antonyo realized his cell phone had fallen from his pocket. He picked it up from the driver's seat before sitting down, noticing he had five missed calls and one voice mail message. He incorrectly assumed all the calls and the message were from Lynn. In reality, only four of the calls were from Lynn. The other call and voice mail message was from an unrecognized number. Antonyo listened to the message, re-listened, and listened one more time to be sure he had heard correctly. The smile spreading across his face grew as wide as the attraction he felt for the caller.

"Hi, Antonyo. This is Keisha Hearn, young adult minister of Trinity Star. I am hosting an event, actually a focus group, this Thursday for young adults between eighteen and twenty-nine at the church. I'm hoping you will attend this first of three sessions. We will begin at 7:00 P.M. I understand you are not an official member of the church . . . yet, but I'll work on that later." Keisha giggled; Antonyo grinned harder. "But membership is not required for this meeting, so please come. I'm praying I'll see you on Thursday. Have a very blessed day, Antonyo."

Wow! Antonyo didn't even know Keisha had his phone number. She must have gotten it from his mother. At any rate, Antonyo knew beyond a shadow of a doubt where he would be spending his Thursday evening as he drove away from his daughter's school. He could not remember a time when he so eagerly anticipated being with a woman. Sure, it wouldn't be an official date; they would more than likely be in a room with several other people. Make no bones about it, however. He resolved to make Minister Keisha Hearn an imperative part of his personal life.

Chapter 18

"Yes, Tony, Greg has been tripping since Toy's first day of school. I've always suspected he was a little jealous of our friendship and the way we parent our daughter together, but ever since that day, he has been on a verbal tirade about us having our own child. Every other sentence from his lips is about how soon we can get pregnant. I'm not against having a baby with my husband, but I want to finish medical school first. I think if you and I are not in each other's presence as much, at least for a little while, he'll calm down."

When Antonyo had picked up LaToya today from Greg and Clarke's house, Greg was downright rude. Normally, Antonyo would go into the house and sit or help prepare his child to leave. Today, however, Greg took a very long time to open the door. Then he closed the door before Antonyo could enter the house, stating he would get the baby ready and bring her out, leaving him standing on the front porch, looking like a confused idiot. He called Clarke for an explanation the moment he stepped through his door.

"Clarke, I've never had a problem with Greg. I can appreciate how he cares for my daughter, but if he starts drama with me about Toy, it is not going to go well for him." Antonyo had become loud when stating his last sentence.

"Tony, please calm down. I don't need you going off the deep end on me too. I will work this out with my husband. Nothing will change between you and your baby girl. I promise."

"Fix it, Clarke. I'll talk to you later. Bye."

Clarke had always felt so blessed to have a relationship with both her husband and the father of her child that worked so well. Now things were starting to fall apart for no apparent reason. "Uggghhh!" Clarke thought aloud. Why did life always have to have complications? The moment the thought crossed her brain, a scripture from Bible study immediately followed the reflection: *I have told you these things, so that in me you may have peace. In this world you will have trouble. But take heart! I have overcome the world.* John 16:33.

Clarke found so much assurance in having God talk to her when she felt distressed. She praised Him for loving her as He did, and she thanked Him. She was thankful to Ms. Trina for taking her to church and Bible study. She knew things would work out beyond a shadow of a doubt.

Thursday had finally arrived. Antonyo sat in the room at the church with about thirteen or fourteen other young adults, anxiously awaiting Keisha's appearance. He'd gotten there about fifteen minutes early, which was about thirteen minutes ago. Two minutes more and his spiritual beauty would walk through the door.

Right on the money, Keisha arrived. She floated in to the room with her Bible in one hand and a thickly padded green folder in the other. "Hello, everyone. It's a blessing to see so many of God's children in the house this evening. I want to thank you for taking time from your busy schedules to spend it with me. I have some light refreshments for you, but I couldn't carry them by myself. Antonyo, would you and Malcolm be so kind as to follow me so we can bring in the snacks?"

Antonyo considered telling Keisha that only his mother

called him by his given name, but decided he liked the way it sounded coming from her lips.

They dutifully followed as requested, both men attracted to the beautiful minister. Antonyo could feel the others man's attraction for "his" woman, and found himself none too happy about the obvious. He wondered if he were as transparent to Malcolm, and if perhaps the other gentleman too carried an envious grudge. No matter. Antonyo had never lost a woman to another man at any other time. He definitely did not plan on this being his first concession to defeat.

Keisha led the men down a lengthy hallway. During their walk, Malcolm engaged the youth minister in meaningless banter, while Antonyo multitasked. He listened to the amateur's weak rap and checked out Keisha's beautifully toned body as she sauntered down the hallway.

Keisha returned Malcolm's conversation, and had the dirty nerve to sound as if she were truly interested in what he was saying. This woman was some kind of special, the kind of special that would make a player burn his card if given the opportunity. He would love to share his daughter with Keisha, to have LaToya in the presence of a woman this dynamic. Clarke was a great role model and mother, but Keisha gave special meaning to the words *phenomenal woman.*

After gathering the snacks and carrying them back to the meeting room, Keisha allowed everyone to partake in the refreshments and then began her discussion while they all snacked and drank.

Keisha hopped up on the countertop and sat down. "Again, I want to thank you all for coming out this evening. I'm sure there are many ways you would have preferred spending your time this Thursday evening. For the married folks in the room, perhaps a romantic evening with the spouse would have been more intriguing. For you single people, such as myself, maybe a date with the significant other, hanging with your boys or your girls, or just a relaxing evening at home would have sufficed. But, yet in still, you came out to lend your ears and voice to little ole me. I appreciate it. Really I do."

Luckily, Antonyo planned on having both: a late-night rendezvous with a not-so-significant other, and the pleasure of spending time with the beautiful minister.

"I've asked you all here tonight to conduct a focus group, if you will. I kind of want to pick your brains a bit about your view on your personal relationship with God. In this folder, I have a brief questionnaire that I put together, which asks some pretty detailed questions. There are no correct answers. I simply want you to share with me, and later with each other, your feelings about the questions I ask. I would like you each to take about twenty minutes to complete the questions, and then we will have some dialogue about your answers.

"I, too, will answer the questions. That way, I can share with you instead of just being the facilitator of our session here. So, why don't we go ahead and get started with the mundane so we can move ahead to the good stuff."

The group of twelve began their written task, all studiously examining their questions, then giving thought-provoking answers; all except Antonyo. He studied the questions, but had no substantial answers to give.

Question 1: How old were you when you initially believed there was a God?

Question 2: Do you remember what triggered your recognition of our Heavenly Father?

Question 3: Do you understand the true concept of the Kingdom of God?

Question 4: What do you think about the Ten Commandments?

Question 5: Where does Jesus fit into your life?

Antonyo was at a complete loss as to how to answer these questions. These were not issues he pondered during his free time. These were not issues he pondered ever. All Antonyo believed for sure was that God was real. He believed that because intellect told him that someone had to create humanity and all its complexities. His thought process didn't go too far beyond that.

Before he realized it, Keisha asked everyone to put down their pencils. Antonyo had not put one letter of the alphabet on his paper. He had never felt so confused in his life. His mother spoke about God as if He were a personal, tangible friend. Clarke talked as if she and God had conversations over tea. Even though he and Minister Keisha had only limited contact with one another, it seemed to Antonyo as if she carried Him with her everywhere she went. Every time he was near Keisha, he felt that she believed God was right there too. Antonyo only knew God existed. He didn't really talk to Him. He didn't eat with Him. He definitely didn't think about Him when he was with his women. He simply knew He existed.

"Okay, good people, let's take some time and discuss our responses, please. We will go over them in order one at a time. Who wants to answer question number one?"

The young adults all looked at one another, each hoping one of the others would speak up so he or she wouldn't have to. Antonyo was surprised to find the apprehension amongst the other people in the room. He was certain he was the only one who had a problem relating to the questions. Minister Keisha also noticed the uneasiness.

"Why don't I start? Feel free to chime in as you began to relate to my experiences." Keisha had come down from her post on the counter and now walked around the room as she spoke. "Question number one: How old were you when you realized there was a God? For me, the answer would be at age eight. At that time, my great-grandmother died. She and I were not very close, but my mother loved her dearly. I had only met her on a couple of occasions because she lived down in Alabama. I watched my mother's sadness over the loss of her grandmother. I felt her sadness inside of me because I loved my mother so much. Then I heard my mother's mother, my grandmother, tell my mother that her grandmother was now with God. At eight years old, I wasn't quite sure what that meant, but my heart was touched by the confidence that my grandmother had when she spoke to my mother about her own mother's death. My grandmother, while sad, was . . . comfortable, shall we say, with her mother dying, because somebody named God now had her. And I remember it like it was yesterday, thinking, 'Wow! I want to know this God.' "

Antonyo listened to Keisha's impassioned speech, wondering if perhaps it took the death of a loved one to bring a person closer to God. He had never lost anyone close to him to death. His own grandmother died when he was three, so he really didn't know her. The rest of his family was still alive and kicking, including deadbeat Sheldon.

Around Antonyo, others had opened up and added to the conversation. Some gave very definite answers to question number one. This also led into question number two. Most people seemed to express feelings kind of like his own uncertainty.

As the dialogue pressed forward and the other questions were being discussed, Antonyo listened intently. While he found most of his peers in the room shared in his confusion, it made him no more comfortable. He was used to being the man in the classroom, in business meetings, with the ladies, everywhere. He usually commanded any environment he was a part of. And if he had anything to do with it, this would be no different in the near future. His perplexity only served to make him determined to learn more about the role God currently played in his life.

In an effort to redeem himself even tonight, he decided to try his hand at giving his thoughts on question number three. The Kingdom of God seemed easy enough to handle.

Keisha resumed her speaking to her group. "Let's not spend too much time on any one question. We have to be out of here in by eight-thirty. Who wants to try number three? What do you know about the Kingdom of God?"

"The Kingdom of God is heaven, right?" Antonyo answered with a confident outward bravado. In truth, he was somewhat nervous about his response. The murmurs from several of the other members of the group signaled agreement with his answer. His certainty level rose with the reactions.

"That is the normal answer to that question." Keisha smiled. Antonyo smiled also. "But it's not quite right." Antonyo's smile disappeared as quickly as doughnuts at a fat camp.

"I know I said there were no right or wrong answers. These questions are supposed to be based on your perceptions and experiences. So, Antonyo, I suppose that answer is based on your perspective. Would you like to elaborate?"

Antonyo prayed Keisha was not intentionally trying to put him on front street, trying to embarrass him. He looked into her eyes, a pair of the most beautiful eyes he'd ever seen, and knew she would never deliberately try to hurt him. "I would like to elaborate, but I'm not sure what to say. I thought I knew what I was talking about when I said God's Kingdom implied heaven. I don't know how old I was when I initially believed God existed. I don't believe I've had a true recognition of God in my life; I'm not sure where Jesus fits, and the only commandment I know is thou shall not kill. Right now, Keisha, I only know two things for sure, but I'll only share one of them with this class. The other I'll share with only you at a later date." The others in the class chuckled, thinking he purposely made a joke. Antonyo, however, spoke with complete seriousness. "I do know there is a God!"

Keisha, moved by Antonyo's heartfelt declaration about his faith that God existed, wanted to hear more from the handsome, self-proclaimed playboy. "How can you be so sure that there is a God if you can't speak of how you have experienced Him personally?"

"I can see God in my mother. I've watched how she has changed since she started going to church. She is happy now. She's getting ready to get married. She is so much better as a result of her finding God."

Keisha felt something inside of her soften toward Antonyo. The minister was not immune to noticing an attractive man when he crossed her path, even taking a second glance on occasion. Antonyo, however, suddenly posed a threat, exposing a palpable stirring she had not experienced in quite some time. Keisha shook off the tremors in order to regain control of her meeting, but it was too late. Antonyo had already taken notice.

He, too, shuddered a little at how real Keisha became at that moment, her authenticity bringing his attraction to her to its highest level ever. He was amazed at how his sincerity had won points with Keisha, while his practiced charm and suaveness had been his claim to fame with other women. What a woman.

Unbeknownst to either of them, because they were simply reacting to each other, most other females in the class had also been affected by Antonyo's transparency.

"We are really running behind schedule, so let's move on. Would anyone else like to comment on any of the questions?" Keisha asked.

"Minister Keisha, you never explained the true concept of the Kingdom of God," one of the group members stated.

Keisha had totally forgotten about where the discussions left off after listening to Antonyo speak. Although a little embarrassed, she was thankful for the reminder. "Oh, yes. I apologize. When we speak about the Kingdom of God, we are actually talking about a body of believers in Jesus Christ. The Kingdom of God is the church; not the building, but us, those of us who believe, who serve Jesus and who witness about Him as we are all doing here tonight. The Kingdom is more a state of being than an actual place.

"The Book of Matthew in your Bible gives great insight to the true meaning of the Kingdom of God. I would like you all to take some time and read about it."

Antonyo mentally thanked tonight's lecturer for that bit of helpful information. He planned on getting his study on. He intended to never get caught totally unaware again on the subject of God.

"That's pretty much all the time we have tonight. I don't want the custodians upset with me for keeping them past their scheduled work time. I certainly appreciate all of you for coming and for your helpful insight. Please leave the questionnaire on the counter on your way out. It doesn't matter how you answered the questions. I just want to get a sense of what you feel. I hope to see each of you in the young adult Bible study on Tuesday at six-thirty. Thank you again so much."

The group members began filing out of the room. Antonyo stayed put, though, as if he were part of the fixtures in the room. He watched Keisha move about, gathering papers, putting desks back in place, restoring order. He got up and began to help just as the last person left.

"Antonyo, you don't have to stay. Your participation was more than enough. It's late. Go home." Keisha valued his assistance, but his nearness caused the sensations from earlier to return. He was a temptation she undoubtedly needed to steer clear of.

"Now, what kind of man would I be if I left a lady to walk to her car alone in the darkness at this late hour? I'm going to wait for you."

The finality of his reply both annoyed and intrigued Keisha. She wanted to be away from him for the sanctity of her libido, but she also enjoyed the authoritative way in which he announced his integrity. The two worked in companionable silence until Keisha turned off the light and they left the room together.

As they walked down the stairs, Antonyo asked, "How old are you, Keisha? Or is it inappropriate for me to address you by your first name? Do I have to say Minister Keisha?"

"You don't have to be so formal when speaking to me. Keisha is fine. If anything is inappropriate, it's that you asked my age." Keisha smiled, letting him know she wasn't really offended. "I'm twenty-seven, Antonyo."

Only one year older than me, Antonyo thought. "Is the invitation to your Bible study class open to the public, or do I have to wait until next semester or something?"

"No. Bible study is an open class. You are welcome to come whenever you want to." Keisha wished she felt as welcoming as she sounded. In truth, she was indeed skeptical about him being in her class. Antonyo did strange things to her thoughts.

"I'll be there next week. Your meeting tonight provoked an interest in me. I didn't like being so uninformed. Ignorance is not my strong suit."

Keisha realized then that it was his pride that motivated his interest in Jesus, not a real desire to have a relationship with Him. Whatever the case, Keisha would accept his wish to be informed as simply the beginning. She recognized that it was merely her responsibility to catch the fish. It was God's job to clean them. Right now, however, she could use some cleansing of her own thoughts. Antonyo was a powerfully potent man.

"I'll be happy to have you. I hope you find what it is you're looking for in class." Keisha grasped the unintended invitation in her statement too late, and Antonyo bit right into the inadvertent bait.

"I'm sure I will. Is this your car?" He stopped walking as Keisha halted by the red old-school Camaro.

"Yes, sir, it is. Thank you for escorting me. I hope to see you in church on Sunday. If not, I'll see you on Tuesday. Good night, Antonyo." Keisha hastily stepped into her car after she unlocked the door.

"Good night, Minister Keisha."

Jessica arrived at Antonyo's right on schedule, just as always. She was one of the most punctual women he had ever dated. No matter how late or early they planned to get together, Jessica never showed late, nor did she ever cancel on him. It often made him wonder what her husband said about her impromptu departures. The other married woman that he dated, Claudia, went on and on about how her husband cheated on her with groupies and hoochies who were always hanging around the Pistons games and players. She complained about how her man never paid any attention to her or the twins. On and on. But not Jessica. She never vented about her marriage.

Antonyo escorted his beautiful companion into his house, greeting her with a very passionate kiss. Jessica was absolutely gorgeous: perfect hair, perfect skin, perfect teeth, perfect waistline, breasts, and backside. Simply perfect in every physical way possible. Jessica's husband was a high school gym teacher, so Antonyo attributed her perfect body to what was probably her husband's fitness regimen. He could not say for sure, however, because other than his name and occupation, Jessica never told Antonyo much else about Scott.

"So, how was your day, Tony?" Jessica asked as she sat down on the sofa in the living room. Immediately, Antonyo thought about Keisha and the vibes that had passed between them that evening. If Jessica knew how quickly that question made him think of another woman, he knew she would have chosen another one to ask.

"My day was interesting, to say the least. I attended a focus group for young adults this evening at my mother's church. The moderator wanted to know how our age group felt about God and our relationship with Him."

"I'm sure you were bored stiff there. Poor baby. Well, Mama's here to completely take your mind off all that religious God mumbo jumbo."

Jessica slid across the couch and began a very skilled performance of seduction. Antonyo, however, could not quite get into the dance. Jessica's assessment of his feelings about the focus group captivated him. He wanted to know what provoked such thoughts with regard to how he would feel about God.

"Wait, Jess. Why would you think I would be bored by such a discussion? And why label God as religious mumbo jumbo? Don't you believe in God?"

Okay, where did all of this come from? Jessica thought as she suddenly halted her foreplay. She stared at Antonyo as if he had two heads, and then blinked twice to be sure her focus was correct, that she indeed sat in the lap of Antonyo Simms. "Tony, you can't possibly sit here and tell me you believe in God and Jesus and all those other religious hoaxes, do you?" Jessica chuckled at the humor those thoughts invoked in her.

Antonyo felt no comedic wit in her statements. He knew he was not a Bible- carrying, gospel-preaching, filled-with-the-Holy-Spirit believer. But neither was he a loud, rebellious agnostic either. "What have I ever said or done that gives you the impression that I don't believe in God, Jessica?"

Jessica, again astonished by this conversation, slowly craw-led from Antonyo's lap. He seemed offended by her assumption, so she decided to tread lightly, hoping there would eventually be a punch line in this discussion. The truth of the matter was, what had he done or said to show he was a believer? That is not what she would say, however. She wanted to keep the peace between them, not get into a religious debate. She also wanted what she came over for: a never-disappointing roll in the hay with him.

"Tony, I certainly did not mean to upset you. I have actually never heard your views one way or the other about religion. It's just that you have no problem having sex and being unmarried. Nor do you discriminate, because you have no problem sleeping with women who are married. I don't know much about this God thing, but I'm pretty sure those two items are high on the no-no list of those who do follow religious practices. So, forgive me for being just a little confused here."

Antonyo thought about Jessica's rebuttal, acknowledging its weight, but only for a second. The fact that he was not perfect gave her no right to assume he did not believe in his Creator simply because she apparently did not. Not that he'd had this discussion with all of the women he slept with, but Antonyo did not realize he even knew anyone who did not believe in God.

"Jess, why don't we change the subject? I guess it's true what they say about religion and politics being subjects to stay away from."

Jessica, being more than happy to oblige, quickly agreed. "I hear you. I mean, who knew this is where our conversations would ever end up going?" She smiled her perfect smile, and business as usual resumed for them.

After their romp, however, Antonyo felt compelled to know more about Jessica and her disbelief, so he underhandedly started the dialogue again. "Jessica, how long have you been married?"

Totally satisfied with what just happened between them, Jessica would have gratified him in any way he asked at the moment. So, she answered his question, though the subject of her marriage was normally off limits. "Four years."

"Do you consider what we do cheating on your marriage, on your husband?"

"Under normal circumstances, I would say yes. But my circumstances are somewhat different."

Okay, now he was confused. He wanted to know why someone who didn't believe in God would partake in the institution of marriage, which God created. But her answer about her circumstances made him curious. His curiosity won out.

"What about your circumstances makes it okay to cheat on your husband?"

Jessica shifted her position on the bed in an effort to put a little distance between her and Antonyo. Having still been on a high from their lovemaking, she didn't realize what she had let slip. She hung out with Antonyo to get away from her "circumstances" at home, in her marriage. She did not want to discuss them with him or anyone else. Not even her mother knew what she lived with every day.

Antonyo noticed the change in her demeanor. What could possibly be so wrong in her marriage that every time the subject came up she became really uncomfortable? "Talk to me, Jess. What's going on at home? Is your husband cheating and his affair bothers you? Is he hurting you? Hitting you?"

Maybe if she told him the entire story she would feel better. Keeping it all to herself surely had not done anything to alleviate her stress. The only person who gave her peace, even temporarily, was Antonyo. Maybe he would understand her pain.

Jessica sat up in the bed, pulling the covers up to shield her nakedness. She stared straight ahead for several long seconds, leaving Antonyo wondering what could be so deep. He, too, sat up, making sure that their bodies did not touch. He wanted Jessica to feel at ease, without the normal sexual parameters of their association. He wanted to truly be a friend, a sounding board for her if she decided to open up to him.

Wow, where had those thoughts come from? He questioned himself. He never thought beyond the bedroom with any of the women he dated. Why, suddenly, had he cared enough to listen to the problems of one of them? Jessica started speaking, and he returned his full attention back to what she had to say.

"Antonyo, Scott and I have an unconventional marriage. It started out normal, at least for me, but about two years ago, things changed drastically.

"I met Scott when we were seniors in high school. I attended a party with my cousin in his neighborhood. That's where we were first introduced. I almost fainted when my cousin's girlfriend told me Scott wanted to meet me. He was so handsome and I was so flattered."

Okay, this was going to be the long version, but it had to be good, so he listened without interruption.

"We started dating and became monogamous very quickly. We were inseparable. I only applied to Oakland University because that is where Scott wanted to go. It was my intention to go to UCLA or Arizona State University. I wanted to get away from the cold and the snow, you know? But once I met Scott, I never wanted to be away from him. I could deal with the harsh winters for the rest of my life as long as I had Scott to keep me warm."

Long and sappy. Man, when is she going to get to the circumstances? Antonyo thought. He decided to intervene in an effort to speed the conversation along. "So, what happened to sour this great love the two of you had?"

"During our sophomore year in college, Scott started exhibiting some strange behavior. For the first two years, we were never apart. Then suddenly, every now and again, Scott would be missing in action. Of course, my initial thoughts were that he had started cheating on me. On a couple of occasions, he disappeared for a day, and when I asked him where he'd been, he said he was having some emotional issues and he needed some alone time to work through things.

"I wanted to believe he would not hurt me by betraying our relationship, so I asked about his issues and why he felt he could not share his pain with me. He simply stated that school was so very challenging, and the pressures to keep up were becoming too much to handle. He then admitted that he began smoking marijuana to relax and didn't want me to see him while he used drugs.

"My cousin, Jordan, the one who introduced us, helped to convince me that Scott had told me the truth. He, too, confessed to smoking weed and stated he and Scott had been hanging out together on some of the times Scott had been away from me. Therefore, I was more than convinced that Scott had not been with another woman, because Jordan would have never stood for it."

Immediately, pictures of a crack-addicted shell of a man appeared before Antonyo's eyes. Is that what—or should he say who—Jessica ran from each time she ran to him? The sound of Jessica's voice continuing her story brought him back from his musings.

"The disappearing acts continued throughout sophomore and junior year. The marijuana and relaxation getaways apparently worked for Scott, because his grades were exemplary. He made the dean's list each semester.

"But still there remained an edge of uneasiness that surrounded Scott. On the first few days after he would return from one of his retreats, which occurred generally about once a month, he would be fine; then for several days after that, he would be sullen. I was confused, but in love. So I just went along with Scott's program, hoping he would eventually get back to normal.

"By the time senior year rolled around, Scott had seemingly come back to himself. Jordan had graduated the previous semester with a degree in sociology and found a job teaching in Atlanta. He proposed to his fiancée. They were married a couple weeks after their graduation, and they moved away to begin their new life together. As far as I knew, Jordan had been Scott's only retreat buddy. Once Jordan left, the retreats ended and I had my man back."

Jessica stopped speaking for a moment. Antonyo could feel the heaviness the story created for her, and decided to help her take a break. "Hey, how about I get us something to drink and grab a little snack." Before she could answer, he jumped up, put on his robe, and headed toward his kitchen.

When he returned, Jessica had put on her oversized blouse to cover her, but she didn't look as if she was preparing to leave. She had gotten comfortable on his bed and awaited his return. He joined her on the bed, handing her a glass of fruit juice, and set a bowl with potato chips and a plate of chocolate chip cookies between them. Jessica sipped from her glass, nibbled at a cookie, and then continued her story.

"By the end of senior year, Scott and I had grown closer than ever. I loved him more than ever. I wanted to be with him forever. And he did not disappoint me. He asked me to marry him three weeks before our graduation ceremony. We celebrated our graduation by driving to Toledo to get married on the same day we received our degrees. It was perfect."

Yeah, yeah, yeah. Perfect. Whatever, Antonyo thought. *Now get to the part that has you running to my bed on a regular basis. Tir-*

ing of the long-winded walk down memory lane, he resolved to again try to push this version along a little. "So, when *exactly* did things fall apart for you two?"

"Two years ago, Scott pulled another Houdini and disappeared on me again, this time for a full two days. I was worried sick, frantic even. At the forty-seventh hour, as I picked up the phone to call the police, Scott walked in the door, looking disheveled, but unharmed. I was both happy and angry at the same time. While I was glad he was alive, I wanted to kill him for not being hurt and worrying me so.

"When I got up from my seat on the sofa, where I practically lived during the hours of his disappearance, I didn't know if I would slap him or hug him. As I approached him, still unsure of how I would put my hands on him, I was immediately attacked by the aroma of marijuana. The anger took over and I slapped him. Hard. Twice. I could not believe he had put me through the hell of the unknown so that he could go somewhere to get high.

"I sat down on the sofa, fearing the worst, knowing he was about to tell me he had been cheating on me when we were in college and that he had started his affair once again. I was not only prepared to hear that he had been dishonoring our marriage, but that he had been betraying me with a woman who used drugs. I sat on the couch, gripped its edge, and stilled myself for the fallout from his lips."

Antonyo sat in eager anticipation of how Scott would explain this all to his wife as well. Jessica had taken all day to get to this point, but now she had prepared him for the climactic end with expectancy. There were a million questions running around in his head. Was this woman the same woman Scott cheated with in college? Were they still seeing each other? What arrangement had Jessica and Scott worked out so that they could still stay together? He waited for Jessica to finish her entire story, though, before he began his interrogation about the current state of her marriage.

"'Well what is it, Scott? What do you have to say for yourself,' I asked. No matter what I thought I was prepared for, nothing could have readied me for what he told me." Jessica paused before repeating the words Scott had said to her.

"He said, 'I was with Matthew. We went to his parents' house up north. Jessica, Matthew and I were at the cabin as lovers this weekend.'"

"What!" Antonyo yelled in astonishment. "Your husband is gay?"

"Tony, I was just as amazed as you are; probably more so considering that I was married to him and deeply in love with him at the time of his declaration."

"Man! This is deep, Jessica. How long has your husband been gay?"

"Get this. Remember I said that when Scott apologized, he stated that he had been deceiving me since we have known each other? When I was finally able to speak again, I asked him to explain his statement. He informed me that he and my cousin, Jordan, had been in an intimate relationship with each other for several years."

Antonyo's eyes grew to the size of saucers. Initially he was too astonished to even speak the words lodged in his throat. When he did finally find his voice, he asked, "But didn't you say that your cousin is now married? What's up with all the gay dudes suddenly deciding they want women? And don't these guys act gay? I mean, how is it that you and your cousin's wife couldn't tell?"

Jessica sat on the bed shaking her head, her look clearly testifying to the fact that she saw no clues. "I searched my mind frantically on that day, trying to recall if there were any signs that I missed or ignored. There were none, Tony. None.

I could have been blinded by love, I guess, but I saw nothing."

Antonyo had very little interaction with gay people, but those he had been around were usually easy to spot. They behaved somewhat feminine, and were generally weird to him. How could Jessica and her cousin have been that blind?

"Does your cousin's wife know the real deal?"

"According to Scott, Tamala, my cousin's wife, is the one who pulled him out of the lifestyle. She supposedly met him, introduced him to Jesus or Christ or whatever, and eventually he decided he did not want to be a homosexual anymore. The two of them fell in love, and as they say, the rest is history."

God? Did He actually change homosexuals to heterosexuals? While Antonyo sat silently musing, Jessica made her opinion on the subject plainly known.

"I think that's all a bunch of bull, though. If there is a God, why would He change Jordan so that he could marry, and not change Scott? Does your God play favorites, Tony?"

Whoa! Where had that come from? Just a little while earlier she had accused him of being such a bad guy that he could not possibly believe in God. Now she wanted him to answer religious questions about God and her gay husband. Antonyo became a bit aggravated by the fact that he was not sure how to answer Jessica, because he wanted to be able to answer her. He hoped the Bible study classes he would attend with Minister Keisha would prepare him for moments like this. He gave it his best shot, though, using what he'd heard in church and what he'd heard his mother say over the years.

"Jessica, I don't think God plays favorites. I'm nowhere near knowledgeable enough to explain why your cousin was changed and not your husband, but if I had to guess, I would say it's because Jordan wanted to change after he found Jesus. Perhaps if Scott developed a relationship with God, he, too, might want to change."

"According to Scott, he's been gay his whole life. So, if that is the case, that means that *your* God made him gay since *your* God created him. Now, are you saying *your* God is expecting Scott to right the wrong He made initially?" The question was rhetorical, so she continued speaking without waiting for an answer. "Whatever! You and your God can kick rocks, Tony. There is supposedly this God who doesn't like gay people, yet He creates gay people? Whatever!"

Antonyo felt even more foolish because he had no rebuttal for Jessica's statements. In all honesty, what she said made absolute sense to him—everything, that is, except her disbelief in God. Despite what she said, Antonyo knew that God existed.

"Jess, I'm sorry you have been hurt by your husband. I'm even sorry that I have no answers to your questions about God. But I'm certain there is a God, and that's all I can say about it. Now, let me ask you a question. Why are you still married to a man that obviously is not attracted to you anymore, if ever he was attracted to you?"

"What makes you so sure he is not attracted to me? Scott still loves me, for your information, and I still love him. It's complicated, and *that's all I can say about it*," she said mockingly.

Oh, my goodness. Did this beautiful, intelligent chick think that a gay man could really be attracted to her? She sounded delusional to him. How could she still possibly love this dude knowing he enjoyed sleeping with men? Dang! Love must be blinder than he'd ever heard. Suddenly, a terrible thought occurred to him, causing him instant panic. He needed Jessica to answer a question quickly. No sarcasm allowed.

"Have you slept with your husband since you found out he was gay?" Antonyo asked.

"What goes on in my bedroom in my home with my husband is none of your business, Tony." Jessica was clearly upset and defensive, but Antonyo couldn't care less at this point. This chick was sadly mistaken if she thought her sexual history with a gay man was none of his business. She came to his home and climbed in his bed, husband or not, at least once a week. They were usually very careful, but passion had preceded precaution on a couple of occasions.

"I beg to differ, Jessica. The antics of your bedroom are very much my business, since you could be putting my life at risk." Now Antonyo had developed a little attitude of his own.

"A little late to be concerned now, isn't it, Mr. Self-righteous?"

Antonyo's ire rose each time Jessica gave him a sarcastic or evasive response, especially those that made sense. Now, after having just had sex with her, was not the best time to inquire about her risk factors, but the fact remained that at this point, if she had continued to have sex with Scott, he, too, was at risk.

For the first time in his life, Antonyo felt the urge to strike a female. He removed himself from the bed to put some distance between them, but his anger did not subside one iota.

Just as he was about to begin yelling, Jessica, too, got up from the bed and began to get dressed while yelling. "Tony, I cannot believe I have told you any of this. This was personal. Private. Between my husband and me. Not that you have a right to know, but I'll tell you anyway. No! I have not had sex with my husband in more than one year.

"Why do you think it was so easy for me to climb in bed with you? You are cute, but you're shallow, Tony. You're irresponsible. You are not the type of man I would normally choose to spend time with, but I needed the physical release you offered. I needed to feel relaxed and take off the edge that I have lived with for more than two years. You may think you are special, Tony. All the other women you screw around with may have you believing you are wonderful, but for me, you were nothing more than a sexual object."

Jessica screamed and sobbed as she put on her clothing. Her frustrations screeched from her throat and poured from her eyes. Her anger did not truly lay with Antonyo. She simply hurled the insults at him because he was the one who had gotten her to talk about her pain, and he was the one who stood there while she openly dealt with it at this moment.

Antonyo's anger lessened as he realized the horror Jessica suffered every day in her marriage. "I'm sorry, Jess. I didn't mean to sound so selfish."

Jessica did not bother to respond. She continued in her mission until she was fully dressed. She left Antonyo's home without a backward glance in his direction.

Chapter 19

"So, how did you enjoy tonight's class, Antonyo?" Minister Keisha asked her handsome student as they sat in the informal Coney Island restaurant near the church, finishing their light snack.

While they read through a great deal of the book of Proverbs, Antonyo seemed interested and intrigued. He was inquisitive, responsive, and eager; however, Keisha knew quite a bit about Antonyo's beguiling charm, so she couldn't be sure if he was genuine in his displayed desire to learn, or just running game to get her into the position she sat in now, having an evening meal with him.

"Minister Keisha, I have always enjoyed school and learning. My grades in both regular education and college have always been well above average. Tonight, however, provided a whole new dimension to learning for me. I can look at you and see that you're wondering if my interest in Bible study is real. You realize that I'm attracted to you, so you believe that this is all a ploy to get you to go out with me."

Keisha's eyes widened in surprise. Antonyo had called her on what she was thinking as if it were written in bold letters across her forehead. His instincts were quite keen, which explained to her why he was so capable of wooing and winning the ladies.

Antonyo smiled at the minister's reaction, thinking to himself, *So beautiful, so brilliant, yet still normal in so many ways.*

"Class tonight was great for me, Minister Keisha. The lessons from Proverbs were informative and easy to follow. You being the instructor is icing on a delicious cake. You being here with me now is like having a big bowl of ice cream with my cake."

Now it was Keisha's turn to smile. "Antonyo, can you please just call me Keisha? Minister Keisha sounds so formal, especially when we are out in a setting such as this."

"I'll drop the Minister and tell you a secret if you agree to go out with me again."

Keisha blushed again, not sure how to answer him. Her attraction to him had apparently been obvious to them both, but her positioning in the church made her wary. She was concerned about a fraternization issue.

She quickly reasoned with herself, however. As an unmarried minister, propriety was certainly expected, but what would be so improper about her enjoying an evening out with a nice, albeit extremely handsome and devastatingly alluring, man? Antonyo was merely her Bible study student, right? And she was here with him now without qualms, so what would be the big deal about accepting his formalized invitation?

Keisha knew the answer to that question before she'd even formed it in her mind. Antonyo Simms caused her to think things about a man she had not thought about in quite some time. Again, she let reasoning kick into gear.

I am strong and I know God's Word and will for my life. Yes, this man is fine, but God is my rock, upon whom I can stand. Keisha looked up to find Antonyo staring at her. Had he again read her mind and deciphered all the thoughts she had going on in her head? She decided to answer him quickly in hopes of avoiding him calling her out again.

"Okay. I'll go out with you again. Now tell me the secret."

Antonyo pulled his wallet from his pocket, preparing to

pay the check the waitress just set before him on their table. This was a foreign concept to him indeed. He could count on less than three fingers the number of times he'd picked up the check for any date he'd had with a woman other than his mother or aunt. For him to even do it without giving it a second thought surprised him. He, too, thought about Keisha's allure, and had to give credence to how special this woman made him feel. The secret he was about to let her in on also added to his assessment of her credibility.

"The secret is this: Up until meeting you, the only woman I tolerated calling me Antonyo was my mother. I prefer to be called Tony, but I honestly like the way my given name sounds when you speak it."

Keisha' s blush was so deep this time, she actually had to lower her eyes away from this expert charmer in an effort to keep herself from turning into a quivering idiot. Antonyo thrilled at her response to him.

"Tony!"

Antonyo and Keisha were so in-tune to one another that neither of them saw the jealous, crazed Lynn approach their table. She had squealed his name so loudly that each and every one of the few patrons and staff in the restaurant halted what they were doing to spy out the person behind the annoying voice.

"What the—heck?" Antony altered his comment out of respect for his companion just before a more vulgar response was uttered.

Lynn's appearance shocked him more than her sudden emergence. He'd never seen her looking so disheveled. She had always been the picture of immaculate perfection. Now, however, she looked as if she had simply awakened, threw on the ragged oversized pink fleece jogging suit, and left the house. Her hair was uncombed, she wore house slippers on her feet, and her normally manicured nails looked as if they had been run through a shredder. Before him stood a terrible alter ego of the bourgeois, pampered princess he had known for years.

This was the first time he had seen Lynn since he slammed the door in her face more than a week ago, the day she left the beautiful watch in his mailbox.

"Lynn, what in the world is wrong with you? What are you doing here?" Antonyo asked.

"No, Tony. The question is what are you doing here with her while you have on the watch I bought you?" Lynn replied.

"What? Are you serious?"

Keisha sat confused and unnerved while watching and listening to the uncomfortable scene unfold in front of her. She should have realized that a man as charming and as good looking as Antonyo would come with lots of drama, which usually equated to lots of crazy women and at least one female stalker. Unsure of what she should do, Keisha decided to sit still and be quiet, hoping that Antonyo was experienced in handling women screaming at him in public places.

"Oh, I'm dead serious, punk! You can't answer *my* calls. You don't want *me* at your house, but you can floss in my watch while entertaining some other chick. And I know I didn't just see you reach for your wallet like you were preparing to pay the bill? You ain't never spent a raggedy dime on me."

Lynn screamed as if only she and Antonyo were in the restaurant. A few of the patrons stared at the confrontation like it was a hit box office movie. Others grabbed their things and made ready to leave, probably hoping to escape the possibility of being an eye witness to what could turn into a crime scene.

"Lynn, you need to check yourself and bounce. You are making a complete fool of yourself in this restaurant." Antonyo remained outwardly calm, while he was actually quite embarrassed.

Keisha listened to the calm in Antonyo's voice, surprised at how he remained calm under the circumstances. He was obviously used to dealing with these types of predicaments.

Lynn moved closer and bent over the table so that she could get within six inches of Antonyo's face. "I will *bounce*, as you so eloquently put it, when you give me my watch back, li'l ghetto boy. I don't know what I ever saw in you in the first place." Lynn stood straight again, but made no move away from the table. She then continued to yell at Antonyo while planting one hand on her hip and waving the other around, making it look as if it would detach from her arm at any moment.

"You got me out here following you around this city just so I can get my property back," Lynn confessed. "That's right. I have been following you around for three days now. I saw you and your little brat leave for church on Sunday. I followed you to and from work on Monday, and then I followed you back to church again today. I thought that church was a strange place for the likes of your low-life behind to be hanging out, but now I see why you all of sudden discovered religion." Lynn made a horrific face at Keisha, staring at her as if she smelled terribly foul.

Keisha used every bit of Holy Ghost power she posed to stay seated. Her flesh screamed to get up and knock this Lynn chick into the middle of next week. Knowing she would not endure any more of this psycho's insults, she figured it best to put some distance between her and Lynn.

"Antonyo, maybe we should leave," Keisha stated with a calm far greater than what she felt. She then began sliding from the booth in an effort to get away from this soap opera mess, hoping Antonyo would follow her advice. She had rid-den to the restaurant with him, leaving her car in the church's parking lot.

Before Keisha could fully extract herself from her seat, Lynn shoved her roughly back into a sitting position. "You can just sit back down, sweetie, 'cause this fool here is not leaving until I get my watch back."

"Lord, give me strength," Keisha stated out loud as she tried to calm herself before speaking directly to Lynn. "Please do not put your hands on me again."

"Girl, you better pray. Pray that I don't kill this fool about my property." Lynn used her forefinger to poke Antonyo dead in the center of his forehead as she spoke her last word, as if she physically needed to demonstrate to Keisha just who she was talking about.

Before she realized it, Keisha stood up, pushed forcefully past Lynn, and said, "And don't put your hands on him again either."

Initially startled by Keisha's show of bravado on Antonyo's behalf, Lynn stood speechless for about five seconds. Antonyo, too, had been shocked into silence by Keisha's defensive stance on his behalf. The shocked expressions were very temporary, however, because Lynn quickly became very animated. She tossed one hand on her hip and somehow managed to get even louder than before as she wagged the forefinger of her free hand in front of Keisha's face.

"Oh, I'm about two seconds from slapping the ugly off your face, Ms. Thang," Lynn spat. "You better just stay out of business that is not yours."

Keisha moved an inch closer and raised her own hand to remove Lynn's hand from in front of her face. Antonyo quickly stopped her from touching Lynn, however, by grabbing that same hand and using it to lead her out of the restaurant. "Come on, Keisha. This fool is not worth it. Let's just leave." Antonyo threw several bills on the table and the couple attempted to leave the diner.

"I said you are not going anywhere until I get my watch, Tony!"

Antonyo never saw Lynn pick up the fork she plunged deeply into his upper back just left of his shoulder blade. The obviously crazed woman then yanked the fork from his skin and stuck him again, this time about an inch and a half up from the first stab wound.

Antonyo fell forward, doing his best to use both arms to break his fall before he hit the tiled floor face first. He was both too shocked and in too much pain to cry out. Blood spurted from both wounds simultaneously, creating a messy pool at Keisha's feet. She immediately fell to the floor on her knees next to Antonyo, trying to see if he was still conscious. Then she began yelling.

"Please! Somebody! Call an ambulance." Tears flowed freely from Keisha's eyes. Fear painfully gripped her heart. "Antonyo, can you hear me? Oh my God! Antonyo, please be okay. God, please! Let him be okay. Father, I pray right now in the name of Jesus. Save him, Lord."

While Keisha held on to Antonyo's left arm, Lynn bent down and snatched the Rolex watch from his right wrist. "I told you, you were not leaving with my watch." Lynn then got up from her crouched position and calmly left the restaurant with the Rolex watch in hand.

Antonyo's eyes fluttered open. His surroundings were unfamiliar to him. His mouth and throat felt as if they had been packed with pounds of sawdust. His body felt as if he had been lying immobile for weeks. His mind was foggy and his thoughts were very confused right now. What had happened to him, he wondered?

"Antonyo! Baby, are you awake?"

Mama? he thought, bewildered. He tried to sit up, using his elbows as leverage to propel him forward. The moment he applied pressure, searing pain shot through his entire body. Every nerve in his being screamed. He, too, screamed out loud, joining them in their song of agony as he slumped back on the stiff mattress. Antonyo had never known hurt like what he was experiencing at that very moment. He would have sworn to anyone willing to listen that his eyelashes even hurt.

"William, go get the nurse!" Trina frantically gestured for her fiancé to leave the room and do as he was told. She stood by her son's bed, wanting to touch him, to hold him while he screamed, but she was too afraid that anything she did would bring him more grief

Nurse? What in the world was going on, Antonyo thought through his haze of torture. "Maaaaaaa, what is happening? Where am I?" He had not stopped screaming, so the questions came out loud.

"Shhh, baby. Just try to calm down. William went to get the nurse, and she will get you something for the pain."

"Where am I?" he asked again, not changing his tone one iota.

"Tony, please calm down. You are in the hospital, so you really need to try and stay calm. You are probably scaring the other patients. You are just waking up from surgery, baby." At that moment, William, the surgeon, and a nurse entered Antonyo's room. Trina moved away from the bed, giving the doctor access to her vacated position.

"Hey, champ. No need for me to ask how you're feeling. This entire floor can hear that you are hurting, man," the doctor said. "But you won't feel this badly for long. The nurse here will take your vitals, and then we can get you some pain medication.

"By the way, I'm Dr. Franklin. I would shake your hand, but then you would probably try to kill me for moving that arm. I performed your surgery this evening to repair the damage done when you were stabbed. We won't go into all the technical details right now. Just know that you are well on your way to being one-hundred percent again. You should be ready to walk out of here in about two days tops. I'll come back in the morning to check on you."

When the doctor left, the nurse inserted a thermometer into Antonyo's mouth and then she gently applied the blood pressure cup to his left arm, the side opposite the surgically repaired shoulder. Once everything beeped to indicate completion, the nurse spoke to Antonyo. "Your blood pressure is normal, but your temperature is still a little spiked. I'll be right back with that pain medication. That should help bring down the fever as well."

Once the nurse left, Antonyo's questions began. This time he spoke without yelling. "I think it's coming back to me. Lynn stabbed me in the back, right?" he surmised.

"More like in the shoulder area, but yes, it was Lynn," La-Trina answered.

"She stabbed me in a restaurant while I was with Minister Keisha, right?"

"Yes," came again from Trina.

"Did Lynn hurt Keisha?"

"No. Minister Keisha is fine. She said that Lynn ran from the restaurant after taking a watch from you. The police picked her up from her home soon after they brought you here to the hospital. She is in custody."

"Minister Keisha is a special lady, Tony. She has been here since they brought you to the hospital. She even rode in the ambulance with you," William chimed in.

The more they all spoke, the more Antonyo began to remember. He was still awake when the paramedics loaded him into the ambulance. He remembered Keisha being with him, alternating between speaking softly to him to reassure him he would be okay and praying to God, asking him to make it so. He recalled being wheeled into the emergency room and the hospital staff telling Keisha she had to wait in the waiting area. He must have passed out after that, because the next thing he remembered was screaming in pain when he awakened a few moments ago.

"Keisha is still here now? Where is she? Can she come in here?" Again Antonyo tried to sit up, but the pain quickly halted his process this time.

"Calm down, baby. I will go get Keisha and send her in here. The staff will only allow two people in the room with you at a time, so William and I will wait downstairs for a little while. I'm going to go down and call your aunt to let her know you're up and okay. I'll come back in about fifteen minutes."

The nurse returned between the time Trina left and Keisha appeared. She came in, administered the pain medication as prescribed by the doctor, then left just as Keisha came into the room. Antonyo could not remember experiencing the joy Keisha's face brought to his heart with any female other than his daughter. Why this woman affected him the way she did astounded him. The fact that she stayed at the hospital the whole time while he was in surgery endeared her to him even more. The pain in his shoulder had lessened considerably, and Antonyo wondered if it was the quick action of the pain medication, or the beauty of his minister friend.

Keisha sat in the chair by the side of the bed, staring for long moments at Antonyo. She was so happy to see him alive. His stab wounds were probably never life threatening, but the blood that poured from his body scared her so badly that at the time of the stabbing, she feared the possibility.

"Thanks for staying here, Keisha, and for contacting my mother. I am so sorry you had to witness that whole ugly scene at the restaurant. Lynn has always been a little nutty, but I have never had this kind of trouble from her before."

"I was so afraid when I saw you bleeding like that. How do you feel now?"

"The moment you walked through that door, the pain in my shoulder began to diminish," he stated honestly.

How in the world could she allow his words to continue to affect her the way they did, especially after witnessing what she had today? "Why did she do this to you? I know she kept screaming about her watch, but it could not have been that simple, could it?"

Antonyo had no idea how to answer Keisha's questions. Yes, Lynn had been ridiculous from day one, but never did he think she would act this crazy. Even when he had tried the monogamy thing with Clarke and stopped seeing her for a while, she didn't go ballistic on him. She just kept up her pursuit. The stabbing was way out there, even for Lynn. The watch was the most expensive gift she had given him at one time thus far; yet and still, he would have never believed she would behave this way.

"Keisha, I am at a loss myself about this whole situation. Lynn has always been a bit of a handful, but she has never stalked me before; at least not to my knowledge. If she had simply showed up and started going off, that would not have surprised me. The stabbing, however, is far more than I would have ever imagined."

"I know you said you are being honest with me. I believe you are, but I need you to continue the trend with your answer to the next question. Have you ever promised that girl anything? In other words, did you ever tell her that you two were in an exclusive relationship?"

"Keisha, I may be a lot of things. Am I a womanizer? Yes. Am I a manipulator? Yes. Have I taken advantage of women and their feelings for me? Yes. But I have never, ever told Lynn that we were anything more than friends. I have been seeing her for the better part of five years now, and never once have I even tried to have anything exclusive with her—or she with me, for that matter."

Antonyo took a pause to see how Keisha absorbed what he'd said thus far. On any other occasion, he'd been able to pretty much discern what she was thinking. Right now, she wore a solid poker face, listening intently to him describe his association with Lynn.

As he watched for Keisha's reaction, Antonyo realized that what she thought truly mattered to him. He wanted to be honest with her, but he also wanted her to look past who he was currently to see what he could become if he had an opportunity with her. So, he kept talking, hoping to impress upon her that Lynn's actions toward him were not warranted.

"I told her that I would never see her again about a week ago, because she violated the rules concerning my daughter. I meant what I said. I have not allowed any of the women I dated to meet my daughter. When Lynn showed up at my house knowing Toy would be there, I knew I had to cut it off for good."

Keisha shook her head, trying to clear some of the fog Antonyo's words had left there. She knew Antonyo wanted to engage her in more than a friendly or ministerial relationship. Honestly, she found herself intrigued at the prospect of seeing him on a more social level. But what did it all mean to him, she wondered? How many women was he currently dating, and did he plan to make her a part of his harem?

Keisha had not dated much since giving her life to Christ. Even before becoming saved, she had only been in one monogamous relationship, which lasted nine months, so her experience was limited when it came to matters of the heart. These feelings she had begun developing for Antonyo confused her, to say the least.

Finally, a reaction, Antonyo thought. Her puzzled look gave him something to work with. "Keisha, tonight had to be terrifying for you. Again, I apologize. I like you, though, Keisha. I like you differently than any other female I have ever dated. I don't want anything material from you. I'm not even thinking about sleeping with you. I know you are not used to hanging out with guys like me. This is different for me, too."

Wow! Antonyo probably did not even realize his God-given gift of discernment, a gift he had obviously used before for not-so-spiritual aspirations. While she appreciated what he said, Keisha felt no less confused. Knowing that God was not the author of confusion, she knew that she needed to put some space between her and Antonyo so she could think clearly.

"Antonyo, I don't even know what to say about any of this. I thank God you are going to be okay, but that is all I know for sure right now." Keisha stood from the chair. She gently rubbed Antonyo's uninjured arm for a moment and then made ready to leave. "I'm going to go home now and get some rest. I'll come back tomorrow to check on you."

"How are you going to get home? Isn't your car still at the church?"

"No. Mr. Rucker took me to the church to get it while you were in surgery. I'll be praying for you, and like I said, I'll come back to see you tomorrow."

"Promise?"

"Yes. Good night, Antonyo."

Three days later, Antonyo had yet to leave the hospital. The fever that had spiked after surgery had hung around, rising and falling, yet never completely going away. His temperature continually hovered between 101 and 104.

Keisha had kept her promise and visited Antonyo the next day and each subsequent day he spent in the hospital. Trina was a constant guest in her son's room, praying and trying hard not to worry. She read to him from the Bible, concentrating on the Psalms, encouraging him to get well and be strong.

LaTreece had come to visit each day as well. Her nephew was important to her. Unlike her sister, all she could do was worry. She believed in God just fine; she just had her own way of doing things. In true Auntie Treecie fashion, she snuck LaToya in to see Antonyo on his second day, because children under aged twelve were not allowed to visit.

The doctors explained to Trina and Antonyo that he had developed an infection near both the wounded areas. They were trying several different antibiotics, working hard at not causing a negative reaction. Nothing they had tried thus far seemed to be working. They were now in the process of running numerous tests. As they ruled things out, they would keep them informed. Antonyo had given his consent for the doctors to do their work to the fullest to find out why he could not shake his fever.

He awoke now to find his mother and his doctor entering his room. Trina looked puzzled, curious even. Dr. Riley looked sullen. Antonyo now looked worried.

Afraid to hear what the doctor had to say, Antonyo addressed his mother. "Mama, what's wrong with me?"

"Antonyo, I don't know. He won't tell me anything because your medical results are confidential," Trina replied with an obvious attitude.

"Antonyo, I think you should ask your mother to leave the room. You are an adult, and as she stated, I can't share any information with her, but I really need to talk to you about some things we found in your test," Dr. Riley stated in a tone laced with professional severity.

"Anything you have to tell me you can say in front of my mother. This sounds serious. I want her here," Antonyo told the doctor.

"Are you sure?"

"Absolutely."

Dr. Riley walked the short distance to the door and closed it. He then returned and got straight to the point. "Antonyo, preliminary testing shows that you are HIV positive. . . . " The doctor continued to speak, giving more information about his diagnosis, but Antonyo had not heard another word beyond the words *HIV positive*.

LaTrina stood stock still, pain and shock radiating from every pore of her body. She wished for that numbness everyone spoke about when hearing terrible news, because she felt all the dreadful rawness of the doctor's announcement. She was so stunned she did not have the presence of mind to even pray at that moment. Before she realized what was happening, Trina landed on the floor as her legs gave way beneath her. She had not fainted. She simply no longer had the strength to stand on her own.

Antonyo jumped from the bed and joined the doctor as he knelt over his mother.

"Ms. Simms!" the doctor called out.

"Ma!" Antonyo said.

The wailing that ensued let both men know that Trina was very much awake. While her state of consciousness was no longer in question, her state of mind left them both wondering. The screams were deafening and tortured. Finally, she began calling on God.

"Lord, please, no. Please, no, Father. Please, Savior, save my baby. Let it not be true, God. Let it not be true," she screamed.

In dealing with his mother's grief, Antonyo had no time to ponder how he felt about the blow the doctor just delivered. He concentrated now solely on getting his mother up from the floor and calmed down. Together with Dr. Riley, they lifted Trina from the floor and into a chair. She depended totally on them to move her body. She was unable to do anything other than cry.

In his weakened condition, Antonyo had tuckered himself out assisting Dr. Riley while they lifted his mother. He stumbled back to his hospital bed, breathing heavily. Dr. Riley saw his patient struggling to pull his legs onto the bed, so he went there to offer his help. He, too, was now worn out from his physical exertion, but he fought to show no outward signs of it. His tiredness, he knew, paled in comparison to the fear and grief this mother and son now experienced. He stood next to the bed, watching his patient struggle with the diagnosis he'd received. Though Antonyo lay in bed with his eyes closed, Dr. Riley could see the turmoil as it radiated throughout his body.

Once he was able to catch his breath, Antonyo asked, "Dr. Riley, what does this all mean for me? Can you tell from your test how advanced my condition is?"

"Right now, Antonyo, I can tell you that your T-cell count is lower than normal. That is why you are unable to fight off the infection. Now that we have isolated the problem, however, we can begin with the proper medications, and we can start fighting the disease itself."

The pain that had been lodged in his chest from the moment he heard the diagnosis now poured from his eyes. It had been many years since he had shed a tear. Now it seemed the dam that stored those tears for all those years broke, and the water that he had held back for so long ran free and unchecked. A strong and magnified fear consumed his body. He wondered what would happen to his daughter when he died. He looked at his mother, who was bent over from the waist in the chair, controlled by her misery. How could he have done this to her?

To Dr. Riley, the scene of the grieving mother and son was nothing new, yet never any easier to witness. "I'll go and order your medications and get the nurses in here to get you started on them. I'll be back in a little while and we can talk further." He left the room to do as he stated he would do.

The hospital room was absent of dialogue, but filled with the noises of despair, anxiety, and uncertainty. Trina had halted her screams, but her sobs were still audible. Antonyo's cries were silent, but it seemed both he and his mother could hear his tears that slid from his face and hid in the bed sheets. The first words spoken since the doctor left the room came from Antonyo.

"I'm sorry, Mama" he choked out. Aloud, but more to the atmosphere than to anyone else, he said, "I'm sorry, Toy."

LaTrina got up from her chair and joined her son on his bed. She held him tightly and for a long while they cried together. Then she halted her tears and spoke softly to her only baby. "Oh, baby, you don't owe me an apology. And I don't believe you owe LaToya an apology either. Sweetheart, right now you just have to turn it all over to God. I can't even begin to try and have all this make sense to you. I can't give you any real answers, and I am not going to blame or condemn you. Antonyo, all I know to do right now is pray."

And that is what she began to do. "Father God, who art in Heaven. Lord, I come to you right now to give you praise even in this our darkest moment. Lord, you are sovereign, and everything you do is good. I am trusting you literally, Father, with my child's life. I turn it over to you, and I count it all joy, the suffering we are facing right now.

"You are the God, my God, who can work miracles and wonders. You are the God who gave us your only Son so that we may have life. You are the Savior who came so that we may be healed. Lord, I proclaim the victory over Satan right now. I name him as defeated, knowing in your sovereignty that we will win this battle, no matter what triumph looks like. This is my prayer in the mighty and matchless name of my Lord and Savior. Amen"

Chapter 20

Antonyo had spent two additional days in the hospital before he was allowed to go home. During those two days, the only person he would grant visitation to was his mother. As much as it pained him, even Minister Keisha had not been permitted access into his room. How could he ever face her again? How could he tell her, the one woman who could change his outlook on relationships and women, that he had been given a death sentence?

Antonyo had become certain that during the time he spent with Keisha, her ministerial armor had cracked and she had begun to look at him as a man. Not for a second did he think that she would renounce her commitment to God for him, but he had definitely touched the woman in her. Just when he had seriously considered giving monogamy his wholehearted effort, for real this time, and had been willing to truly fight against what he believed to be his inherent nature, he was knocked out with one punch. HIV had ended the fight before he could even take his first swing of at least proposing the idea to Keisha.

Trina had spent the majority of those two days in his room with him. She would go home only to sleep, shower, and change clothes. She ate with her son, watched television with him, and reminisced about their life together. Oftentimes during their talks, Antonyo would interrupt his mother in mid-sentence and ask her to pray aloud for him. At the end of each prayer, he would feel a little better and be encouraged by what his mother had said to God on his behalf. He would then remember what Dr. Riley said about being able to live with HIV for many years as long as he took his medications and worked to stay healthy. Dr. Riley stated that science was working continually to discover a cure for this wretched virus. During that conversation, Trina threw in, "And who knows? God could come through with a breakthrough any day."

Upon Antonyo's discharge, Dr. Riley had given him paperwork indicating that he needed to be excused from work for at least six weeks. The doctor cited personal stress and mental fatigue as the diagnosis and reason for the requested time off. Antonyo left the hospital and asked his mother to drive him straight to his employer to get the paperwork started for his short-term disability. After leaving the job, Trina took him to his home. She initially pleaded with him to come and stay with her for a few days so that she could keep an eye on him. Antonyo assured her that he was physically okay, and that he really needed some time to himself to deal with the emotional impact of his disease.

Once they arrived at his house, Trina helped him in. She made sure he was comfortable and prayed with him. She then asked if there was anything she could do for him before she left. Antonyo asked her to call the district attorney's office. The female D.A. had left him a voice mail message asking that he get in touch with her regarding Lynn's criminal case.

When Trina had phoned, she explained who she was and that her son wasn't feeling well. She asked to get the information for him. When Trina got off the phone, she explained to Antonyo what she had been told.

"The D.A. says that Lynn is currently out on a very small bond. She also says the likelihood of her ever seeing the inside of a jail cell as a result of this case is non-existent. This was Lynn's first offense. She's an attorney, and her family has money and a lot of influence in this state. The D.A. says that she will probably be sentenced to a very minimal probation period and face disciplinary action from the State Bar Association."

Amazingly, Antonyo harbored no desire to see Lynn get a harsh punishment. He only hoped that she get some professional help. Trina did not have a vengeful spirit about any of this either. She, too, prayed that Lynn changed her life.

Still not quite convinced it was good idea to leave her son, Trina resolved to let him have his way. "Well, okay. If there is nothing else, I'm going to get ready to leave. Are you sure you don't want to come back to my house with me? Or I could stay here with you for a couple days."

"Ma, I'm good. But if I start to feel overwhelmed in any way, I promise I will call you. Before you leave, though, tell me the Psalm you read to me while I was in the hospital."

"It's Psalm thirty-four, baby. I'll call you later to check on you." Trina left the house with a full heart. While she still felt the sting of her son's disease, she rejoiced in knowing that Antonyo was working his own way to God. She knew that if she continued to trust God, he would heal Antonyo spiritually, giving him more ammunition to fight HIV physically.

Before Trina left, she made her son promise he would call her if he needed her in any way. When his mother was out the door, Antonyo went to his bedroom to retrieve the Bible she had given him for Christmas a few years ago. This Bible was a Message translation, making the Word of God easier for him to comprehend. He returned to the living room, sat on his sofa, and began reading the Psalm.

As he read and reached his favorite parts, verses fifteen through eighteen, he read those aloud. "God keeps an eye on His friends; his ears pick up every moan and groan. God won't put up with rebels; He'll cut them from the pack. Is anyone crying for help? God is listening, ready to rescue you. If your heart is broken, you'll find God right there; if you're kicked in the gut, He'll help you catch your breath." He continued on reading the rest of the Psalm to himself.

After he finished his reading, Antonyo sat and meditated on what he'd just read. Whether it was from sheer desperation or a true sense of belief, he wasn't sure, but Antonyo used the words of the Bible to encourage him and make him believe that he would live a long life even with HIV. He said a silent prayer after he closed his Bible, something he had been doing a lot the past two nights when he was alone once his mother left for the evening.

In his newfound encouragement, Antonyo decided he needed to see his daughter. What he had not yet decided was whether he was prepared to share his news with Clarke. Thus far, the only people who knew about his diagnosis were his mother and Aunt Treecie. As he picked up the phone to call Clarke, he realized that he owed her the truth. The two decided back when LaToya was born that anything that involved their daughter involved both parents. He would wait to tell her in person, versus divulging the information on the phone.

Clarke was happy to hear from Antonyo. It had been more than five days since he last spoke with LaToya. Their daughter had begun to get a little irritable. Clarke knew Antonyo had been stabbed by the lunatic Lynn, but had not been able to get much more information from Trina when she inquired about his condition. When he called and asked if he could pick up the baby, she was more than thrilled to allow him time with his cranky child.

In the past five days, Greg had seemed more relieved than he had since the first day of school for their daughter. Afraid to start up his ranting again, she decided to just bask in the peace. She never even mentioned his contrast in moods to him. Now that Antonyo was on his way over to get LaToya, she wondered if things would get tense again.

The doorbell rang and Clarke went to let Antonyo in the house. When Clarke appeared at the door instead of Greg, Antonyo was very thankful. The last thing he needed right now was to have to deal with a jealous husband and stepfather.

"Come on in, Tony. Clarke is all packed for the next three days. Just let me know if you want to keep her a few extra days and I'll bring over some additional things," Clarke offered.

"I keep telling you that I have everything she needs at my house. You don't even have to send the stuff you packed, but for some reason it makes you feel better, so I'll take the packed bag. If she stays longer, however, it won't be necessary for you to send anything else."

Clarke smiled. "Let me go and get your daughter for you."

"Clarke, wait. Before you get the baby, I need to sit down and talk with you for a moment." Antonyo, deciding to be a really big man, added, "I need to speak with both you and Greg."

Clarke worried a little about having both men together again, but Antonyo sounded serious. She reluctantly called her husband from their bedroom. Assuming she wanted him to bring the baby with him so she could leave with Antonyo, he arrived with LaToya in tow.

As usual, LaToya saw her father and ran to him with her normal call of greeting. "Daaaaddyyy."

"Hey, baby girl. Daddy missed you," Antonyo stated.

"I missed you too, Daddy. Mommy said I'm going to your house. Yeah!"

"Yes, you are, but first I need to talk to Mommy and Greg. I want you to go back in your room and play. I'll come and get you before I leave. Okay?"

"Okay, Daddy. Don't leave me." LaToya scampered away, heading back toward her bedroom.

Neither Greg nor Clarke had a clue as to why Antonyo called this impromptu meeting. Both held puzzled looks as they all walked into the living room and sat down. Clarke and Greg held court on the sofa. Antonyo sat opposite them on the loveseat.

"I need to tell you both something very important. It's about my hospital stay." Antonyo paused for a moment, realizing this would be his first public announcement about his condition. The thought made him a little uncomfortable. He closed his eyes for a moment and sought strength in a silent prayer.

Clarke and Greg noticed Antonyo's distress. This intensified their curiosity. Clarke even became a little fearful. She, too, said a quick silent prayer.

"Guys, I discovered while I was in the hospital after my stabbing that I am HIV positive." Antonyo decided that straight-up was probably the best way to go.

"Oh my God!" Clarke screamed as she bolted up from her seat. Greg just sat there, staring, holding both hands in front of his mouth as if doing his best to not let something escape. The three stayed completely quiet for several seconds.

Finally Clarke sank back onto the sofa next to her husband, unable to control her emotions any longer. She placed her face into Greg's shoulder and began to cry. Greg massaged her shoulder, doing his best to comfort his frightened wife.

Greg was the first to speak. "Tony, man, I don't even know what to say. I'm so sorry to hear that, man."

"Thank you, Greg. I needed to tell you both because this affects LaToya," Antonyo said.

Clarke lifted her head and asked, "What does this mean exactly? I mean, I have never known anyone personally who had this disease. What did the doctors say?"

"Dr. Riley, the doctor I had in the hospital, says that he really could not give me any specific timeframes or lifespan. He says that these days, people were living longer and more normal lives because of advance medicines. As long as I stay healthy and take my medicine, I should be able to fight the disease. My mom says that God could come through with a cure any day." He smiled weakly at the couple as he internally held out hope that she had prophesied the truth.

A sudden fear gripped Greg's heart. He certainly did not mean to be rude at a time like this, but he really needed to know the answer to the question that nearly rendered him motionless. "Tony, was the doctor able to give you an idea about how long you have been carrying the virus?"

Both Clarke and Antonyo knew where Greg was going with his question. Clarke was a little embarrassed by her husband's boldness. Antonyo stared, a little confused. It just hit him that this was the first time he ever thought about that question. Suddenly, Jessica and the story she told him about her gay husband came to mind.

"Greg, they can't pin this thing down to a science, but I will say this: Up until the time I got with Clarke, I was very careful. It was only recently that I stupidly became a little lax; however, it couldn't hurt for both of you to be tested."

Again, he thought about Jessica and Scott. In all honesty, with his own sexual history, it could have been anybody. As the saying went, abstinence was the only surefire safe method. That word had not been in his vocabulary since he was thirteen. He made a mental note to contact Jessica, however. He had not talked to her since the last time he saw her, a couple of weeks ago, when she had left his house angry.

Greg continued to hold his wife while he silently thanked God. The odds of her being HIV positive were slim to none. If she were, LaToya would have more than likely been born infected. But as Antonyo suggested, they would both be tested as soon as possible. He was also thankful and relieved of his insecurities about the special bond shared between Clarke and Antonyo. With this type of information on the table, he was sure there would never be anything more between the two of them. Selfish? Yes. But he would take peace of mind any way he could get it.

"Look, I just wanted to let you both know the real. I don't think LaToya needs to know any of this, though. She's too young to understand. If I get really ill anytime soon, Clarke, I trust you will handle it correctly at that point. But for now, I don't think we should say anything." Greg and Clarke nodded in agreement. "If you don't have any other questions that I could answer, I would like to take LaToya and get back home."

All three adults stood and headed toward the door. Clarke dried her tears and went to get LaToya from her bedroom. She certainly didn't want her daughter to see her distress. She returned with LaToya all ready to go.

Clark and Greg gave the baby their hugs and kisses. Then Clarke hugged Antonyo long and tight. There was not even a hint of romantic feelings in the embrace. It was a hug filled simply with godliness, love, and concern for her child's father.

Once Clarke released Antonyo, Greg gave him a brotherly embrace. "You take care of yourself. All right, man?"

"I will," Antonyo assured him. "Bye."

Before returning to his house, Antonyo took his daughter to her favorite place; McDonald's. She had the chicken nuggets Happy Meal as always, and, for the first time ever, Antonyo ordered a chicken salad. Before learning he was HIV positive, Antonyo was strictly a meat and potatoes man.

Any other time, he would have ordered his favorite Big Mac combo. In an effort to stay healthy, however, he would now begin eating healthier foods. Before leaving the hospital, a nutritionist had counseled him on changing his eating habits to include more fruits and vegetables. The added vitamins would help protect him from things like the common cold, which in his condition could be very dangerous.

The moment his princess finished her last nugget, she hopped from their table and ran straight to the Playscape. Antonyo watched as LaToya walked up and slid down the sliding board. She then swung around on the swinging bars until finding her way to the huge tub of multicolored plastic balls. She took off her little shoes as required and hopped in for a roll. As he watched her play with such carefree abandon, fear began to creep into Antonyo's subconscious. How much longer would he have to see her in her complete innocence? Would he get to see her graduate from high school? Would he get to ward off the would-be imitators of himself who would try to take advantage of his baby girl?

LaToya scurried back to her father after about fifteen minutes, all tuckered out from her playing. Antonyo welcomed her with open arms.

"Are you ready to go, princess?" he asked, kissing her on the cheek.

"Yes, Daddy. I want to go to our house now so I can play with my toys in my room."

"All right. Go back and get your shoes and we will leave."

When the pair arrived at the house, Antonyo unfastened LaToya from her car seat. Before they made it to the front door, an unknown vehicle pulled in to his driveway behind his car. For a moment, Antonyo suspected it might be Lynn coming to do only God knew what. He picked up LaToya and hurried to get her inside the house. He reached the front door and put the key in the lock just as the mystery person stepped from the car.

"Tony, hold up, man."

The voice sounded familiar, but without a doubt, Antonyo knew it could not be who it sounded like. Not after all this time. Not while he was dealing with the uncertain chaos that now doubled as his life. He continued with his task of getting his daughter in the house, and the trespasser made his way up onto his front porch.

"Tony, it's me, Sheldon. Your daddy. I know you haven't forgotten me already, have you?"

When the lock gave way to the key, Antonyo moved through the door with haste. With every fiber of his being, he wanted to slam the door in Sheldon's face, but his mother's face and voice appeared in his head. "Antonyo, Sheldon is your father, *and no matter what, I will not allow you to disrespect him.*" He knew she had to be behind his showing up at the house without warning. Otherwise, how else would the dead-beat know where he even lived? He left the door open, reluctantly allowing Sheldon to enter his home.

"LaToya, go into your room and take your jacket off. Then you can start playing with your toys. I'll come in there in just a minute to check on you," Antonyo ordered his daughter.

LaToya looked up at the stranger and then she glanced at her father. She was instinctively curious about who Sheldon was, but the look on her father's face frightened her, so she did as she was told and hustled her way into her bedroom.

"So that's my granddaughter, huh? Man, she is a cutie pie, for sure." Sheldon smiled as if he beamed with pride over his grandbaby.

How dare he? Antonyo thought. What he said, however, was "Sheldon, man, what are you doing here?"

Before answering, Sheldon removed his jacket and made

himself comfortable on his son's sofa. Antonyo remained standing, figuring he was in the best position to escort the deadbeat to the door in a very short while.

"Look, man, your mama tracked me down through some of my people yesterday. She left a phone number at my cousin Ruby's house saying it was urgent that I call her. When I got the message and called her, she told me about you being HIV positive. Tony, I'm sorry. Your daddy certainly hates to hear that you have to deal with something as heavy as that."

Antonyo knew that was the reason behind his visit. Why his mother insisted on trying to make this man a part of his life was beyond his comprehension. He made it all the way to manhood without him, so what was her obsession about them relating to one another now?

"Look, Sheldon, what I'm dealing with is not your fault, so there is no need for you to apologize. I'm going to handle this disease the way I have handled everything else in my life: without you. So, you can take your day late and dollar short sympathy on back to wherever it is you've been hiding for the past ten years. I'm cool." Antonyo could not believe Sheldon had the nerve to look guilty. *This dude,* he thought.

"Why don't you take a seat, son, so we can talk for a moment? I promise I won't keep you too long."

"Sheldon, I don't want to talk to you, okay? So just leave, please. I don't want to act disrespectfully, but I really need you to get out of my house before—"

"Daddy, you said you were coming to check on me." LaToya barged into the room before Antonyo could finish his sentence. Sheldon held his hand out for LaToya to come to him. Antonyo gently put his hand on his daughter's shoulder to halt her from going near his father. In an effort not to frighten her, he did not apply too much pressure. LaToya kept walking and stopped right in front of her grandfather. "You look like my daddy," she said innocently.

"That's because I'm your daddy's daddy. I'm your grand-daddy," Sheldon informed the child.

"What is your name?"

"My name is Sheldon, but you can call me Grandpa. Is that okay with you?"

LaToya looked to her father for confirmation. "Daddy, can I call your daddy Grandpa?"

The last thing Antonyo wanted was for LaToya to get attached to Sheldon, knowing he would not be around long. How could he explain this to a three-year-old?

"Why don't we start by calling him Mr. Emerson? When you get to know him better you can call him Grandpa."

"Okay, Daddy. I'm going back to my room to wait for you. Bye, Mr. Emerson." LaToya left her newfound friend and her father alone. The innocent child had no idea the tension she left behind in the living room.

"Man, how dare you come up in my house telling my daughter to call you Grandpa? She does not know you, and you do not know her. I will never let you hurt my child with that part-time to no-time bull crap you put me through." Antonyo did his best to control his anger, as well as the level of his voice, for the sake of LaToya, but to heck with the respect his mother felt this punk deserved. His daughter's well-being was at stake, and he would protect her at all costs.

"Tony, I came here to apologize to you for all that, son. I was not a good father to you. I know that, but I want to make up for that."

"Man, I'm twenty-six years old. I don't need a father now. My daughter dang sure don't need no fake grandfather. We are good, sir, so you can pack all that mess you talking and carry it back out the door with you, Sheldon. I am not a silly little kid anymore falling for this act." Antonyo walked to the door and yanked it open, hoping that Sheldon walked through it on his own. At this point, though, he was not beyond tossing this fool out.

Sheldon stood up and headed toward the open door. "Antonyo, I really want us to reconnect. I mean that from the bottom of my heart. Obviously now is not the best time to talk to you, though. But let me at least say this and then I will leave." Sheldon reached out to touch Antonyo's shoulder, but his son pulled away before he was able to make contact. Sheldon continued speaking anyhow. "It looks like you have turned out to be a great father despite my absence from your life. I really wish I could say I was responsible for that, but I can't. I was not there for you, and for that I am sorry." Sheldon then headed outside.

Antonyo came out on the porch just as his dad reached the bottom of the three steps that led to the walkway. "Sheldon, you can trust and believe that you had a lot to do with the type of father I am to my child. I used your example of exactly what not to do. Realize it or not, you are most definitely responsible for how well I treat my daughter." After saying his peace, Antonyo turned and reentered his house, this time slamming the door behind him.

Chapter 21

On the day of Sheldon's unwelcomed visit, Antonyo packed up LaToya and the two of them headed over to his mother's house. He needed to speak with her face to face to inform her once and for all to stay out of his business when it came to Sheldon. The last thing he would do would be to disrespect Trina, but he had to make her understand that he did not want Sheldon in his or his child's life.

When he arrived, Trina opened the door before he had a chance to use his key to enter, beaming like she had won the lottery or something. "Well, how did it go, son? Did you and Sheldon have a good talk?"

Antonyo stared bug-eyed at his mom once he crossed her threshold. Did she really believe that Sheldon could pop up on his doorstep and all would be well with the world once he left? Her unwavering faith was a little misplaced here.

Antonyo's first instinct was to send LaToya to the playroom she had here at her grandmother's house, but he was sure the baby had gotten tired of sitting in bedrooms since he'd picked her up from her mother's, so he decided to let her stay. He took her to the kitchen and made a peanut butter and jelly sandwich for her. While he prepared the snack for her, Trina kept talking in his ear about Sheldon's visit. Antonyo completely ignored his mother, instead concentrating on taking care of his business with his daughter. Once he had the baby settled in her booster seat at the table, he and his mother went into the living room to talk.

"Mama, I need you to let go of this nonsense you have fixed in your head about Sheldon and I becoming bosom buddies or this great father and son duo. I do not want that man in my life. I do not want him around my daughter. Please, Mama, leave it alone. Sheldon is the last person I want to have to deal with while I am dealing with handling this disease. In all honesty, I would not want to deal with him if I were perfectly healthy." Antonyo never raised his voice, but he still hoped his mother did not interpret his speech as rude.

LaTrina stood up from the place where she sat next to her son on the sofa. She left the living room for a few brief moments and returned with her Bible from her bedroom. She resumed her place on the sofa and began flipping through pages.

"Antonyo, I do my very best in this life that I have been blessed with to not make pertinent decisions without first finding out how God feels about them. When I contacted Sheldon and sent him to your house today, I did so with the blessing of God as stated here in His Word.

"Honey, I went to the Word, and this is what it said: 'Do not judge, and you will not be judged. Do not condemn, and you will not be condemned. Forgive, and you will be forgiven.' That's Luke 6:37. 'Be kind and compassionate to one another, forgiving each other, just as in Christ God forgave you.' That's Ephesians 4:23. And while I was there I saw this: 'Children, obey your parents in the Lord, for this is right. Honor your father and mother'—which is the first commandment, with a promise—'that it may go well with you and that you may enjoy long life on earth.'

"Antonyo, you don't know what God has planned and purposed for you as far as this HIV virus goes. But, baby, you need to be prepared for whenever it is that He calls you home. Sweetie, if you want God to forgive you and allow you in heaven, you are going to have to forgive Sheldon. And in an effort to store up days, months, even years, for your life with this disease, you are going to have to start honoring your father. That is what the Word of God says, Antonyo."

Antonyo stared at his mother, pleading with his eyes for her words, or better yet God's, not to be true. He was so anguished by what she'd just read to him, tears began to pour from those same eyes. "Ma, but what about Sheldon never being there for me, or what he put you through by not helping you to take care of me? How am I supposed to just forget about all that?"

"Antonyo, these scriptures do not give conditions. They don't say anything about listening only if you have not been wronged by the person you need to forgive. They don't say honor your father only if he was a good father. You need only to listen and obey. Sheldon's actions have nothing to do with how you are supposed to respond to the Word of God."

LaToya, apparently finished with her sandwich, decided to join the conversation in the living room. "I know Sheldon. He is my daddy's daddy, and he wants me to call him Grandpa. Daddy says I have to wait. I waited, Daddy, so can I call him Grandpa when I see him again?"

Antonyo stared at his mother, who returned his stare with just as much regard. He then slowly turned his eyes to his daughter and said, "Yes. You can call him Grandpa."

That was a few days ago. Now, as Antonyo prepared himself and LaToya for church service this morning, he thought about how he should approach Sheldon for a heart to heart reconciliation. His reservations about doing so were still in place, but he was not willing to risk further disobedience being the cause of any more negative consequences in his life.

Upon his arrival into the sanctuary, the first face he saw, or at least the first he paid attention to, was Minister Keisha Hearn. He had not seen her since the day before his diagnosis. While thinking and spending time with his daughter these past few days, he realized that as crazy as it sounded, especially under the circumstances, he wanted a chance at a real relationship with Keisha. Of course, this would mean full disclosure to her about his disease. He had no idea how she would feel about him after learning that he was HIV positive, but he was willing to take a chance.

Minister Keisha was heavily involved in conversation with some of the congregants, but she felt Antonyo's presence the moment he stepped fully into the sanctuary. Her heartbeat quickened and butterflies danced a routine in her stomach that was probably worthy of the praise dancers to perform. Why did he have such an effect on her? He refused her visits, and had not returned one of the many messages she had left for him.

She glanced in his direction and found Antonyo coming toward her with his daughter in tow. He came only close enough to give her enough room to continue the conversation she was currently engaged in. He stood in the background, waiting patiently for her to finish.

Keisha was glad she was not delivering the message this morning, because she knew she would hardly be able to concentrate on what God wanted her to teach. As it was, she had become unable to even focus on what the people around her were saying ever since he entered the sanctuary. At the risk of being rude, she excused herself from the group she had been chatting with to address Antonyo. "Hello, Mr. Simms. Hello Princess Simms."

"Hi, Minister Keisha. Are you going to peach today?" Both Keisha and Antonyo chuckled at the baby's mispronunciation of the word.

"No, LaToya. I am not *preaching* today." Keisha smiled.

"Well then, perhaps you can come and sit with my daughter and me," Antonyo extended the invitation.

Unable to come up with a good excuse not to, other than the truth—that Antonyo had an overwhelming effect on her, and that sitting with him would only make her think impure thoughts—she simply stated, "Sure."

As the trio turned from the front of the church to find seats, Antonyo spotted his mother and William coming up the aisle with Sheldon in tow. Shock was not a powerful enough word to describe Antonyo's reaction to seeing his dad in church; not to mention the fact that he was hanging with his mom while she walked arm in arm with her man. What an odd vision.

Keisha also noticed the handsome stranger walking with Ms. Simms and Mr. Rucker. Something about him seemed vaguely familiar, though she was sure she had never seen him before. Then she realized that the man looked like Antonyo. Perhaps he was Ms. Simms's brother, which would account for the family resemblance.

"Grandpa!" LaToya shouted just before she took off running toward the trio.

"Grandpa?" Keisha said before she realized she had said it aloud. The gentleman was definitely too young to be Ms. Simms's father, which would mean . . .

"I'll explain everything later. Come on. Let me introduce you to my father," Antonyo told Keisha.

The bug-eyed look he received was priceless. He smiled at the woman he loved—*Whoa! Where did that come from?* he thought. He led Keisha in the direction in which his daughter had sprinted.

He and Keisha approached just as his father scooped La-Toya into his arms and proudly exclaimed, "I see your daddy

has allowed you to call me Grandpa after all, huh, princess?"
LaToya nodded her head in vigorous agreement.

"Keisha, this is my father, Sheldon Emerson. Sheldon, this
is Minister Keisha Hearn. She is the youth and young adult
minister here at Trinity Star," Antonyo introduced.

"Hello, Mr. Emerson. It is nice to meet you."

"Hello, Minister. It is nice to meet you too."

"Well, we all better get to a seat before praise and worship
gets started," Trina directed. She, William, and Sheldon sat
on one side of the church. Sheldon initially started to follow
LaToya, Antonyo, and Keisha as they moved several rows up
on the opposite side of the sanctuary; however, Trina cau-
tioned him to give it a little time yet. She asked him not to
overload Antonyo with his presence all at once.

Pastor Adrian Mitchell, senior pastor of Trinity Star, preached a wonderful message on giving your whole life to Christ.
The message was based on the scripture references of Philippians 4:13; John 4:13 and Romans 8:28. Pastor Mitchell's
message basically said that a person can do anything through
Christ and nothing without Him. Pastor Mitchell even went
so far as to state that even the sin a person commits can be
used to benefit them and others and glorify Christ's Kingdom. As long as they truly love the Lord, they can turn away
in repentance and learn to depend solely on Him.

Antonyo and Keisha were both very impressed with the
message. The two did not speak a word to each other during the sermon. LaToya had fallen asleep nestled between the
two, with her head comfortably resting in her father's lap and
her legs draped across Keisha's lap.

When Pastor extended the invitation to come to the altar
in order for people to give their lives to Christ, Antonyo did
not hesitate to remove his daughter from his person and gently give her to Minister Keisha. He strutted to the front of the

sanctuary, making one of the most certain and sound decisions he had ever made in his life. Trina, William, and even Sheldon stood and applauded loudly as he walked the aisle. Keisha would have stood, too, had it not been for the baby resting in her lap.

After service, the entire clan, including Sheldon and Keisha, got in their respective vehicles and went to Outback Steakhouse on Greenfield Road in Southfield to celebrate Antonyo's remarkable step into his new future.

"I cannot tell you enough how very proud I am of you, Antonyo. You have exasperated me into near psychosis worrying over you for the past several years, but I had complete faith that this day would come," Trina beamed.

"Man, trust me when I tell you, giving your life to Jesus is the best thing you can do for you, and even for little Miss LaToya there," William stated. "Your decision today will bless your family for generations to come, just as you were blessed when your mother made the decision."

Sheldon spoke up as well. "They are right, Tony. When I got saved a few years ago, I felt an inner peace like none other I had ever known. I admit that I am still not where God wants me to be, but at least I know that He is still working on me, and at the end of this life, I have an eternal home with Him. Congratulations, Tony, on making your reservation for heaven today."

Not wanting to be left out of the conversation, LaToya chimed in. "Con-gra-cha-may-tens, Daddy." Everyone laughed at the baby's pronunciation.

Antonyo had no idea that Sheldon was a Christian. Then again, how could he know? He had not seen nor heard from his father in ten years. Again, some of the anger and bitterness welled in him as he thought about his father's absence from his life. He hoped that God would work that out of him soon. He also hoped that *soon* had nothing to do with when he would have to utilize that reservation Sheldon just spoke of.

After dinner, the crew lingered over parking lot conversation for several minutes. Before getting in his car to leave, Sheldon thanked Antonyo for allowing LaToya to call him Grandpa, promising, seriously this time, as he put it, to call him up soon so they could really talk.

Antonyo wasn't sure if he should take Sheldon at his word. He decided he wouldn't worry about it, though. He had done his part by starting the forgiving process. The rest was up to God.

Trina kissed her son and granddaughter good-bye, letting Antonyo know she would be checking on him later that evening. Now, only LaToya, Antonyo and Keisha remained.

"Keisha, I would really like to talk to you today, if that is at all possible. I have some really important news that I need to share with you."

Keisha looked into Antonyo's eyes and saw humility, sincerity, and even a hint of fear. She assumed he wanted to talk more about his decision he'd made to get saved today. "Um, sure. Would you like me to follow you somewhere, or what?"

"No. I have to drop LaToya off with her mother, and then, if it is okay with you, I would like to come to your place." Antonyo thought this would be best. Once he told her the news about being HIV positive, he figured she would at least be at home and not having to drive anywhere with that on her heart.

"Okay. I live on Lindsay, right off of Puritan." She reached in her purse and grabbed a pad and pen to write down her address. She handed him the slip torn from the pad.

Antonyo accepted the paper. "Thank you. I will call you when I am on my way." He walked Keisha to her car and opened her door for her. Once she was securely in, he headed back to his vehicle to take LaToya home.

When he arrived at Clarke and Greg's, he carried his sleeping daughter to her bedroom. When he emerged, the couple stood waiting for him. "Tony, we just wanted you to know we were both tested the other day, and our preliminary results came back negative," Clarke stated.

Antonyo's reaction was that of complete relief. The last thing he wanted was to have physically harmed Clarke, Greg, or LaToya with this disease. "That is great news, Clarke, great for both of you. I am so happy. Thank you, God."

Both Clarke and Greg were a little startled. They had never heard Antonyo publicly speak to God before.

"Thank you, Tony," Clarke said.

"Don't thank me. I'm just glad I did not cause you any damage with my mess. Look, I have to get going. Tell LaToya I will see her on Wednesday for our normal visit. Again, I'm happy for both of you."

On the drive to Keisha's, Antonyo still basked in the relief of not having infected Clarke or Greg, and especially LaToya. This revelation also made him realize that more than likely, he had contracted the disease in the past three years—though there was no surefire way of knowing exactly when he got the disease, since he could have had it for many years. Until meeting Clarke, he had been very careful. After that, he really got lax.

He thought hard, trying to remember all the females he'd slept with since he and Clarke split up. Of course, there was Lynn, but she always insisted on his wearing a condom. Crazy she might have been, but she did not play. In hindsight, he had to respect her tenacity in that area.

There were so many others that he decided to concentrate on those who would be at the highest risk. That would include any of the females that were married, since he knew for a fact they were sleeping with at least one other person while sleeping with him.

Claudia was married to an NBA player, and the whole world knew that sports figures were notorious for their infidelities. Then, of course, there was Jessica and the gay husband. She claimed she had stopped sleeping with him more than a year ago, but who's to say that was the truth? Even if that were true, Scott had been having affairs with men even before he and Jessica were married. She could have been infected who knows how long ago. There were several others, and any one of them, or even more than one could be responsible for his current state of health.

Antonyo picked up his cell phone and called Jessica. He had not spoken with her since she'd left his apartment angry. It would not have surprised him if she did not answer upon seeing his number on her caller ID. When she picked up, he was astonished.

"Hello," she said.

"Jessica, I'm sure you know this is Tony. How are you?"

"I'm cool, Tony. What about yourself?" Jessica responded flatly.

"Well, Jess, I'm not really all that great. This may not be the appropriate way to inform you of this, but, Jessica, I just found out I am HIV positive." There was dead silence for a long time. Antonyo had actually pulled in front of Keisha's house and sat there waiting for Jessica to say something. "Jessica, are you there?"

"Antonyo, I have to call you later." She disconnected the call.

Why did that phone call seem very odd to him? Most women would have had more of a reaction to finding out that a person they were recently sexually active with carried HIV. He knew calling her back would be futile, especially right now.

He also realized there were a few more women he would have to contact in the very near future, but right now he had other things to attend to. So, he went about taking care of the business at hand: telling Keisha about his status.

Antonyo rang the bell, and Keisha answered just seconds afterward. She'd changed from the outfit she wore to church into a comfy-looking royal blue velour two-piece jogging suit. She invited him into the spacious living room of the large two-story house.

"Do you live here alone, Keisha?" Antonyo asked.

"Yes. I know it's big, but my grandmother left it to me when she passed away two years ago. Follow me. Let's go back here into the family room. I'll get you something to drink."

"I'm sorry to hear about your grandmother. You two must have been really close for her to leave her house to you."

"I was raised by my grandmother. My mother died when I was nine years old. I never knew my father, and had no brothers or sisters to call my own. It was basically just me and Grammy. She does have two other daughters who have children, so I do have some first cousins that I am pretty close to.

"Make yourself comfortable on the couch. What would you like to drink?"

"A glass of ice water would be perfect." Antonyo took a seat on the leather sofa. "I take it that it was your grandmother who taught you about God?"

Keisha returned from the kitchen, which was within earshot of the family room. She carried a glass of water with ice for Antonyo, and a glass of orange juice for herself. She sat on the sofa only a few inches away from Antonyo.

"Yes, sir. My grandmother was very spiritual. She was a deacon at Trinity Star. She used to tell me when I was a little girl that I would be a preacher."

"I remember you telling us the story of how you first came

to know God in the focus group. You said that your mother was sad about your great-grandmother's death. You said that you were about eight at the time. So, you mean to tell me that your own mother passed away just a year later?"

"Yes." The one-word answer was a mixture of both melancholy and faith. Antonyo pressed her no further. The last thing he wanted to do was make her very sad before sharing his crazy news with her.

As if picking up on an unspoken cue, Keisha asked, "So, what did you want us to talk about, Antonyo?"

Never before in his life had he been this nervous about talking to a female. When he told Clarke about his status, he held no fear or shame. Even when he announced it to Jessica, there was no anxiety present. Now he trembled from the inside out. He shook so badly that the ice in his glass clanked. Keisha took notice and moved a little closer to him. She began gently rubbing his arm, incorrectly assuming it was his shoulder injury that caused him to shake.

"Are you hurting, Antonyo?" He shook his head, still unable to speak.

Keisha had never seen this suave and charismatic man so unnerved. If it was not shoulder pain, she wondered what in the world had him so fretful.

Antonyo took a large swallow from his water glass. He then took some deep breath and proceeded to let Keisha know why he'd requested today's visit. "Keisha, you are a beautiful woman of God, inside and out. As such, I'm sure He has made you aware of how I feel about you by now." Keisha turned away in a deep blush, but Antonyo forged ahead before he lost his nerve again.

"You are the first woman I have met in my entire life that I wanted to settle down with and try having a normal relationship. I realized just the other day that I have actually fallen in love with you."

The bug-eyed stare that had become signature to Keisha surfaced once again. Her heart flipped so hard she was sure Antonyo could hear it as it thudded against her chest from the inside.

"Antonyo, are you sure—"

He cut her off before she could continue with her entire question. "Keisha, I don't mean to be rude, but I have to finish what I have to say before I can allow you to reply. I need you to know everything before you start telling me that you feel the same way about me."

Antonyo's ability to read her mind astounded her. One day in the near future, she would ask him how he did it. She kept her mouth closed, however, and waited for him to finish.

"While I was in the hospital . . ." Antonyo took a deep breath and blew it out through his mouth slowly. He closed his eyes and counted to three; then he continued without re-opening his eyes. "When I was in the hospital, I discovered I am HIV positive." Finally, he opened his eyes again, prepared to see Keisha with her signature look. What he saw, however, was something else totally. He saw no fear or judgment, simply empathy and concern for his well-being.

"Oh, Antonyo," she said softly. She reached out to hug him. "You must have been terrified when you found out."

Now it was Antonyo who stared bug-eyed. She obviously had not heard him correctly. He pulled away from the embrace and asked, "Keisha, did you hear me? I don't have Swine Flu or some other curable disease. I am HIV positive. And as of right now, it is a definite death sentence." For some odd reason, Antonyo became a little offended by her cavalier attitude in regards to his announcement.

Keisha recognized Antonyo's aggressive tone. She had become quite familiar with it, since she worked quite closely with young adults who were HIV positive. She had been a volunteer with the state health clinic since she was twenty-one years old. Her own mother died of AIDS as a result of a bad blood transfusion after a car accident. Keisha had become well versed on the subject of HIV over the years.

"I heard you, Antonyo. I also understand very clearly what you are dealing with. You expected me to become frightened when you told me, but I'm not." She then went on to describe her experience with the disease.

"Your mom died from this?" he asked, astounded.

"Yes. That was eighteen years ago. Medical research has come a long way since then. People are living much longer now with the virus before it progresses into AIDS. As a matter of fact, I have only known one person to die from this disease since I started working at the clinic, and she had the full-blown disease when I met her. One other person that I met there has since died, but he was killed in the commission of an armed robbery. Medication can help you to live a pretty normal life, even with this virus."

Antonyo stared at Keisha for several long seconds. Then it hit him hard and strong: Meeting Keisha more than four years ago had been part of God's purpose for his life, knowing that he would eventually find himself HIV positive. He had prepared Keisha for him and this time in his life. With the realization came very strong emotions. He covered his face with his hands just as the first tear spilled onto his cheeks. Everything that his mother had been telling him about God loving him, despite his mistakes and lifestyle, had been made so clear at that very second. He sat there on Keisha's sofa, weeping and praising God aloud.

"Thank you, God. Thank you, God," he said over and over again.

Keisha knew better than to interrupt a man when he was in full, sincere praise mode. She let him spill his heart to God in worship and surrender, even though she was anxious to hear him say again that he was in love with her. Keisha had been attracted to Antonyo since the very first time his mother introduced the two in church. That was four years ago. Yes, his HIV status did concern her, but she'd been trained very well on how to handle herself and how to be careful. There would definitely be no sex between them unless this thing, whatever it was, progressed into marriage. For now, though, she wanted to help take care of her friend, who she just so happened to be in love with.

"Keisha, do you know the only other woman who has ever seen me cry in my adult life has been my mother?" Antonyo admitted when he was again able to pull himself together.

"Should I be flattered?" she asked playfully.

"Of course, woman. It is a rare privilege to see Antonyo Ian Demonté Simms express such true emotions," he replied in mock exasperation.

"Speaking of true emotions, what was that you said a few moments ago? Something about how you . . . feel about me?"

"I have no idea what you're talking about. I was under emotional duress, so I cannot be held responsible for anything I said during that time."

Keisha gave him a cockeyed and crazy look, causing him to burst into laughter. He had not felt this carefree or happy since before hearing about his HIV status. He obviously loved this woman dearly, because only a man in love could laugh so wholeheartedly and feel so lighthearted in the face of exposing such a predicament. He knew how she felt about him, but he needed to hear her say it aloud.

"Minister Keisha Hearn, I take back what I said about not being in my right mind when I said I love you. I have never been as sane and sure about anything in my life. I am in love with you. Now I need to hear you tell me how you feel about me."

Keisha stared deeply into his eyes, wanting him to fully understand that she was not afraid of anything he'd told her today. She was not afraid of his HIV status, because she served a sovereign God who made no mistakes. She knew that God would not allow her to feel this way about a man who she was not supposed to be with. She believed, like Antonyo, that God had prepared her, even with the death of her own mom, for such a time as this.

"I love you too, Antonyo. And I am more than prepared to walk with you on this new journey in your life."

The new couple sealed their mutual declaration with a kiss—a kiss filled with promise, potential, purpose, and passion.

Epilogue

Five months later

The entire congregation stood as the bride and her escort made their way down the aisle. The bride had never been more beautifully radiant or happy in her entire life. She seriously considered taking off in a full sprint, dragging her escort down the aisle with her, to hurry to get to the man she would spend the rest of her life with. Only God knew how long that would be.

The eager groom stood antsy and anxious at the altar. He thanked God with every painstakingly slow step his future wife took. The BeBe & CeCe Winan's song, "If Anything Ever Happened to You," which she chose as her bridal march, should have been something more up tempo, like "Living for the Weekend," by the O'Jays. Perhaps that would have helped her to get to him more quickly. And it was definitely appropriate, for he was certainly living for this honeymoon weekend. His bride-to-be had made him wait until their wedding night to fully explore her.

Once they finally made their way to the altar, the bride's escort turned and looked over his left shoulder to steal a look at the woman who was nearly as beautiful as the bride. Each time he saw her, she took his breath away.

After stating the preliminaries and saying a quick prayer, Pastor Mitchell finally asked, "Who gives this woman to be married to this man?"

Antonyo announced proudly, "I do." He then handed his mother over to William and took his seat on the front pew next to Keisha, the love of his life.

After the ceremony, everyone at the wedding reception ate, danced, and had a wonderful time. All in attendance were ecstatically happy for the newly married couple, Trina and William Rucker, but no one was more pleased than Antonyo. His mother deserved every bit of the joy she wore on her face as she danced with her new husband. She had been his rock, his provider, his disciplinarian, and his protector. She had raised him to adulthood, doing the very best she could to see to it that he had everything he needed. She had been patient with him when he would not listen to her, and she had been forgiving when he had to return with his tail tucked between his legs for being hard-headed. Trina Simms had been a very good example of a Jesus clone in his life all the way up until he decided to get to know Jesus for himself. Now Trina Rucker was carving out a piece of happiness just for herself.

Antonyo looked around the room to see all of his family and his mother's wonderful friends. His daughter, LaToya, made a perfect flower girl. Aunt Treecie was the maid of honor, and William's brother served as his best man. The couple had kept it very simple, as this was the total extent of their bridal party.

Sheldon had attended the ceremony at Antonyo's request and with Trina's blessing. Father and son had been in constant contact, just as Sheldon had promised. In getting to know his father again, Antonyo discovered he had two half siblings, a brother and a sister. LaToya adored her grandpa and her new aunt and uncle.

Antonyo also began attending the support group meetings

at the free clinic where Keisha volunteered. He had been so encouraged by those people he met who shared his disease. He met some of the most courageous men and women. They helped him cope when he got down about his disease, and he, in turn, helped others when they were fearful. He would never hesitate to tell them how Jesus had been preparing him and Keisha to deal with his disease even before the two of them ever laid eyes on each other.

One of the hardest parts about being HIV positive thus far had been facing the women he slept with and telling them they were now at risk. Of the nine females he talked to, only one of them had admitted to testing positive. That was Jessica. She, too, had begun attending the support group sessions.

Antonyo had decided, with the permission of Pastor Mitchell, he would start a ministry for young men aged twelve to seventeen to counsel them about sexual awareness and abstinence. He would give them full disclosure of his own status, and be very transparent with them about his former lifestyle. It was his mission to attempt to save other young men from the detrimental mindset he had as a teenager and even into young adulthood.

All of the mistakes he had made in his life with regard to the way he had treated women would now be put to use to prayerfully keep other young men from following his path. While HIV was part of the consequences of his reckless sexual lifestyle, he also understood that God allowed him to continue in his waywardness so that he would be prepared for such a time as this.

He searched around the room, looking to spot his beautiful lady. He saw her not very far away, dancing with his daughter. His heart skipped a beat as he watched the two most important women in his life enjoy each other. He looked up to the sky, closed his eyes, and silently mouthed a short prayer of thanks to God for His awesome grace and mercy. If he had his way and God agreed, he, too, would one day soon be celebrating at his very own wedding reception.

READING GROUP QUESTIONS FOR DISCUSSION

1.   Give your best description of Antonyo and his character before he became saved.

2.   How do you feel about Aunt LaTreece? Do you think she was wrong for starting him on his way to being a womanizer and a user?

3.   How long did it take you to realize that the initials to Antonyo's full name (Antonyo Ian Demonté Simms) spell AIDS?

4.   Describe your feelings about Sheldon and his ten-year absence, and then re-emergence, into his son's life.

5.   Do you find the stories about Antonyo's women and their tolerance of his behavior realistic? Which was your favorite story? Do you know a woman who would fit the description of any of the women Antonyo dated?

6.   If you were LaTrina, would you have continually allowed Antonyo to keep coming back to live with you? Do you feel she enabled him?

7.   Did you find it strange that Minister Keisha would develop an interest in the young playboy? Do you think you could become the significant other and perhaps eventually the wife/husband of a person who you knew to be HIV positive?

8.   Do you think Lynn got off too easily for her assault on Antonyo? Do you think he deserved what she did to him?

9.   Jessica's story was quite disturbing. Would you stay married to a man/woman who admitted to being gay if he told you he wanted to change his life and work toward being in a completely heterosexual relationship with you?

10. Did you find it strange that Antonyo had no male friends?